WITHDRAWN

Enduring Love

Enduring Love

Ian McEwan

Thorndike Press • Chivers Press
Thorndike, Maine USA   Bath, England

This Large Print edition is published by Thorndike Press, USA and by Chivers Press, England.

Published in 1998 in the U.S. by arrangement with Doubleday, a division of Bantam Doubleday Dell Publishing Group, Inc.

Published in 1998 in the U.K. by arrangement with Random House (UK) Ltd.

U.S. Hardcover   0-7862-1447-3   (Basic Series Edition)
U.K. Hardcover   0-7540-1153-4   (Windsor Large Print)
U.K. Softcover   0-7540-2110-6   (Paragon Large Print)

The text of this Large Print edition is unabridged.
Other aspects of the book may vary from the original edition.

Set in 16 pt. Plantin by Rick Gundberg.

Printed in the United States on permanent paper.

British Library Cataloguing in Publication Data available

Library of Congress Cataloging in Publication Data

McEwan, Ian.
    Enduring love : a novel / Ian McEwan.
        p.   cm.
    ISBN 0-7862-1447-3 (lg. print : hardcover : alk. paper)
    1. Obsessive-compulsive disorder — Fiction.   2. Chiltern Hills (England) — Fiction.   3. Large type books.   I. Title.
    [PR6063.C4E53   1998b]
    823'.914—dc21   98-13542

To Annalena

One

The beginning is simple to mark. We were in sunlight under a turkey oak, partly protected from a strong, gusty wind. I was kneeling on the grass with a corkscrew in my hand, and Clarissa was passing me the bottle — a 1987 Daumas Gassac. This was the moment, this was the pinprick on the time map: I was stretching out my hand, and as the cool neck and the black foil touched my palm, we heard a man's shout. We turned to look across the field and saw the danger. Next thing, I was running toward it. The transformation was absolute: I don't recall dropping the corkscrew, or getting to my feet, or making a decision, or hearing the caution Clarissa called after me. What idiocy, to be racing into this story and its labyrinths, sprinting away from our happiness among the fresh spring grasses by the oak. There was the shout again, and a child's cry, enfeebled by the wind that roared in the tall trees along the hedgerows. I ran faster. And there, suddenly, from different points around the field, four other men were converging on the scene, running like me.

I see us from two hundred feet up, through the eyes of the buzzard we had watched earlier, soaring, circling, and dipping in the tumult of currents: five men running silently toward the center of a hundred-acre field. I approached from the southeast, with the wind at my back. About two hundred yards to my left two men ran side by side. They were farm laborers who had been repairing the fence along the field's southern edge where it skirts the road. The same distance beyond them was the motorist, John Logan, whose car was banked on the grass verge with its door, or doors, wide open. Knowing what I know now, it's odd to evoke the figure of Jed Parry directly ahead of me, emerging from a line of beeches on the far side of the field a quarter of a mile away, running into the wind. To the buzzard, Parry and I were tiny forms, our white shirts brilliant against the green, rushing toward each other like lovers, innocent of the grief this entanglement would bring. The encounter that would unhinge us was minutes away, its enormity disguised from us not only by the barrier of time but by the colossus in the center of the field, which drew us in with the power of a terrible ratio that set fabulous magnitude against the puny human distress at its base.

What was Clarissa doing? She said she walked quickly toward the center of the field. I don't know how she resisted the urge to run. By the time it happened, the event I am about to describe — the fall — she had almost caught us up and was well placed as an observer, unencumbered by participation, by the ropes and the shouting, and by our fatal lack of cooperation. What I describe is shaped by what Clarissa saw too, by what we told each other in the time of obsessive reexamination that followed: the aftermath, an appropriate term for what happened in a field waiting for its early summer mowing. The aftermath, the second crop, the growth promoted by that first cut in May.

I'm holding back, delaying the information. I'm lingering in the prior moment because it was a time when other outcomes were still possible; the convergence of six figures in a flat green space has a comforting geometry from the buzzard's perspective, the knowable, limited plane of the snooker table. The initial conditions, the force and the direction of the force, define all the consequent pathways, all the angles of collision and return, and the glow of the overhead light bathes the field, the baize and all its moving bodies, in reassuring clarity. I think that while we were still converging, before we made contact, we were in a state of mathematical grace. I linger on our dispositions, the relative distances and the compass point — because as far as these occurrences were concerned, this was the last time I understood anything clearly at all.

What were we running toward? I don't think any of us would ever know fully. But superficially the answer was a balloon. Not the nominal space that encloses a cartoon character's speech or thought, or, by analogy, the kind that's driven by mere hot air. It was an enormous balloon filled with helium, that elemental gas forged from hydrogen in the nuclear furnace of the stars, first step along the way in the generation of multiplicity and variety of matter in the universe, including our selves and all our thoughts.

We were running toward a catastrophe, which itself was a kind of furnace in whose heat identities and fates would buckle into new shapes. At the base of the balloon was a basket in which there was a boy, and by the basket, clinging to a rope, was a man in need of help.

Even without the balloon the day would have been marked for memory, though in the most pleasurable of ways, for this was a reunion after a separation of six weeks, the longest Clarissa and I had spent apart in our seven years. On the way out to Heathrow I had made a detour into Covent Garden and found a semilegal place to park, near Carluccio's. I went in and put together a picnic whose centerpiece was a great ball of mozzarella, which the assistant fished out of an earthenware vat with a wooden claw. I also bought black olives, mixed salad, and focaccia. Then I hurried up Long Acre to Bertram Rota's to take delivery of Clarissa's birthday present. Apart from the flat and our car, it was the most expensive single item I had ever bought. The rarity of this little book seemed to give off a heat I could feel through the thick brown wrapping paper as I walked back up the street.

Forty minutes later I was scanning the screens for arrival information. The Boston flight had only just landed and I guessed I had a half-hour wait. If one ever wanted proof of Darwin's contention that the many expressions of emotion in humans are universal, genetically inscribed, then a few minutes by the arrivals gate in Heathrow's Terminal Four should suffice. I saw the same joy, the same uncontrollable smile, in the faces of a Nigerian earth mama, a thin-lipped Scottish granny, and a pale, correct Japanese businessman as they wheeled their trolleys in and recognized a figure in the expectant crowd. Observing human variety can give pleasure, but so too can human sameness. I kept hearing the same sighing sound on a downward note, often breathed through a name as two people pressed forward to go into their embrace. Was it a major second or a minor third, or somewhere in between? Pa-pa! Yolan-ta! Ho-bi! Nz-e! There was also a rising note, crooned into the solemn, wary faces of babies by long-absent fathers or grandparents, cajoling, beseeching an immediate return of love. Han-nah? Tom-ee? Let me in!

The variety was in the private dramas: a father and a teenage son, Turkish perhaps, stood in a long silent clinch, forgiving each other, or mourning a loss, oblivious to the baggage trolleys jamming around them; identical twins, women in their fifties, greeted each other with clear distaste, just touching hands and kissing without making contact; a small American boy, hoisted onto

12

the shoulders of a father he did not recognize, screamed to be put down, provoking a fit of temper in his tired mother.

But mostly it was smiles and hugs, and in thirty-five minutes I experienced more than fifty theatrical happy endings, each one with the appearance of being slightly less well acted than the one before, until I began to feel emotionally exhausted and suspected that even the children were being insincere. I was just wondering how convincing I myself could be now in greeting Clarissa when she tapped me on the shoulder, having missed me in the crowd and circled round. Immediately my detachment vanished, and I called out her name, in tune with all the rest.

Less than an hour later we were parked by a track that ran through beech woods in the Chiltern Hills, near Christmas Common. While Clarissa changed her shoes I loaded a backpack with our picnic. We set off down our path arm in arm, still elated by our reunion; what was familiar about her — the size and feel of her hand, the warmth and tranquillity in her voice, the Celt's pale skin and green eyes — was also novel, gleaming in an alien light, reminding me of our very first meetings and the months we spent falling in love. Or, I imagined, I was

13

another man, my own sexual competitor, come to steal her from me. When I told her, she laughed and said I was the world's most complicated simpleton, and it was while we stopped to kiss and wondered aloud whether we should not have driven straight home to bed that we glimpsed through the fresh foliage the helium balloon drifting dreamily across the wooded valley to our west. Neither the man nor the boy was visible to us. I remember thinking, but not saying, that it was a precarious form of transport when the wind rather than the pilot set the course. Then I thought that perhaps this was the very nature of its attraction. And instantly the idea went out of my mind.

We went through College Wood toward Pishill, stopping to admire the new greenery on the beeches. Each leaf seemed to glow with an internal light. We talked about the purity of this color, the beech leaf in spring, and how looking at it cleared the mind. As we walked into the wood the wind began to get up and the branches creaked like rusted machinery. We knew this route well. This was surely the finest landscape within an hour of central London. I loved the pitch and roll of the fields and their scatterings of chalk and flint, and the paths that dipped across them to sink into the darkness of the beech stands, certain neglected, badly drained valleys where thick iridescent mosses covered the rotting tree trunks and where you occasionally glimpsed a muntjak blundering through the undergrowth.

For much of the time as we walked westward we were talking about Clarissa's research — John Keats dying in Rome in the house at the foot of the Spanish Steps where he lodged with his friend, Joseph Severn. Was it possible there were still three or four unpublished letters of Keats's in existence? Might one of them be addressed to Fanny Brawne? Clarissa had reason to think so and had spent part of a sabbatical term traveling around Spain and Portugal, visiting houses known to Fanny Brawne and to Keats's sister Fanny. Now she was back from Boston, where she had been working in the Houghton Library at Harvard, trying to trace correspondence from Severn's remote family connections. Keats's last known letter was written almost three months before he died, to his old friend Charles Brown. It's rather stately in tone and typical in throwing out, almost as parenthesis, a brilliant description of artistic creation: "the knowledge of contrast, feeling for light and shade, all that information (primitive sense) necessary for a poem, are great enemies to the recovery of the stomach." It's the one with the famous farewell, so piercing in its reticence and courtesy: "I can scarcely bid you good-bye, even in a letter. I always made an awkward bow. God bless you! John Keats." But all the biographies agree that Keats was in remission from tuberculosis when he wrote this letter, and remained so for a further ten days. He visited the Villa Borghese and strolled down the Corso. He listened with pleasure to Severn playing Haydn, he mischievously tipped his dinner out the window in protest at the quality of the cooking, and he even thought about starting a poem. If letters existed from this period, why would Severn or, more likely, Brown have wanted to suppress them? Clarissa thought she had found the answer in a couple of references in correspondence between distant relations of Brown's written in the 1840s, but she needed more evidence, different sources.

"He knew he'd never see Fanny again," Clarissa said. "He wrote to Brown and said that to see her name written would be more than he could bear. But he never stopped thinking about her. He was strong enough those days in December, and he loved her so much. It's easy to imagine him writing a letter he never intended to send."

I squeezed her hand and said nothing. I knew little about Keats or his poetry, but I thought it possible that in his hopeless situation, he would not have wanted to write precisely because he loved her so much. Lately I'd had the idea that Clarissa's interest in these hypothetical letters had something to do with our own situation, and with her conviction that love that did not find its expression in a letter was not perfect. In the months after we met and before we bought the apartment, she had written me some beauties, passionately abstract in their exploration of the ways our love was different from and superior to any that had ever existed. Perhaps that's the essence of a love letter, to celebrate the unique. I had tried to match hers, but all that sincerity would permit me were the facts, and they seemed miraculous enough to me: a beautiful woman loved and wanted to be loved by a large, clumsy, balding fellow who could hardly believe his luck.

We stopped to watch the buzzard as we were approaching Maidensgrove. The balloon may have recrossed our path while we were in the woods that cover the valleys around the nature reserve. By the early afternoon we were on the Ridgeway Path,

17

walking north along the line of the escarpment. Then we struck out along one of those
broad fingers of land that project westward
from the Chilterns into the rich farmland
below. Across the Vale of Oxford we could
make out the outlines of the Cotswold Hills
and beyond them, perhaps, the Brecon Bea-
cons rising in a faint blue mass. Our plan
had been to picnic right out on the end,
where the view was best, but the wind was
too strong by now. We went back across
the field and sheltered among the oaks along
the northern side. And it was because of
these trees that we did not see the balloon's
descent. Later I wondered why it had not
been blown miles away. Later still I discovered that the wind at five hundred feet was
not the same that day as the wind at ground
level.

The Keats conversation faded as we un-
packed our lunch. Clarissa pulled the bottle
from the bag and held it by its base as she
offered it to me. As I have said, the neck
touched my palm as we heard the shout. It
was a baritone, on a rising note of fear. It
marked the beginning and, of course, an
end. At that moment a chapter — no, a
whole stage — of my life closed. Had I
known, and had there been a spare second
or two, I might have allowed myself a little

nostalgia. We were seven years into a child-less marriage of love. Clarissa Mellon was also in love with another man, but with his two hundredth birthday coming up, he was little trouble. In fact, he helped in the com-bative exchanges that were part of our equi-librium, our way of talking about work. We lived in an art deco apartment block in North London with a below-average share of worries — a money shortage for a year or so, an unsubstantiated cancer scare, the divorces and illnesses of friends, Clarissa's irritation with my occasional and manic bouts of dissatisfaction with my kind of work — but there was nothing that threatened our free and intimate existence.

What we saw when we stood from our picnic was this: a huge gray balloon, the size of a house, the shape of a teardrop, had come down in the field. The pilot must have been halfway out of the passenger basket as it touched the ground. His leg had become entangled in a rope that was attached to an anchor. Now, as the wind gusted and pushed and lifted the balloon toward the escarpment, he was being half dragged, half carried across the field. In the basket was a child, a boy of about ten. In a sudden lull, the man was on his feet, clutching at the basket, or at the boy. Then there was another gust, and the pilot was on his back, bumping over the rough ground, trying to dig his feet in for purchase or lunging for the anchor behind him in order to secure it in the earth. Even if he had been able, he would not have dared disentangle himself from the anchor rope. He needed his weight to keep the balloon on the ground, and the wind could have snatched the rope from his hands.

As I ran I heard him shouting at the boy, urging him to leap clear of the basket. But the boy was tossed from one side to another as the balloon lurched across the field. He regained his balance and got a leg over the edge of the basket. The balloon rose and fell, thumping into a hummock, and the boy dropped backward out of sight. Then he was up again, arms stretched out toward the man and shouting something in return — words or inarticulate fear, I couldn't tell.

I must have been a hundred yards away when the situation came under control. The wind had dropped; the man was on his feet, bending over the anchor as he drove it into the ground. He had unlooped the rope from his leg. For some reason — complacency, exhaustion, or simply because he was doing what he was told — the boy remained where he was. The towering balloon wavered and tilted and tugged, but the beast was tamed. I slowed my pace, though I did not stop. As the man straightened, he saw us — or at least the farmworkers and me — and he waved us on. He still needed help, but I was glad to slow to a brisk walk. The farm laborers were also walking now. One of them was coughing loudly. But the man with the car, John Logan, knew something we didn't and kept on running. As for Jed Parry, my view of him was blocked by the balloon that lay between us.

The wind renewed its rage in the treetops just before I felt its force on my back. Then it struck the balloon, which ceased its innocent, comical wagging and was suddenly stilled. Its only motion was a shimmer of strain that rippled out across its ridged surface as the contained energy accumulated. It broke free, the anchor flew up in a spray of dirt, and balloon and basket rose ten feet in the air. The boy was thrown back, out of sight. The pilot had the rope in his hands and was lifted two feet clear off the ground. If Logan had not reached him and taken hold of one of the many dangling lines, the balloon would have carried the boy away. Instead, both men were now being pulled across the field, and the farmworkers and I were running again.

I got there before them. When I took a rope, the basket was above head height. The boy inside it was screaming. Despite the wind, I caught the smell of urine. Jed Parry was on a rope seconds after me, and the two farmworkers, Joseph Lacey and Toby Greene, caught hold just after him. Greene was having a coughing fit, but he kept his grip. The pilot was shouting instructions at us, but too frantically, and no one was listening. He had been struggling too long, and now he was exhausted and emotionally out of control. With five of us on the lines the balloon was secured. We simply had to keep steady on our feet and pull hand over hand to bring the basket down, and this, despite whatever the pilot was shouting, was what we began to do.

By this time we were standing on the escarpment. The ground dropped away sharply at a gradient of about twenty-five percent and then leveled out into a gentle slope toward the bottom. In winter this is a favorite tobogganing spot for local kids. We were all talking at once. Two of us, myself and the motorist, wanted to walk the balloon away from the edge. Someone thought the priority was to get the boy out. Someone else was calling for the balloon to be pulled down so that we could anchor it firmly. I saw no contradiction, for we could be pulling the balloon down as we moved back into the field. But the second opinion was prevailing. The pilot had a fourth idea, but no one knew or cared what it was.

I should make something clear. There may have been a vague communality of purpose, but we were never a team. There was no chance, no time. Coincidences of time and place, a predisposition to help, had brought us together under the balloon. No one was in charge — or everyone was, and we were in a shouting match. The pilot, red-faced, bawling, and sweating, we ignored. Incompetence came off him like heat. But we were beginning to bawl our own instructions too. I know that if I had been uncontested leader, the tragedy would not have happened. Later I heard some of the others say the same thing about themselves. But there was not time, no opportunity for force of character to show. Any leader, any firm plan, would have been preferable to none. No human society, from the hunter-gatherer to the postindustrial, has come to the attention of anthropologists that did not have its leaders and the led; and no emergency was ever dealt with effectively by democratic process.

It was not so difficult to bring the passenger basket down low enough for us to see inside. We had a new problem. The boy was curled up on the floor. His arms covered his face and he was gripping his hair tightly. "What's his name?" we said to the red-faced man.

"Harry."

"Harry!" we shouted. "Come on, Harry. Harry! Take my hand, Harry. Get out of there, Harry!"

But Harry curled up tighter. He flinched each time we said his name. Our words were like stones thrown down at his body. He was in paralysis of will, a state known as learned helplessness, often noted in laboratory animals subjected to unusual stress; all impulses to problem-solving disappear, all instinct for survival drains away. We pulled the basket down to the ground and managed to keep it there, and we were just leaning in to try and lift the boy out when the pilot shouldered us aside and attempted to climb in. He said later that he told us what he was trying to do. We heard nothing for our own shouting and swearing. What he was doing seemed ridiculous, but his intentions, it turned out, were completely sensible. He wanted to deflate the balloon by pulling a cord that was tangled in the basket.

"Yer great pillock!" Lacey shouted. "Help

us reach the lad out."

I heard what was coming two seconds before it reached us. It was as though an express train were traversing the treetops, hurtling toward us. An airy, whining, whooshing sound grew to full volume in half a second. At the inquest, the Met office figures for wind speeds that day were part of the evidence, and there were some gusts, it was said, of seventy miles an hour. This must have been one, but before I let it reach us, let me freeze the frame — there's a security in stillness — to describe our circle.

To my right the ground dropped away. Immediately to my left was John Logan, a family doctor from Oxford, forty-two years old, married to a historian, with two children. He was not the youngest of our group, but he was the fittest. He played tennis to county level and belonged to a mountaineering club. He had done a stint with a mountain rescue team in the western Highlands. Logan was a mild, reticent man, apparently, otherwise he might have been able to force himself usefully on us as a leader. To his left was Joseph Lacey, sixty-three, farm laborer, odd-job man, captain of his local bowls team. He lived with his wife in Watlington, a small town at the foot of the escarpment. On his left was his mate, Toby

Greene, fifty-eight, also a farm laborer, un-married, living with his mother at Russell's Water. Both men worked for the Stonor estate. Greene was the one with the smoker's cough. Next around the circle, try-ing to get into the basket, was the pilot, James Gadd, fifty-five, an executive in a small advertising company who lived in Reading with his wife and one of their grownup children, who was mentally handi-capped. At the inquest, Gadd was found to have breached half a dozen basic safety pro-cedures, which the coroner listed tonelessly. Gadd's ballooning license was withdrawn. The boy in the basket was Harry Gadd, his grandson, ten years old, from Camberwell, London. Facing me, with the ground slop-ing away to his left, was Jed Parry. He was twenty-eight, unemployed, living on an in-heritance in Hampstead.

This was the crew. As far as we were concerned, the pilot had abdicated his authority. We were breathless, excited, de-termined on our separate plans, while the boy was beyond participating in his own survival. He lay in a heap, blocking out the world with his forearms. Lacey, Greene, and I were attempting to fish him out, and now Gadd was climbing over the top of us. Logan and Parry were calling out their own suggestions. Gadd had placed one foot by his grandson's head and Greene was cussing him when it happened. A mighty fist socked the balloon in two rapid blows, one-two, the second more vicious than the first. And the first was vicious. It jerked Gadd right out of the basket onto the ground, and it lifted the balloon five feet or so, straight into the air. Gadd's considerable weight was removed from the equation. The rope ran through my grip, scorching my palms, but I managed to keep hold, with two feet of line spare. The others kept hold too. The basket was right above our heads now, and we stood with arms upraised like Sunday bell ringers. Into our amazed silence, before the shouting could resume, the second punch came and knocked the balloon up and westward. Suddenly we were treading the air with all our weight in the grip of our fists.

Those one or two ungrounded seconds occupy as much space in memory as might a long journey up an uncharted river. My first impulse was to hang on in order to keep the balloon weighted down. The child was incapable, and was about to be borne away. Two miles to the west were high-voltage power lines. A child alone and needing help. It was my duty to hang on, and I thought we would all do the same.

Almost simultaneous with the desire to stay on the rope and save the boy, barely a neuronal pulse later, came other thoughts, in which fear and instant calculations of logarithmic complexity were fused. We were rising, and the ground was dropping away as the balloon was pushed westward. I knew I had to get my legs and feet locked around the rope. But the end of the line barely reached below my waist, and my grip was slipping. My legs flailed in the empty air. Every fraction of a second that passed increased the drop, and the point must come when to let go would be impossible or fatal. And compared with me, Harry was safe, curled up in the basket. The balloon might well come down safely at the bottom of the hill. And perhaps my impulse to hang on was nothing more than a continuation of what I had been attempting moments before, simply a failure to adjust quickly.

And again, less than one adrenally incensed heartbeat later, another variable was added to the equation: someone let go, and the balloon and its hangers-on lurched upward another several feet.

I didn't know, nor have I ever discovered, who let go first. I'm not prepared to accept that it was me. But everyone claims not to have been first. What is certain is that if we had not broken ranks, our collective weight would have brought the balloon to earth a quarter of the way down the slope as the gust subsided a few seconds later. But as I've said, there was no team, there was no plan, no agreement to be broken. No failure. So can we accept that it was right, every man for himself? Were we all happy afterward that this was a reasonable course? We never had that comfort, for there was a deeper covenant, ancient and automatic, written in our nature. Cooperation — the basis of our earliest hunting successes, the force behind our evolving capacity for language, the glue of our social cohesion. Our misery in the aftermath was proof that we knew we had failed ourselves. But letting go was in our nature too. Selfishness is also written on our hearts. This is our mammalian conflict: what to give to the others and what to keep for yourself. Treading that line, keeping the others in check and being kept in check by them, is what we call morality. Hanging a few feet above the Chilterns escarpment, our crew enacted morality's ancient, irresolvable dilemma: us, or me.

Someone said *me*, and then there was nothing to be gained by saying *us*. Mostly, we are good when it makes sense. A good society is one that makes sense of being good. Suddenly, hanging there below the basket, we were a bad society, we were disintegrating. Suddenly the sensible choice was to look out for yourself. The child was not my child, and I was not going to die for it. The moment I glimpsed a body falling away — but whose? — and I felt the balloon lurch upward, the matter was settled; altruism had no place. Being good made no sense. I let go and fell, I reckon, about twelve feet. I landed heavily on my side; I got away with a bruised thigh. Around me — before or after, I'm not so sure — bodies were thumping to the ground. Jed Parry was unhurt. Toby Greene broke his ankle. Joseph Lacey, the oldest, who had done his National Service with a paratroop regiment, did no more than wind himself.

By the time I got to my feet, the balloon was fifty yards away and one man was still dangling by his rope. In John Logan, husband, father, doctor, and mountain rescue worker, the flame of altruism must have burned a little stronger. It didn't need much. When four of us let go, the balloon, with six hundred pounds shed, must have surged upward. A delay of one second would have been enough to close his options. When I stood up and saw him, he was a hundred feet up and rising, just where the ground itself was falling. He wasn't struggling, he wasn't kicking or trying to claw his way up. He hung perfectly still along the line of the rope, all his energies concentrated in his weakening grip. He was already a tiny figure, almost black against the sky. There was no sight of the boy. The balloon and its basket lifted away and westward, and the smaller Logan became, the more terrible it was, so terrible it was funny, it was a stunt, a joke, a cartoon, and a frightened laugh heaved out of my chest. For this was preposterous, the kind of thing that happened to Bugs Bunny or Tom or Jerry, and for an instant I thought it wasn't true, and that only I could see right through the joke, and that my utter disbelief would set reality straight and see Dr. Logan safely to the ground.

I don't know whether the others were standing or sprawling. Toby Greene was probably doubled up over his ankle. But I do remember the silence into which I laughed. No exclamations, no shouted instructions as before. Mute helplessness. He was two hundred yards away now, and perhaps three hundred feet above the ground. Our silence was a kind of acceptance, a death warrant. Or it was horrified shame, because the wind had dropped, and barely stirred against our backs. He had been on the rope so long that I began to think he might stay there until the balloon drifted down or the boy came to his senses and found the valve that released the gas, or until some beam, or god, or some other impossible cartoon thing, came and gathered him up. Even as I had that hope, we saw him slip down right to the end of the rope. And still he hung there. For two seconds, three, four. And then he let go. Even then, there was a fraction of time when he barely fell, and I still thought there was a chance that a freak physical law, a furious thermal, some phenomenon no more astonishing than the one we were witnessing, would intervene and bear him up. We watched him drop. You could see the acceleration. No forgiveness, no special dispensation for flesh, or bravery, or kindness. Only ruthless gravity. And from somewhere, perhaps from him, perhaps from some indifferent crow, a thin squawk cut through the stilled air. He fell as he had hung, a stiff little black stick. I've never seen such a terrible thing as that falling man.

Two

Best to slow down. Let's give the half-minute after John Logan's fall careful consideration. What occurred simultaneously or in quick succession, what was said, how we moved or failed to move, what I thought — these elements need to be separated out. So much followed from this incident, so much branching and subdivision began in those early moments, such pathways of love and hatred blazed from this starting position, that a little reflection, even pedantry, can only help me here. The best description of a reality does not need to mimic its velocity. Whole books, whole research departments, are dedicated to the first half-minute in the history of the universe. Vertiginous theories of chaos and turbulence are predicated upon the supremacy of initial conditions, which need painstaking depiction.

I've already marked my beginning, the explosion of consequences, with the touch of a wine bottle and a shout of distress. But this pinprick is as notional as a point in

Euclidean geometry, and though it seems right, I could have proposed the moment Clarissa and I planned to picnic after I collected her from the airport, or when we decided on our route, or the field in which to have our lunch and the time we chose to have it. There are always antecedent causes. A beginning is an artifice, and what recommends one over another is how much sense it makes of what follows. The cool touch of glass on skin and James Gadd's cry — these synchronous moments fix a transition, a divergence from the expected: from the wine we didn't taste (we drank it that night to numb ourselves) to the summons, from the delightful existence we shared and expected to continue to the ordeal we were to endure in the time ahead.

When I let the wine bottle fall to run across the field toward the balloon and its bumping basket, toward Jed Parry and the others, I chose a branching in the path that foreclosed a certain kind of easeful life. The struggle with the ropes, the breaking of ranks, and the bearing away of Logan — these were the obvious, large-scale events that shaped our story. But I see now that in the moments immediately after his fall there were subtler elements exerting powerful sway over the future. The moment

34

Logan hit the ground should have been the end of this story rather than one more beginning I could have chosen. The afternoon could have ended in mere tragedy.

In the second or two it took for Logan to reach the ground I had a sense of déjà vu, and I immediately knew its source. What came back to me was a nightmare I had occasionally in my twenties and thirties, from which I used to shout myself awake. The setting varied, but the essentials never did. I found myself in a prominent place watching from far off the unfolding of a disaster — an earthquake, a fire in a sky-scraper, a sinking ship, an erupting volcano. I could see helpless people, reduced by distance to an undifferentiated mass, scurrying about in panic, certain to die. The horror was in the contrast between their apparent size and the enormity of their suffering. Life was revealed as cheap; thousands of scream-ing individuals, no bigger than ants, were about to be annihilated, and I could do nothing to help. I did not think about the dream then so much as experience its emo-tional wash — terror, guilt, and helplessness were the components — and feel the nausea of a premonition fulfilled.

Down below us, where the escarpment leveled out, was a grassy field used for pasture, bounded by a line of pollarded willows. Beyond them was a larger pasture, where sheep and a few lambs were grazing. It was in the center of this second field, in our full view, that Logan landed. My impression was that at the moment of impact the little stick figure flowed or poured outward across the ground, like a drop of viscous fluid. But what we saw in the stillness, as though reconstituted, was the compact dot of his huddled figure. The nearest sheep, twenty feet away, barely looked up from its chewing.

Joseph Lacey was attending to his friend, Toby Greene, who could not stand. Right next to me was Jed Parry. Some way off behind us was James Gadd. He was less interested than we were in Logan. He was shouting about his grandson, who was being carried away in the balloon across the Vale of Oxford toward the line of pylons. Gadd pushed past us and went a few paces down the hill, as if intending to go in pursuit. *Such is his genetic investment,* I remember thinking stupidly. Clarissa came up behind me and looped her arms around my waist and pressed her face into my back. What surprised me was that she was already crying — I could feel the wetness on my shirt — whereas to me, sorrow seemed a long way off.

Like a self in a dream, I was both first and third persons. I acted, and saw myself act. I had my thoughts, and I saw them drift across a screen. As in a dream, my emotional responses were nonexistent or inappropriate. Clarissa's tears were no more than a fact, but I was pleased by the way my feet were anchored to the ground and set well apart, and the way my arms were folded across my chest. I looked out across the fields and the thought scrolled across: *That man is dead.* I felt a warmth spreading through me, a kind of self-love, and my folded arms hugged me tight. The corollary seemed to be *And I am alive.* It was a random matter, who was alive or dead at any given time. I happened to be alive. This was when I noticed Jed Parry watching me. His long, bony face was framed around a pained question. He looked wretched, like a dog about to be punished. In the second or so that this stranger's clear gray-blue eyes held mine, I felt I could include him in the self-congratulatory warmth I felt in being alive. It even crossed my mind to touch him comfortingly on the shoulder. My thoughts were up there on the screen: *This man is in shock. He wants me to help him.*

Had I known what this glance meant to him at the time, and how he was to construe it later and build around it a mental life, I would not have been so warm. In his pained, interrogative look was that first bloom, of which I was entirely ignorant. The euphoric calm I felt was simply a symptom of my shock. I honored Parry with a friendly nod and, ignoring Clarissa at my back — I was a busy man, I would deal with them all one at a time — I said to him in what I thought was a deep and reassuring voice, "It's all right."

This flagrant untruth reverberated so pleasantly between my ribs that I almost said it again. Perhaps I did. I was the first one to have spoken since Logan hit the ground. I reached into my trouser pocket and withdrew, of all things to have out here at this time, a mobile phone. I read the fractional widening of the young man's eyes as respect. It was what I felt for myself, anyway, as I held the dense little slab in my palm and with the thumb of the same hand jabbed three nines. I was in the world, equipped, capable, connected. When the emergency operator came on, I asked for police and ambulance and gave a lucid, minimal account of the accident and the balloon drifting away with the boy, and our position and the nearest access by road. It was all I could do to hold my excitement in. I wanted to shout something — commands, exhortations, inarticulate vowel sounds. I was brittle, speedy; perhaps I looked happy.

When I turned off the phone, Joseph Lacey said, "He won't need no ambulance."

Greene looked up from his ankle. "They'll need that to take him away."

I remembered. Of course. This was what I needed: something to do. I was wild by now, ready to fight, run, dance, you name it. "He might not be dead," I said. "There's always a chance. We'll go down and take a look."

As I was saying this I became aware of a tremor in my legs. I wanted to stride away down the slope, but I did not trust my balance. Uphill would be better. I said to Parry, "You'll come." I meant it as a suggestion, but it came out as a request, something I needed from him. He looked at me, unable to speak. Everything, every gesture, every word I spoke, was being stored away, gathered and piled, fuel for the long winter of his obsession.

I unclasped Clarissa's arms from my waist and turned. It didn't occur to me that she was trying to hold me steady. "Let's go down," I said quietly. "There may be something we can do." I heard my softening of tone, the artful lowering of volume. I was in a soap opera. *Now he's talking to his woman.* It was intimacy, a tight two-shot.

Clarissa put her hand on my shoulder. She told me later that it crossed her mind to slap my face. "Joe," she whispered. "You've got to slow down."

"What's up?" I said in a louder voice. A man lay dying in a field and no one was stirring. Clarissa looked at me, and though her mouth looked set to frame the words, she wouldn't tell me why I should slow down. I turned away and called to the others, who stood about on the grass waiting for me, so I thought, to tell them what to do. "I'm going down to him. Is anyone coming?" I didn't wait for an answer but set off down the hill, conscious of the watery looseness in my knees and taking short steps. Twenty seconds later I glanced back. No one had moved.

As I carried on down, the mania began to subside and I felt trapped and lonely in my decision. Also there was the fear, not quite in me but there in the field, spread like a mist, and denser at the core. I was walking into it without choice now, because they were watching me, and to turn back would have meant climbing up the hill, a double humiliation. As the euphoria lifted, so the fear seeped in. The dead man I did not want to meet was waiting for me in the middle of the field. Even worse would be finding him alive and dying. Then I'd have to face him alone with my first aid techniques, like so many silly party tricks. He wouldn't be taken in. He would go ahead and die anyway, and his death would be in and on my hands. I wanted to turn and shout for Clarissa, but they were watching me, I knew, and I had blustered so much up there I was ashamed. This long descent was my punishment.

I reached the line of pollarded willows at the bottom of the hill, crossed a dry ditch, and climbed through a barbed wire fence. By now I was out of their sight and I wanted to be sick. Instead, I urinated against a tree trunk. My hand was trembling badly. Afterward I stood still, delaying the moment when I would have to set out across the field. Being out of view was a physical relief, like being shaded from a desert sun. I was conscious of Logan's position, but even at this distance I didn't care to look.

The sheep that had barely glanced up at the impact stared and backed away into faltering runs as I strode among them. I was feeling slightly better. I kept Logan at the periphery of vision, but even so, I knew he was not flat on the ground. Something protruded at the center of the field, some stumpy antenna of his present or previous self. Not until I was twenty yards away did I permit myself to see him. He was sitting upright, his back to me, as though meditating, or gazing in the direction in which the balloon and Harry had drifted. There was calmness in his posture. I went closer, instinctively troubled to be approaching him unseen from behind but glad I could not yet see his face. I still clung to the possibility that there was a technique, a physical law or process of which I knew nothing, that would permit him to survive. That he should sit there so quietly in the field, as though he were collecting himself after his terrible experience, gave me hope and made me clear my throat stupidly and say, knowing that no one else could hear me, "Do you need help?" It was not so ridiculous at the time. I could see his hair curling over his shirt collar and sunburned skin along the tops of his ears. His tweed jacket was unmarked, though it drooped strangely, for his shoulders were narrower than they should have been. They were narrower than any adult's could be. From the base of the neck there was no lateral spread. The skeletal structure had collapsed internally to produce a head on a thickened stick. And seeing that, I became aware that what I had taken for calmness was *absence*. There was no one there. The quietness was that of the inanimate, and I understood again, because I had seen dead bodies before, why a prescientific age would have needed to invent the soul. It was no less clear than the illusion of the evening sun sinking through the sky. The closing down of countless interrelated neural and biochemical exchanges combined to suggest to a naked eye the illusion of the extinguished spark, or the simple departure of a single necessary element. However scientifically informed we count ourselves to be, fear and awe still surprise us in the presence of the dead. Perhaps it's life we're really wondering at.

These were the thoughts with which I tried to protect myself as I began to circle the corpse. It sat within a little indentation in the soil. I didn't see Logan dead until I saw his face, and what I saw I only glimpsed. Though the skin was intact, it was hardly a face at all, for the bone structure had shattered, and I had the impression, before I looked away, of a radical, Picassoesque violation of perspective. Perhaps I only imagined the vertical arrangement of the eyes. I turned away and saw Parry coming toward me across the field. He must have been following me down closely, for he was already within talking distance. He must have seen when I paused in the shelter of the trees.

I watched him over Logan's head as he slowed and called out to me, "Don't touch him, please don't touch him."

I hadn't intended to, but I said nothing. I was looking at Parry as though for the first time. He stood with his hands resting on his hips, staring not at Logan but at me. Even then, he was more interested in me. He had come to tell me something. He was tall and lean, all bone and sinew, and he looked fit. He wore jeans and box-fresh trainers tied with red laces. His bones fairly burst out of him, the way they hadn't with Logan. His knuckles, brushing against his leather belt, were big and tight-knobbed under the skin, which was white and stretched tight. The cheekbones were also tight and high-ridged and together with the ponytail gave him the look of a pale Indian brave. His appearance was striking, even slightly threatening, but the voice gave it all away. It was feebly hesitant, neutral as to region but carrying a trace, or acknowledgment, of Cockney — a discarded past or an affectation. Parry had his generation's habit of

44

making a statement on the rising inflection of a question — in humble imitation of Americans or Australians or, as I heard one linguist explain, too mired in relative judgments, too hesitant and apologetic to say how things were in the world.

Of course, I didn't think of any of this at the time. All I heard was a whine of powerlessness, and I relaxed. What he said was "Clarissa's really worried about you? I said I'd come down and see if you're all right?"

My silence was hostile. I was old enough to dislike his presumption of first names and, for that matter, of claiming to know Clarissa's state of mind. I didn't even know Parry's name at this point. Even with a dead man sitting between us, the rules of social engagement prevailed. As I heard it later from Clarissa, Parry had come over to her to introduce himself, then turned away to follow me down the hill. She had said nothing to him about me.

"Are you all right?"

I said, "There's nothing we can do but wait," and I gestured in the direction of the road, one field away.

Parry took a couple of steps closer and looked down at Logan, then back to me. The gray-blue eyes gleamed. He was excited, but no one could ever have guessed to what extent. "Actually, I think there is something we can do."

I looked at my watch. It was fifteen minutes since I had phoned the emergency services. "You go ahead," I said. "Do what you like."

"It's something we can do together?" he said as he looked about for a suitable place on the ground. The wild thought came to me that he was proposing some form of gross indecency with a corpse. He was lowering himself and with a look was inviting me to join him. Then I got it. He was on his knees.

"What we could do," he said with a seriousness that warned against mockery, "is to pray together?" Before I could object, which for the moment was impossible because I was speechless, Parry added, "I know it's difficult. But you'll find it helps. At times like this, you know, it really does help."

I took a step away from both Logan and Parry. I was embarrassed, and my first thought was not to offend a true believer. But I got a grip on myself. He wasn't concerned about offending me.

"I'm sorry," I said pleasantly. "It's not my thing at all."

Parry tried to speak reasonably from his

diminished height. "Look, we don't know each other and there's no reason why you should trust me. Except that God has brought us together in this tragedy and we have to, you know, make whatever sense of it we can?" Then, seeing me make no move, he added, "I think you have a special need for prayer?"

I shrugged and said, "Sorry. But you go right on ahead." I Americanized my tone to suggest a lightheartedness I did not feel.

Parry wasn't giving up. He was still on his knees. "I don't think you understand. You shouldn't, you know, think of this as some kind of duty. It's like, your own needs are being answered? It's got nothing to do with me, really, I'm just the messenger. It's a gift."

As he pressed harder, so the last traces of my embarrassment disappeared. "Thanks, but no."

Parry closed his eyes and breathed in deeply, not praying so much as gathering his strength. I decided to walk back up the hill. When he heard me moving away, he got to his feet and came over. He really didn't want to let me go. He was desperate to persuade me, but he was not going to drop the patient, understanding manner. So he seemed to smile through a barrier of pain

47

as he said, "Please don't dismiss this. I know it's not something you'd normally do. I mean, you don't have to believe in anything at all, just let yourself do it and I promise you, I promise —"

As he tripped over the terms of his promise, I interrupted him and stepped back. I suspected that at any moment he would be reaching out to touch me. "Look, I'm sorry. I'm going back up to see my friend." I couldn't bring myself to share Clarissa's name with him.

He must have known his only chance of keeping me now was a radical change of tone. I was already several steps away when he called sharply, "Okay, fine. Please just have the courtesy to tell me this."

It was irresistible. I stopped and turned.

"What is it, exactly, that stands in your way? I mean, are you able to tell me, do you actually know yourself what it is?"

For a moment I thought I wouldn't answer him — I wanted him to know that his faith laid no obligations on me. But then I changed my mind and said, "Nothing. Nothing's standing in my way."

He was coming toward me again, with his arms hanging loose at his side and with the palms turned up and the fingers spread in a little melodrama of the reasonable man perplexed. "Then why don't you take a chance on it?" he said through a worldly laugh. "You might see the point of it, the strength it can give you. Please, why don't you?"

Again, I hesitated and almost said nothing. But I decided he ought to know the truth. "Because, my friend, no one's listening. There's no one up there."

Parry's head was cocked, and the most joyous of smiles was spreading slowly across his face. I wondered if he had heard me right, because he looked as though I had just told him I was John the Baptist. It was then that I noticed over his shoulder two policemen climbing over a five-barred gate. As they ran across the field toward us, one of them used a hand to keep his hat in place, Keystone Kops style. They were coming to set in motion the official processing of John Logan's fate and, as I saw it, to deliver me from the radiating power of Jed Parry's love and pity.

Three

By six that evening we were back home, in our kitchen, and everything looked the same — the railway clock above the door, Clarissa's library of cookbooks, the flowery copperplate of a note left by the cleaning lady the day before. The unaltered array of my breakfast coffee cup and newspaper seemed blasphemous. While Clarissa carried her luggage into the bedroom, I cleared the table, opened the picnic wine, and set out two glasses. We sat facing each other and began.

We hadn't said much in the car. It had seemed enough to be coming through the traffic unharmed. Now it came out in a torrent, a postmortem, a reliving, a debriefing, the rehearsal of grief and the exorcism of terror. There was so much repetition that evening of the incidents, and of our perceptions, and of the very phrases and words we honed to accommodate them, that one could only assume that an element of ritual was in play, that these were not only descriptions but incantations also. There was comfort in reiteration, just as there was in the familiar weight of the wineglasses and in the grain of the deal table, which had once belonged to Clarissa's great-grandmother. There were smooth, shallow indentations in its surface near the knife-scarred edges, worn by elbows like ours, I always thought; many crises and deaths must already have been considered around this table.

Clarissa told the beginning of her story in a rush, of the swaying, blundering tangle of ropes and men, of the shouting and cursing, and of how she had gone forward to help but could not find a spare line to hang on to. Together we heaped curses on the pilot, James Gadd, and his incompetence, but this could not protect us for long from thoughts of all the things we should have done to avert Logan's death. We jumped forward to the moment he let go, as we did many other times that evening. I told her how he seemed to hang in the air before dropping, and she told me how a scrap of Milton had flashed before her: *Hurl'd headlong flaming from th'Ethereal Sky.* But we backed away from that moment again and again, circling it, stalking it, until we had it cornered and began to tame it with words. We went back to the struggle with the balloon and the ropes. I felt the sickness of guilt, something I couldn't yet bear to talk about. I showed Clarissa the rope burn on my hands. We had finished the Gassac in less than half an hour. Clarissa raised my hands to her lips and kissed my palms. I was looking in her eyes, that beautiful loving green, but the moment couldn't hold, we were not permitted that kind of peace. She winced as she cried out, "But, oh God, when he fell!" and I stood up hurriedly to reach for a bottle of Beaujolais from the rack.

We were back with the fall, and how long it had taken him to reach the ground, two seconds or three. Immediately we backed off into the peripheries: the police; the ambulance men, one of whom was not strong enough to hold his end of the stretcher carrying Greene and had to be helped across the field by Lacey; and the garage breakdown truck that had towed away Logan's car. We tried to imagine it, the delivery of this empty car to the home in Oxford where Mrs. Logan waited with her two children. But this was unbearable too, so we returned to our own stories. Along the narrative lines there were knots, tangles of horror that we could not look at the first time but could only touch before retreating, and then return. We were prisoners in a cell, running at the walls, beating them back with our heads. Slowly our prison grew larger.

Strange to recall that with Jed Parry we felt on safer ground. She told me how he had walked over to her and said his name and she had said hers. They hadn't shaken hands. Then he had turned and followed me down the hill. I told the prayer story as comedy and made Clarissa laugh. She locked her fingers into mine and squeezed. I wanted to tell her I loved her, but suddenly between us there sat the form of Logan, upright and still. I had to describe him. It was far worse in recollection than it had been at the time. Shock must have dulled my responses then. I began to tell her how his features appeared to hang in all the wrong places, and I broke off my description to tell her of the difference between then and now, and how a certain dream logic had made the unbearable quite ordinary, how I had thought nothing of carrying on a conversation with Parry while Logan sat shattered on the ground. And even as I was saying this it occurred to me that I was still avoiding Logan, that I had shied away from the description I had begun because I still could not absorb the facts, and I wanted to tell Clarissa this fact too. She watched me patiently as I spiraled into a regress of memory, emotion, and commentary. It wasn't that I couldn't find the words: I couldn't fit the speed of my thoughts. Clarissa pushed back her chair and came round my side of the table. She drew my head against her breasts. I shut up and closed my eyes. I caught in the fibers of her sweater the tang of the open air and imagined I saw the sky spread before me.

A little later we were back in our seats, leaning over the table like dedicated craftsmen at work, grinding the jagged edge of memories, hammering the unspeakable into forms of words, threading single perceptions into narrative, until Clarissa returned us to the fall, to the precise moment when Logan had slid down the rope, hung there one last precious second, and let go. This was what she had to get back to, the image to which her shock had attached itself. She said it all again, and repeated the lines from *Paradise Lost*. Then she told me that she too had willed deliverance, even as he was in midair. What had come to mind were angels — not Milton's reprobates hurled from heaven, but the embodiment of all goodness and justice in a golden figure swooping from the cloud base to gather the falling man in its arms. In that delirious thought-rich second it had seemed to her that Logan's fall was a challenge no angel could resist, and his death denied their existence. Did it need denying, I wanted to ask, but she was gripping my hand and saying, "He was a good man," with a sudden pleading note, as though I were about to condemn him. "The boy was in the basket, and Logan wouldn't let go. He had children of his own. He was a good man."

In her early twenties a routine surgical procedure had left Clarissa unable to bear children. She believed her medical notes had been confused with another woman's, but this was impossible to prove, and a long legal action foundered in delays and obstructions. Slowly she had buried the sadness, and built her life again, and ensured that children remained a part of it. Nephews, nieces, godchildren, the children of neighbors and old friends all adored her. She remembered all their birthdays and Christmases. We had a room in our flat, part nursery, part teenage den, where children or young adults sometimes stayed. Friends considered Clarissa to be successful and happy, and most of the time they were right. But occasionally something happened to stir the old sense of loss. Five years before the balloon accident, when we had lived together for two years, Marjorie, a good friend from her university days, had lost her four-week-old baby to a rare bacterial infection. Clarissa had been to Manchester to see the baby when it was five days old and had spent a week there helping to look after it. The news of the baby's death cut her down. I had never witnessed such disabling grief. Central to it was not so much the baby's fate as Marjorie's loss, which she experienced as her own. What was revealed was Clarissa's own mourning for a phantom child, willed into half-being by frustrated love. Marjorie's pain became Clarissa's. A few days later her defenses were back in place, and she dedicated herself to being as useful as she could to her old friend.

This was an extreme example. Other times, the unconceived child barely stirred before the moment passed. Now, in John Logan she saw a man prepared to die to prevent the kind of loss she felt herself to have sustained. The boy was not his own, but he was a father and he understood. His kind of love pierced Clarissa's defenses. With that pleading note — "He was a good man" — she was asking her own past, her ghost child, to forgive her.

The impossible idea was that Logan had died for nothing. The boy, Harry Gadd, turned out to be unharmed. I had let go of the rope. I had helped kill John Logan. But even as I felt the nausea of guilt return, I was trying to convince myself I was right to let go. If I hadn't, Logan and I might have dropped together, and Clarissa would have been sitting here alone tonight. We had heard from the police late in the afternoon that the boy had come down safely twelve miles to the west. Once he had realized he was on his own, he'd had to stir to save himself. No longer frightened by his grandfather's panic, he had taken control and done all the right things. He let the balloon rise high over the power lines and then released the gas valve to make a gentle descent onto a field by a village.

Clarissa had gone quiet. She was supporting her chin on her knuckles and staring down into the grain of the table. "Yes," I said finally. "He wanted to save that kid." She shook her head slowly, acknowledging some unspoken thought. I waited, content to escape my own feelings in order to help her with her own. She was aware of me watching her and glanced up. "It must mean something," she said dully.

I hesitated. I'd never liked this line of thinking. Logan's death was pointless — that was part of the reason we were in shock.

Good people sometimes suffered and died, not because their goodness was being tested but precisely because there was nothing, no one, to test it. No one but us. I was silent too long, for she added suddenly, "Don't worry, Joe. I'm not going weird on you. I mean, how do we begin to make sense of this?"

I said, "We tried to help and we failed."

She smiled and shook her head. I went and stood by her chair and put my arms around her and protectively kissed the top of her head. With a sigh she pressed her face against my shirt and looped her arms around my waist. Her voice was muffled. "You're such a dope. You're so rational sometimes you're like a child . . ."

Did she mean that rationality was a kind of innocence? I never found out, because her hands were working lightly across my buttocks toward my perineum. She caressed my balls and, keeping one hand there, loosened my belt, pulled my shirt clear, and kissed my belly. "I'll tell you one thing it means, dummkopf. We've seen something terrible together. It won't go away, and we have to help each other. And that means we'll have to love each other even harder."

Of course. Why didn't I think of this? Why didn't I think *like* this? We needed love. I had been trying to deny myself even the touch of her hand, assuming that affection was inappropriate, an indulgence, an irreverence in the face of death. Something we would come back to later, when all the talking and confronting was done. Clarissa had effected a shift to the essential. We went hand in hand into the bedroom. She sat on the edge of the bed and I undressed her. When I kissed her neck she pulled me toward her. "I don't mind what we do," she whispered. "We don't have to do anything. I just want to hold you." She got under the blankets and lay with her knees drawn up while I undressed. When I got in she put her arms around my neck and brought my face close to hers. She knew I was a fool for this kind of encirclement. It made me feel that I belonged, that I was rooted and blessed. I knew that she loved to close her eyes and let me kiss them, and then her nose and cheeks, as though she were a child at bedtime, and only at last find her lips.

We often told ourselves off for wasting time in chairs, fully dressed, talking, when we could be doing the same lying down in bed, face to face and naked. That precious time before lovemaking is ill served by the pseudo-clinical term *foreplay*. The world would narrow and deepen, our voices would sink into the warmth of our bodies, the conversation would become associative and unpredictable. Everything was touch and breath. Certain simple phrases came to me, which I didn't say out loud because they sounded so banal — *Here we are,* or *This again,* or *Yes, this.* Like a moment in a recurring dream, these spacious, innocent minutes were forgotten until we were back inside them. When we were, our lives returned to the essentials and began again. When we fell silent, we would lie so close we were mouth to mouth, delaying the union that bound us all the more because of this prelude.

So there we were, this again, and it was deliverance. The darkness beyond the gloom of the bedroom was infinite and cold as death. We were a pinprick of warmth in the vastness. The events of the afternoon filled us, but we banished them from conversation. I said, "How do you feel?"

"Scared," she said. "Really scared."

"But you don't look it."

"I feel I'm shivering inside."

Rather than follow the path that must lead us back to Logan, we told shivering and shaking stories, and as often happened in these talks, childhood was central. When Clarissa was seven, she went to Wales on a family holiday. One of her cousins, a girl of five, had gone missing on a rainy morning and six hours later had still not been found. The police came, bringing with them two tracker dogs. Villagers were out combing the bracken, and for a while a helicopter hovered above the higher ground. Just before nightfall the girl was found in a barn, asleep under some sacking. Clarissa remembered a general celebration in the rented farmhouse that evening. Her uncle, the girl's father, had just shown the last of the policemen to the door. As he came back into the room, his step faltered and he sat back heavily in an armchair. His legs were shaking violently, and the children watched in fascination as Clarissa's aunt knelt by him and pressed her palms soothingly along his thighs. "At the time I didn't connect it with the search for my cousin. It was just one of those odd things you observe neutrally as a child. I thought this might be what they meant by drunkenness, those two knees dancing up and down inside his trousers."

I told the story of my first public performance on the trumpet, when I was eleven. I was so nervous and my hands were shaking so badly that I could not keep the mouthpiece against my lips, nor could I stretch my lips in the proper way to make a note.

So I put the whole mouthpiece between my teeth and bit hard to hold it in place, and half sang, half tooted my part. In the general cacophony of a children's Christmas orchestra, nobody noticed. Clarissa said, "Even now you do a good imitation of a trumpet in the bath."

From shaking we came to dancing (I hate it, she loves it) and from there we came to love. We told each other what lovers never tire of hearing and needing to say. "I love you more now I've seen you go completely mad," she said. "The rationalist cracks at last!"

"It's just the beginning," I promised. "Stick around."

This reference to my behavior after Logan hit the ground broke the spell, but only for half a minute or so. We drew closer and kissed. What eventually followed was heightened by all the emotional rawness of a reconciliation, as though a calamitous week-long row with threats and insults were sweetly resolved in mutual forgiveness. We had nothing to forgive, unless, I suppose, we were absolving each other of the death, but those were the feelings that broke with each wave of sensation. A high price had been paid for this ecstasy, and I had to repel an image of a dark house in Oxford, isolated, as if set in a desert, where from an upstairs window two baffled children watched their mother's somber visitors arrive.

Afterward we fell asleep, and when we woke, after an hour or so, we were hungry. It was while we were back in the kitchen in our dressing gowns, raiding the fridge, that we discovered a need for company. Clarissa went to the phone. Emotional comfort, sex, home, wine, food, society — we wanted our whole world reasserted. Within half an hour we were sitting with our friends Tony and Anna Bruce, eating a Thai takeaway I had ordered and telling our story. We told it in the married style, running alone with it for a stretch, talking through the partner's interruption sometimes, at others giving way and handing over. There were also times when we talked at once, but for all that, our story was gaining in coherence; it had shape, and now it was spoken from a place of safety. I watched our friends' wary, intelligent faces droop at our tale. Their shock was a mere shadow of our own, resembling more the goodwilled imitation of that emotion, and for this reason it was a temptation to exaggerate, to throw a rope of superlatives across the abyss that divided experience from its representation by anecdote. Over the days and weeks, Clarissa and I told our story many times to friends, colleagues, and relatives. I found myself using the same phrases, the same adjectives in the same order. It became possible to recount the events without reliving them in the faintest degree, without even remembering them.

Tony and Anna left at one in the morning. When I came back from seeing them out, I noticed that Clarissa was glancing through some lecture notes. Of course, her sabbatical was over. Tomorrow was Monday and she was due to start teaching. I went into my study and looked at my diary, even though I knew precisely what was there: two meetings, and a piece to be finished by five. In a sense we were well defended against this catastrophe. We had each other, as well as numerous old friends. And we had the demands and absorption of interesting work. I stood in the light of my desk lamp staring at the half-dozen or so unanswered letters that lay in an untidy pile, and felt reassured by them.

We stayed up another half an hour talking, but only because we were too tired to set about going to bed. At two o'clock we managed it. The light had been out five minutes when the phone rang and snatched me from the beginnings of sleep.

I have no doubt that I remember his words correctly. He said, "Is that Joe?" I didn't reply. I had already recognized the voice. He said, "I just wanted you to know, I understand what you're feeling. I feel it too. I love you."

I hung up.

Clarissa murmured into the pillow, "Who was that?"

It may have been exhaustion, or perhaps my concealment was protective of her, but I know I made my first serious mistake when I turned on my side and said to her, "It was nothing. Wrong number. Go to sleep."

Four

Though we woke the next morning with these events still ringing in the air above our bed, the day with its blend of obligations was a balm to us. Clarissa left the house at eight-thirty to give an undergraduate seminar on Romantic poetry. She attended an administrative meeting in her department, had lunch with a colleague, marked term papers, and gave a supervisory hour to a postgraduate who was writing on Leigh Hunt. She came home at six, while I was still out. She made phone calls, took a shower, and went out to have supper with her brother, Luke, whose fifteen-year-old marriage was falling apart.

I had my shower at the beginning of the day. I took a flask of coffee into my study and for a quarter of an hour thought I might succumb to the freelancer's temptations — newspapers, phone calls, daydreams. I had plenty of subject matter for wall gazing. But I pulled myself together and made myself finish a piece about the Hubble telescope for an American magazine.

This project had interested me for years. It embodied an unfashionable heroism and grandeur, served no military or immediate commercial purpose, and was driven by a simple and noble urge: to know and understand more. When it was discovered that the eight-foot primary mirror was ten thousandths of an inch too flat, the general reaction down on Earth was not disappointment. It was glee and gloating, rejoicing and falling-about hilarity on a planetary scale. Ever since the *Titanic* sank we've been hard on our technicians, cynical about their extravagant ambitions. Here was our biggest toy in space so far, as tall, they said, as a four-story building, set to bring marvels to our retinas — images of the origins of the universe, our very own beginnings at the beginning of time. It had failed, not through some algorithmic arcana in the software but because of an error everybody could understand: short sight, the stuff of old-fashioned grind and polish. Hubble became the staple of TV stand-up routines, it rhymed with trouble and rubble, it proved America's terminal industrial decline.

Hubble was grand in conception, but the rescue operation was technologically sublime. Hundreds of space-walking hours, ten correcting mirrors placed around the rim of the faulty lens with inhuman precision, and down at control a Wagnerian-scale orchestra of scientists and computer power. Technically, it was more difficult than putting a man on the moon. The mistake was put right, the twelve-billion-year-old pictures came in true and sharp, the world forgot its scorn and marveled — for a day — then went about its business.

I worked without a break for two and a half hours. What bothered me that morning as I typed up my piece was a disquiet, a physical sensation I could not quite identify. There are certain mistakes that no quantity of astronauts can right. Like mine, yesterday. But what had I done, or not done? If it was guilt, where exactly did it begin? At the ropes under the balloon, letting go, afterward by the body, on the phone last night? The unease was on my skin and beyond. It was like the sensation of not having washed. But when I paused from my typing and thought the events through, guilt wasn't it at all. I shook my head and typed faster. I don't know how I was able to push back all thought of that late-night phone call. I managed to merge it with all the trouble of the day before. I suppose I was still in shock, I was trying to soothe myself by remaining busy.

I finished the piece, corrected it, printed it up, and faxed it to New York, five hours short of my deadline. I phoned the police station in Oxford, and after being transferred through three departments, I learned that there was to be an inquest into John Logan's death, that the coroner's court was likely to sit in six weeks' time, and that we were all expected to attend.

I took a taxi to Soho to meet a radio producer who showed me into his office and told me he wanted me to do a program on supermarket vegetables. I said they weren't my thing. Then the producer, whose name was Eric, surprised me by getting to his feet and making a passionate speech. He said that the demand for year-round snow peas, strawberries, and the like was wrecking the environments and local economies in various African countries. I said it was not my field, and I gave the names of some people he might try. And then, even though I barely knew him, or perhaps because of that, I returned the passion and gave him the full story. I couldn't help myself. I had to be saying it to someone. Eric listened patiently, making appropriate sounds and shakes of his head but looking at me as though I were contaminated, the bearer into his office of a freshly mutated virus of ill fortune. I could have broken off, or made an artificial ending. I pressed on because I couldn't stop. I was telling it for myself, and a goldfish would have served me as well as a producer. When I had done, he said his goodbyes hurriedly — he had another meeting, he'd be in touch with another idea for me — and as I stepped out into the filth of Meard Street I felt tainted. The unnamed sensation returned, this time in the form of a pricking along my nape and a rawness in my gut, which resolved itself, for the third time that day, into an unreliable urge to crap.

I spent the afternoon in the reading room of the London Library, looking up some of Darwin's more obscure contemporaries. I wanted to write about the death of anecdote and narrative in science, my idea being that Darwin's generation was the last to permit itself the luxury of storytelling in published articles. Here was a letter to *Nature* dated 1904, a contribution to a long-running correspondence about consciousness in animals, in particular whether higher mammals like dogs could be said to have awareness of the consequences of their actions. The writer, one Mr. —, had a close friend whose dog favored a particular comfortable chair near the library fire. Mr. — witnessed an occasion after dinner when he and his friend had retired there for a glass of port. The dog was shooed from its chair and the master sat down in its place. After a minute or two sitting in contemplative silence by the fire, the dog went to the door and whined to be let out. Its master obligingly rose and crossed the room, whereupon the pooch darted back and took possession once more of the favored place. For a few seconds it wore about its muzzle a look of undisguised triumph.

The writer concluded that the dog must have had a plan, a sense of the future, which it attempted to shape by the practice of a deliberate deceit. And its pleasure in success must have been mediated by an act of memory. What I liked here was how the power and attractions of narrative had clouded judgment. By any standards of scientific inquiry, the story, however charming, was nonsense. No theory evinced, no terms defined, a meaningless sample of one, a laughable anthropomorphism. It was easy to construe the account in a way that would make it compatible with an automaton, or a creature doomed to inhabit a perpetual present: ousted from its chair, it takes the next best place, by the fire, where it basks (rather than schemes) until it becomes aware of a need to urinate, then goes to the door as it has been trained to do, suddenly notices that the prized position is vacant again, forgets for the moment the signal from its bladder, and returns to take possession, the look of triumph being nothing more than the immediate expression of pleasure, or a projection in the mind of the observer.

I myself was comfortable within a large, smooth-armed leather chair. In my line of vision were three other members, each with a book or magazine on his lap, and all three asleep. Outside, the raucous traffic in St. James's Square, even the dispatch motorbikes, was soporific in the way that other people's frantic motion can be. Indoors, the murmur of water along unseen ancient pipes and, nearer, a creaking of floorboards as someone, invisible behind the magazine rack, moved a couple of paces, paused for a minute or two, and then moved again. This sound, I realized in retrospect, had been perched on the outer edges of my awareness for almost half an hour. I wondered if I could reasonably ask this person to keep still, or suggest he take a pile of magazines and go and sit in silence. My tormentor stirred — four leisurely squeaking steps, and then there was peace. I tried to continue with Mr. — and the mental capacity of dogs, but now I was distracted. When there was movement across the room, I made a point of not looking up from my page, even though I was taking nothing in. Then I gave way, and all I saw was a flash of a white shoe and something red and the closing of the sighing swing doors that led out of the reading room onto the stairs.

Now that the restless time-waster had left, I transferred my irritation to the management. The building was notorious for its noise, above all the buzzing fluorescent lighting in the stacks, which no one could fix. Perhaps I'd be happier at the Wellcome library. The science collection here was laughable. The assumption appeared to be that the world could be sufficiently understood through fictions, histories, and biographies. Did the scientific illiterates who ran this place, and who dared call themselves educated people, really believe that literature was the greatest intellectual achievement of our civilization?

This inner rant may have lasted for as long as two minutes. I was enclosed by it, invisible to myself. I came to by the simple assertion of a self-consciousness that even Mr. — could not have claimed for his friend's dog. It was, of course, not a squeaking floorboard or the library management that agitated me. It was my emotional condition, the mental-visceral state I had yet to understand. I sat back in my chair and gathered my notes. At that stage I still had not grasped the promptings of footwear and color. I stared at the page on my lap. The last words I had written before losing control of my thoughts had been "intentionality, intention, tries to assert control over the future." These words referred to a dog when I wrote them, but rereading them now, I began to fret. I couldn't find the word for what I felt. Unclean, contaminated, crazy, physical but somehow moral. It is clearly not true that without language there is no thought. I possessed a thought, a feeling, a sensation, and I was looking for its word. As guilt was to the past, so, what was it that stood in the same relation to the future? Intention? No, not influence over the future. Foreboding. Anxiety about, distaste for the future. Guilt and foreboding, bound by a line from past to future, pivoting in the present — the only moment it could be experienced. It wasn't fear, exactly. Fear was too focused, it had an object. Dread was too strong. Fear of the future. Apprehension, then. Yes, there it was, approximately. It was apprehension.

In front of me the three sleepers did not stir. The swing doors had moved in diminishing pendulum movement, and now there was nothing but molecular reverberation, one step up from the imaginary. Who was the person who had just left? Why so suddenly? I stood up. It was apprehension, then. All day long I had been in this state. It was simple, it was a form of fear. A fear of outcomes. All day I'd been afraid. Was I so obtuse, not to know fear from the start? Wasn't it an elemental emotion, along with disgust, surprise, anger, and elation, in Ekman's celebrated cross-cultural study? Was not fear and the recognition of it in others associated with neural activity in the amygdala, sunk deep in the old mammalian part of our brains, from where it fired its instant responses? But my own response had not been instant. My fear had held a mask to its face. Pollution, confusion, gabbling. I was afraid of my fear, because I did not yet know the cause. I was scared of what it would do to me and what it would make me do. And I could not stop looking at the door.

It may have been an illusion caused by visual persistence, or a neurally tripped delay of perception, but it seemed to me that I was still slumped in my smooth leather chair staring at that door even while I was moving toward it. I took the broad red carpeted stairs two at a time, swung myself on the newel post round the half-landing, took the final flight in three strides, and burst into the clerkly, predigital calm of the booking and catalogue hall. I dodged past fellow members, past the suggestion book and the schoolboyish tangle of satchels and coats, through the main door, and out into the street. St. James's Square was gridlocked, and empty of pedestrians. I was looking for a pair of white shoes, trainers with red laces. I threaded quickly among the jammed vehicles throbbing patiently. I knew exactly where I myself would have stood to keep the library doors covered: on the northeastern corner across from the old Libyan Embassy. As I went, I glanced to my left up Duke of York Street. The pavements were empty, the streets were full. Cars were our citizens now. I reached the corner, by the railings. There was no one, not even a drunk in the park. I stood there awhile, looking about me and getting my breath. I was right on the spot where the policewoman Yvonne Fletcher had been shot dead by a Libyan from a window across the road. At my feet was a little bunch of marigolds tied with wool, such as a child might bring.

The jam jar they had arrived in had been knocked over and had a little water inside. Still glancing about me, I knelt and returned the flowers to the jar. I couldn't help feeling as I pushed the jar closer to the railings, where it might escape being kicked over again, that it might bring me luck, or rather protection, and that on such hopeful acts of propitiation, fending off mad, wild, unpredictable forces, whole religions were founded, whole systems of thought unfurled.

Then I went back indoors to the reading room.

Five

I had a second meeting that day — I was on a jury judging a science book prize — and by the time I got home Clarissa had left to meet her brother. I needed to talk to her. The effort of appearing sane and judicious for three hours had rather unhinged me. In our comfortable, almost tasteful apartment, the familiar mass and tone of the rooms looked tighter, and somehow dusty. I made a gin and tonic and drank it by the answering machine. The last of the messages was a breathless pause followed by the rattle of a receiver being replaced. I had to talk to Clarissa about Parry. I had to tell her about his call the night before and how he had followed me into the library, and about this discomfort, this apprehension I had. I thought of going to find her in the restaurant, but I knew that by now her adulterous brother would have begun the relentless plainsong of the divorce novitiate — the pained self-advocacy that hymns the trans-mutations of love into hatred or indifference. Clarissa, who was fond of her sister-in-law, would be listening in shock.

To calm myself I turned to that evening clinic of referred pain, the TV news. Tonight, a mass grave in a wood in central Bosnia, a cancerous government minister with a love nest, the second day of a murder trial. What soothed me was the format's familiarity: the war-beat music, the smooth and urgent tones of the presenter, the easeful truth that all misery was relative, then the final opiate, the weather. I returned to the kitchen to mix a second drink and sat with it at the kitchen table. If Parry had been trailing me all day, then he knew where I lived. If he hadn't, then my mental state was very frail. But it wasn't, fundamentally, and he had, and I had to think this through. I could put down his late-night call to stress and solitary drinking, but not if he had been following me about today. And I knew he had, because I had seen the white of his trainer and its red lace. Unless — and the habit of skepticism was proof of my sanity — unless the redness was imagined, or visually conflated. The library carpet, after all, was red. But I had seen the color woven into the glimpse of shoe. I had sensed him behind me even before I saw him. The unreliability of such intuition I was prepared to concede. But it was him. Like many people living a safe life, I immediately imagined the worst. What reason had I given him for murdering me? Did he think I had mocked his faith? Perhaps he had phoned again . . .

I picked up the cordless and dialed last number recall. The computerized female voice intoned an unfamiliar London number. I called it and listened and shook my head. However reasonable my suspicions, confirmation was still a surprise. Parry's machine said, "Please leave your message after the tone. And may the Lord be with you." It was him, and it was two sentences. That his faith should have such reach, into the shallows of his answering machine, into the angles of his prose. What had he meant when he said he felt it too? What did he want?

I looked toward the gin and decided against. A more immediate problem was how to spend the evening until Clarissa's return. If I didn't make conscious choices now, I knew I would brood and drink. I didn't want to see friends, I had no need of entertainment, I wasn't even hungry. Voids like these were familiar, and the only way across them was work. I went into my study, turned on the lights and the computer, and spread out my library notes. It was eight-fifteen. In three hours I could break the back of my piece on narrative in science. I already had the outlines of a theory — not one that I believed in, necessarily, but I could hang my piece around it. Propose it, evince the evidence, consider the objections, reassert it in conclusion. A narrative in itself — a little tired, perhaps, but it had served a thousand journalists before me.

Working was an evasion; I didn't even doubt it at the time. I had no answers to my questions, and thinking would get me no further. My guess was that Clarissa would not be back before midnight, so I abandoned myself to my serious, flimsy argument. Within twenty minutes I had drifted into the desired state, the high-walled infinite prison of directed thought. It doesn't always happen to me, and I was grateful that night. I didn't have to defend myself against the usual flotsam — the scraps of recent memory, the tokens of things not done or ghostly wrecks of sexual longing. My beach was clean. I didn't trick myself from my chair with promises of coffee, and despite the tonic I had no need to urinate.

It was the nineteenth-century culture of

the amateur that nourished the anecdotal scientist. All those gentlemen without careers, those parsons with time to burn. Darwin himself, in pre-*Beagle* days, dreamed of a country living where he could pursue in peace his collector's passion, and even in the life that genius and chance got him, Downe House was more parsonage than laboratory. The dominant artistic form was the novel, great sprawling narratives that not only charted private fates but made whole societies in mirror image and addressed the public issues of the day. Most educated people read contemporary novels. Storytelling was deep in the nineteenth-century soul.

Then two things happened. Science became more difficult, and it became professionalized. It moved into the universities; parsonical narratives gave way to hard-edged theories that could survive intact without experimental support and that had their own formal aesthetic. At the same time, in literature and in other arts, a new-fangled modernism celebrated formal, structural qualities, inner coherence, and self-reference. A priesthood guarded the temples of this difficult art against the trespasses of the common man.

Likewise in science. In physics, say, a

small elite of European and American initiates accepted and acclaimed Einstein's General Theory long before the confirming observational data were in. The Theory, which Einstein presented to the world in 1915 and '16, made the proposition, offensive to common sense, that gravitation was simply an effect caused by the curvature of space-time wrought by matter and energy. It was predicted that light would be deflected by the gravitational field of the sun. An expedition had already been mounted to the Crimea to observe an eclipse in 1914 to test this out, but the war intervened. Another expedition set out in 1919 to two remote islands in the Atlantic. Confirmation was flashed around the world, but inaccurate or inconvenient data were overlooked in the desire to embrace the theory. More expeditions set out to observe eclipses and check Einstein's predictions, in 1922 in Australia, in '29 in Sumatra, in '36 in the USSR, and in '47 in Brazil. Not until the development of radio astronomy in the fifties was there incontrovertible experimental verification, but essentially these years of practical striving were irrelevant. The theory was already in the textbooks, from the twenties onward. Its integral power was so great, it was too beautiful to resist.

So the meanderings of narrative had given way to an aesthetics of form; as in art, so in science. I typed on into the evening. I had spent too much time on Einstein, and I was casting about for another example of a theory accepted for reasons of its elegance. The less confident I became about this argument, the faster I typed. I found a kind of inverted argument from my own past: quantum electrodynamics. This time round there was a mass of experimental verification on hand for this set of ideas about electrons and light, but the theory, especially as propounded by Dirac in its original form, was slow to gain general acceptance. There were inconsistencies, there was lopsidedness. In short, the theory was unattractive, inelegant, it was a song sung out of tune. Acceptance withheld on grounds of ugliness.

I had been working for three hours and I had written two thousand words. I could have done with a third example, but my energy was beginning to fail. I printed out the pages and stared at them in my lap, astonished that such puny reasoning, such forced examples, could have held my attention for so long. Counterarguments welled from between the neat lines of text. What possible evidence could I produce to suggest that the novels of Dickens, Scott, Trollope,

Thackeray, etc., had ever influenced by a comma the presentation of a scientific idea? Moreover, my examples were fabulously skewed. I had compared life sciences in the nineteenth century (the scheming dog in the library) to hard sciences in the twentieth. In the annals of Victorian physics and chemistry alone there was no end of brilliant theory that displayed not a shred of narrative inclination. And what, in fact, were the typical products of the twentieth-century scientific or pseudo-scientific mind? Anthropology, psychoanalysis — fabulation run riot. Using the highest methods of storytelling and all the arts of priesthood, Freud had staked his claim on the veracity, though not the falsifiability, of science. And what of those behaviorists and sociologists of the 1920s? It was as though an army of white-coated Balzacs had stormed the university departments and labs.

I fixed my twelve pages with a paper clip and balanced their weight in my hand. What I had written wasn't true. It wasn't written in pursuit of truth, it wasn't science. It was journalism, magazine journalism, whose ultimate standard was readability. I wagged the pages in my hand, trying to devise further consolations. I had usefully distracted myself, I could make a separate coherent piece out of the counterarguments (the twentieth century saw the summation of narrative in science, etc.), and anyway, it was a first draft, which I would rewrite in a week or so. I tossed the pages onto the desk, and as they landed I heard, for the second time that day, the creak of a floorboard behind me. There was someone at my back.

The primitive, so-called sympathetic nervous system is a wondrous thing we share with all other species that owe their continued existence to being quick on the turn, fast and hard into battle, or fiery in flight. Evolution has culled us all into this efficiency. Nerve terminals buried deep in the tissue of the heart secrete their noradrenaline, and the heart lurches into accelerated pumping. More oxygen, more glucose, more energy, quicker thinking, stronger limbs. It's a system so ancient, developed so far back along the branchings of our mammalian and premammalian past, that its operations never penetrate into higher consciousness. There wouldn't be time anyway, and it wouldn't be efficient. We only get the effects. That shot to the heart appears to occur simultaneously with the perception of threat: even as the visual or auditory cortex is sorting and resolving into awareness what fell upon eye or ear, those potent droplets are falling.

My heart had made its first terrifying cold pop even before I started to turn and rise from my chair and raise my hands, ready to defend myself, or even to attack. I would guess that modern humans, with no natural predators but themselves and with all their toys and mental constructs and cosy rooms, are relatively easy to creep up on. Squirrels and thrushes can only look down on us and smile.

What I saw coming toward me rapidly across the room, with arms outstretched like a cartoon sleepwalker, was Clarissa, and who knows by what complex intervention of higher centers I was able to convert plausibly my motions of primitive terror into a tenderly given and received embrace and to feel, as her arms locked round my neck, a pang of love that was in truth inseparable from relief.

"Oh Joe," she said, "I've missed you all day, and I love you, and I've had such a terrible evening with Luke. And oh God, I love you."

And oh God, I loved her. However much I thought about Clarissa, in memory or in anticipation, experiencing her again — the feel and sound of her, the precise quality of love that ran between us, the very animal presence — always brought, along with the familiarity, a jolt of surprise. Perhaps such amnesia is functional — those who could not wrench their hearts and minds from their loved ones were doomed to fail in life's struggles and left no genetic footprints. We stood in the center of my study, Clarissa and I, on the yellow diamond at the middle of the Bokhara rug, kissing and embracing, and I heard through and between kisses the first fragments of her brother's folly. Luke was leaving his kindly, beautiful wife and bonny twin daughters and Queen Anne house in Islington to live with an actress he had met three months before. Here was amnesia on a grander scale. He was considering, he had said over the seared scallops, quitting his job and writing a play, a monologue in fact, a one-woman show, which stood a chance of being put on in a room over a hairdresser's in Kensal Green.

"Before we go to Paradise," I began, and Clarissa finished, "By way of Kensal Green."

"Reckless courage," I said. "He must be living inside a hard-on."

"Courage to shite!" She drew her breath sharply and shot me a beam of angry green. "An actress! He's living inside a cliché!"

For a second I had become her brother. In recognition of that she drew me close again and kissed me. "Joe. I've wanted you all day. After yesterday, and last night . . ."

Still hanging on to each other, we walked from study to bedroom. While Clarissa continued to tell me more tales from the ruined household and I described the piece I had written, we made preparations for our night journey into sex and sleep. I had already traveled some distance that evening from the time I had come in and had wanted only to talk to Clarissa about Parry. Work had settled on me a veil of abstracted contentment, and her arrival home, for all the sad story, had restored me completely. I felt frightened of nothing. Would it have been right, then, as we lay down face to face as we had the night before, to intrude on our happiness with an account of Parry's phone call? Given what we had witnessed the day before, could I have destroyed our tenderness with fretful suspicions of being followed? The lights were dimmed; soon they would be out. John Logan's ghost was still in the room, but it no longer threatened us. Parry was for tomorrow. All urgency had gone. With closed eyes I traced in double darkness Clarissa's beautiful lips. She bit down on my knuckle, playfully hard. There

are times when fatigue is the great aphro-
disiac, annihilating all other thoughts, grant-
ing sensuous slow motion to heavy limbs,
urging generosity, acceptance, infinite aban-
donment. We tumbled out of our respective
days like creatures shaken from a net.

By our bedside in the dark, the phone
remained silent. I'd unplugged it many
hours before.

Six

There was a time this century when ships, white oceangoing liners such as luxuriously plowed the Atlantic swell between London and New York, became the inspiration for a form of domestic architecture. In the twenties something resembling the *Queen Mary* ran aground in Maida Vale, and all that remains now is the bridge, our apartment building. It gleams a peeling white among the plane trees. Its corners are rounded; there are portholes in the lavatories and lighting the shallow spirals of the stairwells. The steel-framed windows are low and oblong, strengthened against the squalls of urban life. The floors are oak parquet and could accommodate any number of jazzy quick-stepping couples.

The two apartments on the top have the advantage of several skylights and one and a half twists of an iron staircase that leads onto a flat roof. Our neighbors, a successful architect and his boyfriend, who keeps house, have made a fantasy garden in their portion, with clematis severely wound round poles and austere spiky leaves poking between large smooth stones collected from a riverbed and retained, Japanese style, in open black wooden boxes.

In the frenetic month after moving in, Clarissa and I exhausted our small reserve of decorating and nesting energies on the apartment itself, so there's nothing on our side of the roof apart from a plastic table and four plastic chairs, bolted down in case of high winds. Here you can sit among the TV aerials and dishes, the roofing pitch underfoot wrinkled and dusty like an elephant's hide, and look toward the greenery of Hyde Park and hear the tranquillizing thunder of West London's traffic. From the other side of the table you have the best possible view of our neighbors' shrine to orderly growth, and beyond, the dusky roofs of the infinite northward suburbs. This was where I sat the following morning at seven. I had left Clarissa sleeping and brought with me my coffee, the paper, and my pages from the night before.

But instead of reading myself or others, I thought about John Logan and how we had killed him. Yesterday the events of the day before had dimmed. This morning the blustery sunshine illumined and animated the whole tableau. I could feel the rope in my hands again as I examined the welts. I made calculations. If Gadd had stayed in the basket with his grandson, and if the rest of us had hung on, and if we assumed an average weight of a hundred and sixty pounds each, then surely eight hundred pounds would have kept us close to the ground. If the first person had not let go, then surely the rest of us would have stayed in place. And who was this first person? Not me. Not me. I even said the words aloud. I remembered a plummeting mass and the sudden upward jerk of the balloon. But I could not tell whether this mass was in front of me or to my left or right. If I knew the position, I would know the person.

Could this person be blamed? As I drank my coffee, the rush hour below began its slow crescendo. It was hard to think this through. Phrases, well worn and counterweighted, occurred to me, resolving nothing. On the one hand, the first pebble in an avalanche, and on the other, the breaking of ranks. The cause, but not the morally responsible agent. The scales tipping, from altruism to self-interest. Was it panic, or rational calculation? Had we killed him really, or simply refused to die with him? But if we had been with him, stayed with him, no one would have died.

Another question was whether I should visit Mrs. Logan and tell her what happened. She deserved to know from a witness that her husband was a hero. I saw us sitting face to face on wooden stools. She was draped in black, in pantomime widow's weeds, and we were in a prison cell with a high-barred window. Her two children stood close by her side, clinging to her knees, refusing to meet my eye. My cell, my guilt? The image came to me from a half-forgotten painting in the late Victorian narrative style, in the idiom of "And when did you last see your father?" Narrative — my gut tightened at the word. What balls I had written the night before. How was it possible to tell Mrs. Logan of her husband's sacrifice without drawing her attention to our own cowardice? Or was it his folly? He was the hero, and it was the weak who had sent him to his death. Or we were the survivors and he was the miscalculating dolt.

I was so lost in this that I did not notice Clarissa until she sat down on the other side of the table. She smiled and mouthed a kiss. She warmed her hands around a coffee mug.

"Are you thinking about it?"

I nodded. Before her kindness and our love got the better of me, I had to tell her.

"Do you remember, the day it happened, just as we were falling asleep the phone rang?"

"Mmm. Wrong number."

"It was that guy with the ponytail. You know, the one who wanted me to pray. Jed Parry."

She frowned. "Why didn't you say? What did he want?"

I didn't pause. "He said he loved me."

For a fraction of time the world froze as she took this in. Then she laughed. Easily, merrily.

"Joe! You didn't tell me. You were embarrassed? You clot!"

"It was just one more thing. And then I felt bad about not telling you, so it got harder. And then I didn't want to interrupt last night."

"What did he say? Just 'I love you,' like that?"

"Yeah. He said, 'I feel it too. I love you . . .'"

Clarissa put her hand over her mouth, little-girl style. I hadn't expected delight. "A secret gay love affair with a Jesus freak! I can't wait to tell your science friends."

"All right, all right." But I felt lightened to have her teasing me. "There's more, though."

"You're getting married."

"Listen. Yesterday he was following me."

"My God. He's got it bad."

I knew I had to prise her from this levity, for all the comfort it gave. "Clarissa, it's scary." I told her about the presence in the library and how I had run out into the square. She interrupted me.

"But you didn't actually see him in the library."

"I saw his shoe as he went out the door. White trainers with red laces. It had to be him."

"But you didn't see his face."

"Clarissa, it was him!"

"Don't get angry with me, Joe. You didn't see his face, and he wasn't in the square."

"No. He'd gone."

She was looking at me in a new way now and was moving through the conversation with the caution of a bomb disposal expert. "Let me get this straight. You had this idea you were being followed even before you saw his shoe?"

"It was just a feeling, a bad feeling. It wasn't until I was in the library with time to think about it that I realized how it was getting to me."

"And then you saw him."

"Yeah. His shoe."

She glanced at her watch and took a pull from her mug. She was going to be late for work.

"You should go," I said. "We can talk this evening."

She nodded, but she did not rise. "I don't really understand what's upsetting you. Some poor fellow has a crush on you and is trailing you about. Come on, it's a joke, Joe! It's a funny story you'll be telling your friends. At worst it's a nuisance. You mustn't let it get to you."

I felt a childish pang of sorrow when she got to her feet. I liked what she was saying. I wanted to hear it again in different ways. She came round to my side of the table and kissed me on the head. "You're working too hard. Go easy on yourself. And remember that I love you. I *love* you." We kissed again, deeply.

I followed her downstairs and watched as she prepared to leave. Perhaps it was the worried smile she gave me as she bustled past to pack her briefcase, perhaps it was the solicitous way she told me she would be back at seven and would phone me during the day, but standing there on the polished dance-floor parquet I felt like a mental patient at the end of visiting hours. *Don't leave me here with my mind,* I thought. *Get them to let me out.* She put on her coat, opened the front door, and was about to speak to me, but the words never left her. She had remembered a book she needed. While she was fetching it, I lingered by the door. I knew what I wanted to say, and perhaps there was still time. This wasn't "some poor fellow." It was a man bound to me, like the farm laborers, by an experience, and by a shared responsibility for, or at the very least a shared involvement in, another man's death. This was also a man who wanted me to pray with him. Perhaps he felt insulted. Perhaps he was some kind of vengeful fanatic.

Clarissa was back with her book, stuffing it into her briefcase while she held some papers between her teeth. She was halfway out the door. When I started to say my piece, she set the case down to free her hands and mouth. "I can't, Joe, I can't. I'm already late. It's a lecture." She hesitated, agonizing. Then she said, "Go on, tell it to me quick." Just then the phone rang, and I was relieved. I had thought she was giving a supervision, not a lecture, and letting her off the hook would have wasted even more of her time.

"I'll get it, you go," I said cheerily. "I'll tell you this evening."

She blew me a kiss and was gone. I heard her footsteps on the stairs as I reached the phone. "Joe?" said the voice. "It's Jed."

It was perverse of me to be surprised and, for a moment, speechless. He had phoned the day before, after all, and he was on my lips, on my mind. On my mind to such an extent that I had forgotten that he was also out there, a physical entity capable of operating the phone system.

He had paused after his name; now he spoke into my silence. "You phoned me." We all had last number recall. The telephone was not what it was. Pitiless ingenuity was making it needlingly personal.

"What do you want?" Even as I said the words, I wanted them back. I did not want to know what he wanted, or rather, I did not want to be told. It was not really a question anyway, more a gesture of hostility. So too was "And who gave you my number?"

Parry sounded pleased. "That's quite a story, Joe. I went to the —"

"I don't want your story. I don't want you phoning me." I almost said, "Or following me," but something held me back.

"We need to talk."

"I don't."

I heard Parry's intake of breath. "I think

you do. At least, I think you need to listen."

"I'm going to hang up. If I hear from you again, I'm calling the police."

The phrase sounded fatuous, the sort of meaningless thing people say, like "I'll sue the bastards." I knew the local station. They were hard pressed down there, and they had their priorities. This was the sort of thing the citizenry was supposed to sort out for itself.

Parry spoke immediately into my threat. His voice was pitched higher and his words came faster. He had to get this out before I cut him off. "Look, I'm making you a promise. Just see me this once, just once and hear me out and you'll never have to hear from me again. That's a promise, a solemn promise."

Solemn. More like panicky. I calculated: perhaps I should see him, let him see me and let him understand that I was distinct from the creature of his fantasy world. Let him speak. The alternative was more of this. Perhaps I could muster a little detached curiosity. When this story was closed, it would be important to know something about Parry. Otherwise he would remain as much a projection of mine as I was of his. It crossed my mind to make him bring down his god to underwrite his solemn promise.

But I did not want to provoke him.

I said, "Where are you?"

He hesitated. "I can come to you."

"No. Tell me where you are."

"I'm in the phone box at the end of your road?"

He said it, he asked it, without shame. I was shocked, but determined to conceal it. "Okay," I said. "I'll be along." I hung up, put on my coat, took my keys, and left the apartment. It was a comfort to discover that Clarissa's scent, Diorissimo, still hung in the air on the stairs, all the way down.

Seven

Outside our apartment building, running straight on rising ground, was an avenue of plane trees just coming into leaf. As soon as I stepped out onto the pavement I saw Parry standing under a tree at the corner, a hundred yards away. When he saw me he took his hands out of his pockets, folded his arms, then let them droop. He began to come toward me, changed his mind, and went back to his tree. I walked toward him slowly and felt my anxiety dropping away.

As I went closer Parry retreated further under his tree, leaned back against its trunk, and tried to look nonchalant by hooking a thumb into his trouser pocket. In fact he looked abject. He appeared smaller, all knobs and bones, no longer the sleek Indian brave, despite the ponytail. He wouldn't meet my eye as I came up, or rather his eyes made a nervous pass across my face and then turned down. As I put out my hand, I was feeling quite relieved. Clarissa was right: he was a harmless fellow with a strange notion, a nuisance at most, hardly the threat I had made him out to be. He looked a sorry sight now, cringing under the fresh plane leaves. It was the accident and the afterwaves of shock that had distorted my understanding. I had translated farce into indefinable menace. His hand, when it shook mine, exerted no pressure. I spoke to him firmly, but with a little kindness too. He was just about young enough to be my son. "You'd better tell me what this is all about."

He said, "There's a coffee place . . ." and he nodded in the direction of the Edgware Road.

"We'll be fine right here," I said. "I don't have a lot of time."

The wind had got up again and seemed sharpened by the thin sunlight. I drew my coat around me and tightened its belt, and as I did so I glanced at Parry's shoes. No trainers today. Soft brown leather shoes, handmade perhaps. I went and leaned against a nearby wall and folded my arms.

Parry came away from the tree and stood in front of me, staring at his feet. "I'd rather we went inside," he said, with a hint of a whine.

I said nothing and waited. He sighed and looked down the street to where I lived, and then his gaze tracked a passing car. He looked up at the piles of towering cumulus, and he examined the nails of his right hand, but he could not look at me. When he spoke at last, I think his sight line was on a crack in the pavement.

"Something's happened," he said.

He wasn't going to continue, so I said, "What's happened?"

He breathed in deeply through his nose. He still would not look at me. "You know what it is," he said sulkily.

I tried to help him. "Are we talking about the accident?"

"You know what it is, but you want me to say it."

I said, "I think you'd better. I have to go soon."

"It's all about control, isn't it?" He had flashed a look of adolescent defiance at me and now his gaze was down again. "It's so stupid to play games. Why don't you just say it? There's nothing to be ashamed of."

I looked at my watch. This was my best time of day for work, and I had yet to get into central London to collect a book. An empty taxi was coming toward us. Parry saw it too.

"You think you're being cool about this, but it's ridiculous. You won't be able to keep it up, and you know it. Everything's changed now. Please don't put on this act. Please . . ."

We watched the taxi go past. I said, "You asked me to meet you because you had something to say."

"You're very cruel," he said. "But you've got all the power." He inhaled deeply through his nose again, as though preparing himself for some difficult circus feat. He managed to look at me as he said simply, "You love me. You love me, and there's nothing I can do but return your love."

I said nothing. Parry drew another deep breath. "I don't know why you've chosen me. All I know is that I love you too now, and that there's a reason for it, a purpose."

An ambulance with a whooping siren went by and we had to wait. I was wondering how to respond, and whether a show of anger might see him off, but in the few seconds that it took for the din to recede I decided to be firm and reasonable. "Look, Mr. Parry —"

"Jed," he said urgently. "It's Jed." His interrogative style had deserted him.

I said, "I don't know you, I don't know where you live or what you do or who you are. I don't particularly want to know, either. I've met you once before, and I can

105

tell you now that I have no feelings for you either way —"

Parry was speaking over me in a series of gasps. He was pushing his hands out before him, as though to repel my words. "Please don't do this . . . It doesn't have to be this way, honestly. You don't have to do this to me."

We both paused suddenly. I wondered whether to leave him now and walk up the road to find a taxi. Perhaps talking was making matters worse.

Parry crossed his arms and adopted a worldly, man-to-man tone. I thought perhaps I was being parodied. "Look. You don't have to go about it like this. You could save us both so much misery."

I said, "You were following me yesterday, weren't you?"

He looked away and said nothing, which I took as confirmation.

"What possible reason would you have for thinking I love you?" I tried to make the question sound sincere and not merely rhetorical. I was quite interested to know, although I also wanted to get away.

"Don't," Parry said in a whisper. "Please don't." His lower lip was trembling.

But I pressed on. "As I remember it, we spoke at the bottom of the hill. I can understand if you felt strange after the accident. I certainly did."

At this point, to my great surprise, Parry put his hands over his face and started to cry. He was also trying to say something, which I could not hear at first. Then I made it out. "Why? Why? Why?" he kept on saying. And then, when he had recovered a little, he said, "What have I done to you? Why are you keeping this up?" The question made him cry again. I moved from the wall where I had been standing and walked a few paces away from him. He stumbled after me, trying to regain his voice. "I can't control my feelings the way you can," he said. "I know this gives you power over me, but there's nothing I can do about it."

"Believe me, I have no feelings to control," I said.

He was watching my face with a kind of hunger, a desperation. "If it's a joke, it's time to stop. It's doing us both damage."

"Look," I said. "I've got to go now. I don't expect to hear from you again."

"Oh God," he wailed. "You say that, and then you make that face. What is it you *really* want me to do?"

I was feeling suffocated. I turned and walked away quickly toward the Edgware Road. I heard him come running up behind me. Then he was plucking at my sleeve and trying to take my arm. "Please, please," he said in a gabble. "You can't leave it like that. Tell me something, give me one little thing. The truth, or just a part of the truth. Just say that you're torturing me. I won't ask the reason. But please tell me that's what you're doing."

I pulled my arm away and stopped. "I don't know who you are. I don't understand what you want, and I don't care. Now, will you leave me alone?"

Suddenly he was bitter. "Very funny," he said. "You're not even trying to be convincing. That's what's so insulting about it."

He put his hands on his hips, and for the first time I found myself calculating the physical danger he presented. I was bigger, and I still worked out, but I've never hit anyone in my life and he was twenty years younger, with big jointed knuckles and a desperate cause, whatever it was. I straightened my back to make myself taller.

"It hadn't occurred to me to insult you," I said. "Until now."

Parry moved his hands from his hips and presented his open palms. What was so exhausting about him was the variety of his emotional states and the speed of their transitions. Reasonableness, tears, desperation, vague threat — and now honest supplication. "Joe, please, look at me, remember who I am, remember what moved you in the first place."

The whites of his eyes were exceptionally clear. He held my stare for a second before looking away. I was beginning to see the pattern of a tic he suffered when he spoke. He caught your eye, then turned his head to speak as though addressing a presence at his side, or an invisible creature perched on his shoulder. "Don't deny us," he said to it now. "Don't deny what we have. And please don't play this game with me. I know you'll find it a difficult idea, and you'll resist it, but we've come together for a purpose."

I should have walked on, but his intensity held me for the moment and I had just sufficient curiosity to echo him. "Purpose?"

"Something passed between us up there on the hill, after he fell. It was pure energy, pure light?" Parry was beginning to come alive, and now that his immediate distress was behind him, the interrogative inflection had returned to his statements. "The fact that you love me," he continued, "and that I love you is not important. It's just the means . . ."

The means?

He addressed my frown, as though explaining the obvious to a simpleton. "To bring you to God, through love. You'll fight this like mad, because you're a long way from your own feelings? But I know that the Christ is within you. At some level you know it too. That's why you fight it so hard with your education and reason and logic and this detached way you have of talking, as if you're not part of anything at all? You can pretend you don't know what I'm talking about, perhaps because you want to hurt me and dominate me, but the fact is I come bearing gifts. The purpose is to bring you to the Christ that is in you and that *is* you. That's what the gift of love is all about. It's really very simple?"

I listened to this speech, trying not to gape. The fact was that he was so earnest and harmless, he looked so crushed, and he was speaking such nonsense that I felt genuinely sorry for him.

"Look," I said, as pleasantly as I could. "What is it you want, exactly?"

"I want you to open yourself up to —"

"Yes, yes. But what do you actually want from me? Or with me."

This was difficult for him. He squirmed inside his clothes and looked at the thing on his shoulder before saying, "I want to see you?"

"And do what, exactly?"

"Talk . . . get to know each other."

"Just talk? Nothing else?"

He wouldn't answer or look at me.

I said, "You keep using the word *love*. Are we talking about sex? Is that what you want?"

He seemed to think this was unfair. The whining note was back in his voice. "You know very well we can't talk about it like this. I've already told you, my feelings are not important. There's a purpose you can't be expected to know at this stage."

He said more along these lines, but I was only half listening. How extraordinary it was, to be standing on my own street in my coat, this cold Tuesday morning in May, talking to a stranger in terms more appropriate to an affair, or a marriage on the rocks. It was as if I had fallen through a crack in my own existence, down into another life, another set of sexual preferences, another past history and future. I had fallen into a life in which another man could be saying to me, *We can't talk about it like this*, and *My own feelings are not important*. What also amazed me was how easy it was not to say, *Who the fuck are you? What are you talking about?* The language Parry was using set off responses in me, old emotional subroutines. It took an act of will to dismiss the sense that I owed this man, that I was being unreasonable in holding something back. In part I was playing along with this domestic drama, even though our household was no more than this turd-strewn pavement.

I also wondered if I was going to need help. Parry knew where I lived, but I knew nothing about him. I interrupted him and said, "You'd better give me your address." It was a remark he was bound to misinterpret. He took a card from his pocket, which had his name printed on it and an address in Frognal Lane, Hampstead. I put the card in my wallet and set off at a quick pace. I had seen another taxi turning my way. I still felt sorry for Parry in a way, but it was clear that talking to him was not going to help. He was hurrying at my side.

"Where are you going now?" He was like a curious child.

"Please don't bother me again," I said as I raised my arm for the cab.

"I know what your real feelings are. And if this is some kind of test, it's completely unnecessary. I'd never let you down."

The taxi stopped and I opened the door, feeling slightly mad. I went to pull it shut and discovered that Parry had hold of it.

He wasn't trying to get in, but he did have one last thing to say.

"I know your problem," he leaned in and confided over the diesel's throb. "It's because you're so kind. But Joe, the pain has to be faced. The only way is for the three of us to talk."

I had decided to say nothing more to him, but I couldn't help myself. "Three?"

"Clarissa. It's best to deal with this head on —"

I didn't let him finish. "Drive on," I said to the cabbie, and I used two hands to wrench the door from Parry's grasp.

As we pulled away, I looked back. He was standing in the road, waving to me forlornly but looking, without question, like a man blessed in love.

Eight

I told the driver to take me to Bloomsbury. As I settled back to calm myself, I recalled my incoherent feelings the day before when I had run out into St. James's Square looking for Parry. Then he represented the unknown, into which I projected all kinds of inarticulate terrors. Now I considered him to be a confused and eccentric young man who couldn't look me in the eye, whose inadequacies and emotional cravings rendered him harmless. He was a pathetic figure, not a threat after all but an annoyance, one that might frame itself, just as Clarissa had said, into an amusing story. Perhaps it was perverse, after such an intense encounter, to be able to drive it from my mind. At the time it seemed reasonable and necessary — I had wasted enough of my morning already. Before my taxi had covered a mile, my thoughts had drifted to the work I intended to do that day, to the piece that had begun to take shape while I had waited for Clarissa at Heathrow.

114

I had set aside this day to start on a long piece about the smile. A whole issue of an American science magazine was to be dedicated to what the editor was calling an intellectual revolution. Biologists and evolutionary psychologists were reshaping the social sciences. The postwar consensus, the standard social-science model, was falling apart, and human nature was up for reexamination. We do not arrive in this world as blank sheets, or as all-purpose learning devices. Nor are we the "products" of our environment. If we want to know what we are, we have to know where we came from. We evolved, like every other creature on earth. We come into this world with limitations and capacities, all of them genetically prescribed. Many of our features — our foot shape, our eye color — are fixed, and others, like our social and sexual behavior and our language learning, await the life we live to take their course. But the course is not infinitely variable. We have a nature. The word from the human biologists bears Darwin out: the way we wear our emotions on our faces is pretty much the same in all cultures, and the infant smile is one social signal that is particularly easy to isolate and study. It appears in !Kung San babies of the Kalahari at the same time it does in American children of Manhattan's Upper West Side, and it has the same effect. In Edward O. Wilson's cool phrase, it "triggers a more abundant share of parental love and affection." Then he goes on, "In the terminology of the zoologist, it is a social releaser, an inborn and relatively invariant signal that mediates a basic social relationship."

A few years ago, science book editors could think of nothing but chaos. Now they were banging their desks for every possible slant on neo-Darwinism, evolutionary psychology, and genetics. I wasn't complaining — business was good — but Clarissa had generally taken against the whole project. It was rationalism gone berserk. "It's the new fundamentalism," she had said one evening. "Twenty years ago you and your friends were all socialists and you blamed the environment for everyone's hard luck. Now you've got us trapped in our genes, and there's a reason for everything!" She was perturbed when I read Wilson's passage to her. Everything was being stripped down, she said, and in the process some larger meaning was lost. What a zoologist had to say about a baby's smile could be of no real interest. The truth of that smile was in the eye and heart of the parent, and in the unfolding love that only had meaning through time.

We were having one of our late-night kitchen table sessions. I told her I thought she had spent too much time lately in the company of John Keats. A genius, no doubt, but an obscurantist too, who had thought science was robbing the world of wonder when the opposite was the case. If we value a baby's smile, why not contemplate its source? Are we to say that all infants enjoy a secret joke? Or that God reaches down and tickles them? Or, least implausibly, that they learn smiling from their mothers? But then, deaf-and-blind babies smile too. That smile must be hard-wired, and for good evolutionary reasons. Clarissa said that I had not understood her. There was nothing wrong in analyzing the bits, but it was easy to lose sight of the whole. I agreed. The work of synthesis was crucial. Clarissa said I still did not understand her, she was talking about love. I said I was too, and how babies who could not yet speak got more of it for themselves. She said no, I still didn't understand. There we had left it. No hard feelings. We had had this conversation in different forms on many occasions. What we were really talking about this time was the absence of babies from our lives.

I collected my book from Dillon's and spent twenty minutes browsing. Because I was eager to start writing, I took a taxi home. As I turned away from paying off the driver, I saw Parry waiting for me outside the apartment building, right by the entrance. What was I expecting? That he would vanish because I was thinking about something else? He looked a little shamefaced as I approached, but he held his ground.

He began speaking while I was some distance off. "You said wait, so I waited."

I had the keys in my hand. I hesitated. I wanted to tell him I had said no such thing and to remind him of his "solemn promise." I wondered too if it might be to my advantage to hear him out again and discover more about his state of mind. But the prospect of being drawn into another domestic drama, this time on a narrow brick path between shaved clumps of privet, appalled me.

I showed him my key and said, "You're in the way."

He continued to block my view of the entrance. He said, "I want to talk about the accident."

"Well, I don't." I took another two paces toward him, as though he were a ghost and

I might slip the extended key right through him to the lock.

He was back to whining. "Look, Joe. We've got so much to talk about. I know it's on your mind too. Why don't we sit down together now and see what we can work out."

I shouldered my way into him with a curt "Excuse me." I was surprised that he melted at the touch. He was lighter than I had thought. He let himself be shoved to one side and I was able to open the door.

"The thing is," he said, "I'm coming at this from the angle of forgiveness."

I stepped inside, ready to block his attempt to follow me. But he remained where he was, and when I closed the door I saw him through the unbreakable glass mouthing a word at me that may have been *forgiveness* again. I took the lift up, and I had just arrived outside the apartment door when I heard the phone ring. I thought it might be Clarissa, calling in as she had promised. I hurried into the hallway and snatched up the receiver.

It was Parry. "Please don't run from this, Joe," he began.

I hung up and left the phone off the hook. Then I changed my mind and replaced it. I turned off the ring tone and set the answering machine. It clicked into action even as I was crossing the living room to the window. Parry was out there, across the street where he could be seen, and he had a mobile to his ear. I heard his voice on the monitor echo in the hall behind me. "Joe, God's love will seek you out." He looked up and must have glimpsed me before I stepped behind the curtain. "I know you're there, I can see you. I know you're listening."

I went back to the hall and turned the monitor volume down. In the bathroom I splashed my face with cold water and looked in the mirror at my dripping features, wondering what it would be like to be obsessed by someone like me. This moment, as well as the one in the field when Clarissa handed me the bottle of wine, might serve as a starting point, for I think it was then that I really began to understand that this was not going to be over by the end of the day. As I went out into the hallway, back toward the answering machine, I thought, I'm in a *relationship*.

I raised the lid on the machine. The recording tape was still turning. I pushed the volume wheel up a notch and heard Parry's voice faintly intoning, ". . . to walk away from it, Joe, but I love you. You've set this in motion. You can't turn your back on it now . . ."

I walked quickly into my study, picked up the fax phone, and called the police. In the seconds before I was connected I realized that I had no idea what to say. A woman's voice came on, laconic and skeptical, hardened against a workaday deluge of panic and woe.

I spoke in the gruff and reasoned tone of a responsible citizen. "I'd like to report a case of harassment, systematic harassment." I was transferred to a man whose voice showed the same wary calm. I repeated my statement. There was only a fractional hesitation before the first question.

"Are you the person being harassed?"

"Yes. I've been —"

"And is the person causing the nuisance with you now?"

"He's standing outside my place this very minute."

"Has he inflicted any physical harm on you?"

"No, but he —"

"Has he threatened you with harm?"

"No." I understood that my grievance would have to be poured into the available bureaucratic mold. There was no facility refined enough to process every private narrative. Denied the release of complaint, I tried to take comfort in having my story assimilated into a recognizable public form. Parry's behavior had to be generalized into a crime.

"Has he made threats against your property?"

"No."

"Or against third parties?"

"No."

"Is he trying to blackmail you?"

"No."

"Do you think you could prove that he intends to cause you distress?"

"Er, no."

The voice slipped out of official neutrality into a near-genuine query. I thought I caught a Yorkshire accent. "Can you tell me what he's doing, then?"

"He phones me at all hours. He talks to me in the —"

The voice was quick to move back to his default position, the interrogative flowchart. "Is he using obscene or insulting behavior?"

"No. Look, officer. Why don't you let me explain? He's a crank. He won't let me alone."

"Are you aware of what he actually wants?"

I paused. For the first time I was aware

of other voices behind the man's. Perhaps there were banks of police officers like him with headsets and, all day long, muggings, murders, suicides, knife-point rapes. I was in there with the rest: attempted daylight religious conversion.

I said, "He wants to save me."

"Save you?"

"You know, convert me. He's obsessed. He simply won't leave me alone."

The voice cut in, impatience taking hold at last. "I'm sorry, caller. This is not a police matter. Unless he harms you or your property or threatens the same, he's committing no offense. Trying to convert you is not against the law." Then he terminated our emergency conversation with his own little stricture. "We do have religious freedom in this country."

I went back to the living room window and looked down at Parry. He was no longer talking to my machine. He stood there with his hands in his pockets facing the building, as stolid as a Stasi agent.

I made a flask of coffee and some sandwiches and retreated into my study, which faces out across another street, and sat there reading, or rather shuffling, my notes. My concentration was ruined. Being hounded by Parry was aggravating an older dissatisfaction. It comes back to me from time to time, usually when I'm unhappy about something else, that all the ideas I deal in are other people's. I simply collate and digest their research and deliver it up to the general reader. People say I have a talent for clarity. I can spin a decent narrative out of the stumblings, backtrackings, and random successes that lie behind most scientific breakthroughs. It's true, someone has to go between the researcher and the general public, giving the higher-order explanations that the average laboratory worker is too busy, or too cautious, to indulge. It's also true I've made a lot of money swinging spider-monkey-style on the tallest trees of the science fashion jungle — dinosaurs, black holes, quantum magic, chaos, superstrings, neuroscience, Darwin revisited. Beautifully illustrated hardback books, with TV documentary spinoffs and radio discussion panels and conferences in the pleasantest places on the planet.

In my bad moments the thought returns that I'm a parasite and I probably would not feel this way if I did not have a good physics degree and a doctorate in quantum electrodynamics. I should have been out there myself, carrying my own atomic increment to the mountain of human knowledge. But when I left university I was restless after seven years' disciplined study. I traveled, widely, recklessly, and for far too long. When I finally got back to London, I went into business with a friend. The idea was to market a device, basically a cunningly phased set of circuits, that I had worked on in my spare time during my postgraduate days. This tiny item was supposed to enhance the performance of certain microprocessors, and the way it looked to us then, every computer in the world was going to need one. A German company flew us out to Hanover, first class, and for a couple of years we thought we were going to be billionaires. But the patent application failed. A team from a science park outside Edinburgh was there before us with better electronics. Then the computer industry stormed off in another direction anyway. Our company never even traded, and the Edinburgh people went bust. By the time I got back to quantum electrodynamics, the hole in my curriculum vitae was too big, my math was rusting up, and I was looking too old, in my late twenties, for this very competitive game.

When I emerged from my last interview, I already knew — by the emphatic kindness with which my old professor showed me out

— that my academic career was sunk. I walked down Exhibition Road in the rain, wondering what to do. As I passed the Natural History Museum the rain became torrential, and with a few dozen other people I ran into the museum to shelter. I sat myself down by the full-scale model of the diplodocus, and as I dried out I fell into a strangely contented state of crowd-watching. Frequently, large groups provoke in me a vague misanthropy. This time, however, the curiosity and wonder I saw in people seemed to ennoble them. All who walked in, whatever their age, were drawn to come and stand and marvel at that magnificent beast. I overheard conversations, and what interested me, apart from the enthusiasm, was the general level of ignorance. I heard a ten-year-old boy ask the three grownups he was with whether a creature like this one would have chased and eaten people. It was clear from the ready answers he received that the adults' evolutionary timetable was badly out of kilter.

As I sat there, I began to think through the few disparate things I myself knew about dinosaurs. I remembered Darwin's account, in the *Voyage of the Beagle*, of finding large fossilized bones in South America, and how crucial to his theory was the question of their age. He had been impressed by the arguments put forward by the geologist Charles Lyell. The earth was a lot older than the four thousand years defended by the church. In our own time, the cold-blooded/warm-blooded contest was being settled in favor of the latter. There was new geological evidence of various cataclysms that had disturbed life on Earth. That vast crater in Mexico could well have been caused by the meteor that ended the dinosaurs' empire and gave the little ratlike creatures that scuttled at the monsters' feet the chance to expand their niche and so permit the mammals — and therefore ultimately the primates — to flourish. There was also an attractive idea around that the dinosaurs had not been exterminated at all. They had bowed to environmental necessity and evolved into the harmless birds we feed in our back gardens.

By the time I left the museum I had a scheme for a book scrawled on the back of my interview appointment letter. I did three months' reading and six months' writing. The sister of my failed business partner was a picture researcher who kindly agreed to defer her fee. The book came out at a time when no dinosaur book could fail, and mine did well enough for me to be signed up for black holes. My working life began, and as the successes rolled in, so all other possibilities in science closed down on me. I was a journalist, a commentator, an outsider to my own profession. I would never get back to those days, heady in retrospect, when I was doing original doctoral research on the magnetic field of the electron, when I attended conferences on the problem of infinities in the renormalizable theories — not as an observer but as an active, though minor, participant. Now no scientist, not even a lab technician or college porter, would ever take me seriously again.

On this particular day, in my study with my coffee and sandwiches, and my failure to make progress with the smile, and Parry standing guard on the pavement, it came back to me again how I had ended up with this. From time to time I heard the click of the answering machine engaging. Every hour or so I went into the living room to check, and he was always there, staring at the entrance like a dog tied up outside a shop. On only one occasion was he talking on the phone to me. Mostly he stood still, feet slightly apart, hands in pockets, the expression on his face, as far as I could tell, suggesting concentration, or perhaps imminent happiness.

When I looked out at five o'clock, he had gone. I lingered by the window, imagining that I could see his outline in vacated space, a pillar of absence glowing in the late afternoon's diminishing light. Then I went and stood by the machine. The red LED showed thirty-three messages. I used the scan function to skip through them and found Clarissa's voice. She hoped I was all right, she'd be back at six, and she loved me. There were three work messages, leaving Parry's score at twenty-nine. Even as I contemplated that figure, the tape began to turn. I pushed the volume wheel. It sounded like he was calling from a taxi. "Joe. Brilliant idea with the curtains. I got it straightaway? All I wanted to say is this again. I feel it too. I really do." On these last words emotion pitched his voice a little higher.

The curtains? I returned to the living room and looked. They hung as they always did. We never drew them. I pulled one aside, foolishly expecting to find a clue.

Then I sat again in my study, not working but brooding and waiting for Clarissa, and again my thoughts returned to how I came to be what I was, and how it might have been different, and, ridiculously, how I might find my way back to original research and achieve something new before I was fifty.

Nine

It would make more sense of Clarissa's return to tell it from her point of view. Or at least from that point as I later construed it. She arrives up three flights of stairs, bearing five kilograms of books and papers in her leather bag, which she has carried half a mile from the tube station. At her back, a bad day. First thing, the student she supervised yesterday, a raw girl from Lancaster, phoned her in tears and shouting incoherently. When Clarissa calmed her down, the girl accused her of setting her impossible reading tasks and of sending her up blind alleys of research. The Romantic poetry seminar went badly because the two students appointed to give discussion papers had prepared nothing and the rest of the kids had not bothered with the reading. At the end of the morning she discovered that her appointment diary was missing. All through lunch a colleague complained that her husband was too gentle with her in bed and lacked the necessary sexual aggression to overpower her and deliver the quality of orgasm she knew she deserved. For three hours during the afternoon Clarissa sat on a senate committee and found herself maneuvered into voting for the least bad option, a seven percent reduction in the budget of her own department. She went straight from that to a performance and efficiency interview conducted by the management, where she was reminded that she had been consistently late in filing her workload quota schedules and that her teaching, research, and administration ratios were showing an uneven distribution.

As she lugs her bag up the stairs, she feels it is costing her more effort than it should, and she thinks she might be getting a cold. There's a tenderness over the bridge of her nose, and her eyes are pricking. There's also a widening ache in the small of her back, always a reliable sign in her of viral infection. Worst of all, the memory of the balloon accident is back with her. It's never been far from her mind, but for a good part of the day she has kept it at one remove, anecdotalized, in its own compartment. Now it has broken out, it is right inside her. It's like a smell on the end of her fingers. The image that has been with her since the late afternoon is of Logan letting go. The feeling that went with it, the horrified helplessness, has been with her too and seems to have generated the physical symptoms of a cold or flu. Talking the events over with friends no longer seems to help, because, she thinks, she has reached a core of senselessness. As she comes up the last flight of stairs, she notes that the ache is spreading to her knee joints. Or is this what happens to you when you haul books upstairs and you are no longer in your twenties? As she puts the key in the front door, she experiences a little lift of the spirits when she remembers that Joe will be home and is always good at looking after her when she needs it.

When she steps into the hall, he is waiting for her by the door of his study. He has a wild look about him that she has not seen in some time. She associates this look with overambitious schemes, excited and usually stupid plans that very occasionally afflict the calm, organized man she loves. He's coming toward her, talking before she's even through the door. Without a kiss or any form of greeting, he's off on a tale of harassment and idiocy behind which there appears to be some kind of accusation, perhaps even anger against her, for she was quite wrong, he says, but now he is vindicated. Before she can ask him what he's talking about, in fact before she has even put down her bag, he is on another tack, telling her about a conversation he's just had with an old friend in the Particle Physics Unit on Gloucester Road, and how he thinks that this friend there might wangle him an appointment with the professor. All Clarissa wants to say is *Where's my kiss? Hug me! Take care of me!* But Joe is pressing on like a man who has seen no other human for a year.

He is for the moment conversationally deaf and blind, so Clarissa raises both hands, palms turned outward in surrender, and says, "That's great, Joe. I'm going to take a bath." Even then he does not stop, and probably has not heard. As she turns to go toward the bedroom, he walks behind her, and follows her in, telling her over and over in different ways that he has to get back into science. She's heard this before. In fact, last time around, a real crisis two years ago, he ended by concluding that he was reconciled to his life and that it wasn't a bad one after all — and that was supposed to be the close of the matter. He's raising his voice over the thunder of the taps, back now with the harassment tale, and she hears the name Parry and remembers. Oh yes, that. She thinks she understands Parry well enough. A lonely, inadequate man, a Jesus freak who is probably living off his parents and dying to connect with someone, anyone, even Joe.

Joe is hanging in the frame of the bathroom door like some newly discovered nonstop talking ape. Talking, but barely self-aware. She pushes past him to get back into the bedroom. She would like to ask him to bring her a glass of white wine, but she thinks he would be likely to pour himself one too and sit with her while she takes her bath, when all she wants now, if he is not going to take care of her, is to be alone. She sits on the edge of the bed and begins to unlace her boots. If she were really ill, she could say so. She's a borderline case, no more than tired perhaps, and upset by Sunday, and it's not her style to make a fuss, so instead she raises her foot and Joe drops to one knee, the better to ease off her boot — and he doesn't stop talking all the while. He wants to be back in theoretical physics, he wants the support of a department, he's happy to do whatever teaching would get him in, he's got ideas on the virtual photon.

She stands in her stocking feet, unbuttoning her blouse. The exposure, and the sensation on her soles of thick carpet through the silk, excites her vaguely, and she remembers last night and the night before, the sorrow and the seesawing emotions and the sex, and she remembers too that they love each other and happen to be in very different mental universes now, with very different needs. That's all. It will change, and there is no reason to draw significant conclusions, which is what her current mood is prompting her to do. She removes her blouse, touches the fastener on her bra, and then changes her mind. She feels better, but not quite good enough, and she does not want to give Joe a wrong signal, assuming he would even notice. If she could be alone in the bath for half an hour, then she could listen to him, and he could listen to her. All this talking and listening that's supposed to be good for couples. She crosses the room to hang her skirt, then sits on the bed again to take off her stockings, and while she's half listening to Joe she's thinking about Jessica Marlowe, the woman who complained to her at lunch about her husband: too mild, too sexually bland. Who you get, and how it works out — there's so much luck involved, as well as the million branching consequences of your unconscious choice of mate, that no one and no amount of talking can untangle it if it turns out unhappily.

Joe is telling her that it no longer matters that his math is far behind because these days the software can take care of it. Clarissa has seen Joe at work, and she knows that like a poet, all a theoretical physicist needs besides talent and a good idea is a sheet of paper and a sharp pencil — or a powerful computer. If he wanted, he could go in his study now and "get back into science." The department, the professors and the peers and the office he says he needs are irrelevant, but they're his protection against failure, because they will never let him in. (She herself is sick of university departments.) She puts on her dressing gown over her underwear. He is back with this old frenzied ambition because he's upset — Sunday is getting to him in different ways too. The trouble with Joe's precise and careful mind is that it takes no account of its own emotional field. He seems unaware that his arguments are no more than ravings, they are an aberration and they have a cause. He is therefore vulnerable, but for now she cannot make herself feel protective. Like her, he has reached the senseless core of Logan's tragedy, but he has reached it unaware. Whereas she wants to lie quietly in soapy hot water and reflect, he wants to set about altering his fate.

Back in the bathroom she stirs cold water into the hot with a back brush and adds pine oil and lilac crystals and, as an afterthought, an essence, a Christmas gift from a goddaughter, used by the ancient Egyptians, so the label claims, and known to impart to the bather wisdom and inner peace. She empties in the whole bottle. Joe has lowered the lid of the lavatory and is settling there. Theirs is the kind of relationship in which it is perfectly possible to ask to be left alone without incurring consequences, but his intensity is inhibiting her. Especially now that he is back on Parry. As Clarissa eases into the green water, she allows her concentration to settle fully on what he is saying. The police? You phoned the police? Thirty-three messages on the machine? But she saw it as she came in, the indicator said zero. He wiped them, he insists, at which Clarissa sits up in the water and takes another look at him and he returns her stare full on. When she was twelve, her father died of Alzheimer's, and it's always been a fear that she'll live with someone who goes crazy. That's why she chose rational Joe.

Something in this look, or the sudden straightening of her aching back, or the way astonishment loosens the hinge of her jaw, causes Joe to stumble over a word — *phenomenon* — then slow into a short silence, after which he speaks in a lower tone. "What is it?"

She doesn't take her eyes off him as she says, "You've been talking at me nonstop since I came in. Slow down a moment, Joe. Take a few deep breaths."

It touches her that he is prepared to do exactly as she asks.

"How do you feel?"

Staring at the floor in front of him, he rests his hands on his knees and sighs loudly on the exhalation. "Agitated."

She waits for him to go on, to go on being agitated, but he's waiting for her. They hear the arrhythmic tick of the hot water pipe contracting behind the bath. She says, "I know I've said this before, so don't get angry. Do you think it's possible that you're making too much of this man Parry? That he's really not that much of a problem? I mean, ask him in for a cup of tea and he'll probably never bother you again. He's not the cause of your agitation, he's a symptom." As she says this, she thinks of the thirty-three messages that got erased. Perhaps Parry, or the Parry described by Joe, does not exist. She shivers and lowers herself back into the water, keeping her gaze on him.

He seems to consider carefully what she has said. "Symptom of what, exactly?"

There's a warning chill in his last word that makes her lighten her tone. "Oh, I don't know. This old frustration about not doing original research." She hopes it's only that.

Again he considers carefully. Answering her questions has made him seem suddenly tired. He looks like a child at bedtime, sitting there on the lavatory without inhibition while she takes her bath. He says, "It's the other way round. There's this ridiculous situation I can't do anything about. I get pissed off and start thinking about my work, the work I ought to be doing."

"Why do you say you can do nothing about it — about this guy, I mean?"

"I've just told you. After I spoke to him, he stood outside our place and hardly moved for seven hours. He was phoning all day long. The police say it's not their business. So what do you want me to do?"

Clarissa feels the little cold thump to the heart she always gets when anger is directed at her. But at the same time she's aware that she has done the very thing she wanted to resist. She has let herself be drawn into Joe's mental state, his problems, his dilemma, his needs. She has been helpless before the arousal of her protective impulses. Her careful questions were designed to help him, and now she is being rewarded by his aggression while her own needs go unnoticed. She was prepared to look after herself, given that he was not up to it, but even that recourse has been denied her. She speaks quickly, deflecting his question with her own. "Why did you wipe the messages off the tape?"

This throws him. "What are you saying?"

"It's a simple question. Thirty messages would be evidence of harassment you could take to the police."

"The police aren't —"

"All right. *I* could listen to them. They'd be evidence for me." She stands in the bath and snatches a towel to cover herself. The sudden movement makes her dizzy. Perhaps there is something wrong with her heart.

Joe is on his feet too. "I thought we were coming to this. You don't believe me."

"I don't know what to think." She is toweling herself with unusual vigor. "What I know is that I come back from a terrible day and walk straight into yours."

" 'Terrible day.' You think this is about a terrible day?"

They are both back in the bedroom now.

She is already wondering if she has gone too far. But here she is, prematurely out of her bath, looking for her underwear, and the aching in her back is still spreading. They rarely row, Clarissa and Joe. She is especially bad at arguments. She has never been able to accept the rules of engagement, which permit or require you to say things that you do not mean, or are distorted truths or not true at all. She can't help feeling that every hostile utterance of hers takes her further not only from Joe's love but from all the love she's ever had, and makes her feel that a buried meanness has been exposed that truly represents her.

Joe has another kind of problem. His emotions are slow to shift to anger in the first place, and even when they have, he has the wrong kind of intelligence, he forgets his lines and cannot score the points. Nor can he break the habit of responding to an accusation with a detailed, reasoned answer instead of coming back with an accusation of his own. He is easily outmaneuvered by a sudden irrelevance. Irritation blocks his understanding of his own case, and it is only later, when he is calm, that an articulate advocacy unrolls in his thoughts. Also, it's particularly hard to be harsh to Clarissa, because she is so easy to wound. Angry words leave an instant mark of pain across her face.

But now they seem cast in a play they cannot stop, and a terrible freedom is in the air. "The guy's ridiculous," Joe continues. "He's fixated." Clarissa begins to speak, but he waves her down. "I can't get you to take this seriously. Your only concern is I'm not massaging your damned feet after your hard day." This reference to a recent tender half-hour shocks Joe as much as Clarissa. He had no resentment at the time; in fact, he enjoyed it.

She turns her head away but manages to hang on to what she was going to say. "You were so intense about him as soon as you met him. It's like you invented him."

"Right! I get it. I brought it down on myself. I made my own fate. It's my karma. I thought even you were above this kind of New Age drivel."

This *even* comes from nowhere, a rhythmic filler, a reckless little intensifier. Clarissa has never expressed the remotest interest in the New Age package. She looks at him, surprised. The insult has in turn set her free. "You ought to be asking yourself which way this fixation runs."

The suggestion that it is he who is obsessed by Parry appears so monstrous to Joe that he can think of nothing to say but "Christ!" Motiveless energy impels him to stride across the room to the window. There's no one out there. With such anger in the air it makes Clarissa feel vulnerable to be half dressed, so she takes advantage of the movement her remark has caused to snatch a skirt from a coat hanger. Two other coat hangers drop to the floor, but she does not pick them up as she usually would.

Joe takes a deep breath and turns from the window to exhale. He makes a deliberate show of calming himself, of starting again from a reasonable premise, of being a reasonable man refusing to be driven to extremes. He speaks in a quiet, breathy tone, exaggeratedly slow. Where do we learn such tricks? Are they inscribed, along with the rest of our emotional repertoire? Or do we get them from the movies? He says, "Look, there's this problem out there" — he gestures to the window — "and all I wanted from you was your support and help."

But Clarissa does not hear reason. The husky voice, the tense of *wanted,* suggest to her self-pity and accusation and make her angry. She does not need to tell him that he's always had her support and help. Instead she comes at him from a new place, inventing a grievance and recalling it in a single mental act. "The first time he phoned and told you he loved you, you admitted you lied to me about it."

Joe is so astonished he can only stare at her, and while his mouth is struggling to frame a word, Clarissa, unseasoned as she is in this kind of battle, feels a pulse of triumph that is easily confused with vindication. In that moment she honestly feels she has been betrayed and therefore is entitled to add, "So what am I meant to think? You tell me. Then we'll see what kind of support and help you need." As she says this she is slotting her feet into her mules.

Joe is beginning to find his voice. He has so many simultaneous protesting thoughts that his mind is fogged. "Wait a minute. Are you really suggesting . . ."

Clarissa, aware that her remarks might not bear up under discussion, is getting out while she's ahead, leaving the room while it's still delicious to feel wronged. "Well, fuck off, then," Joe shouts to her departing back. He feels he wouldn't mind picking up the dressing table stool and throwing it through the window. He is the one who should be walking out. After some seconds' hesitation, he hurries out of the room, passing Clarissa in the hallway, snatches his coat from its peg, and goes out, slamming the door hard behind him and glad that she was close by to hear its full force.

As he leaves the apartment building, he is surprised at how dark it has become. It's raining, too. He gathers his coat about him and tightens the belt, and when he sees Parry waiting for him at the end of the brick path, he does not even break his stride.

Ten

My impression was that the rain intensified the moment I stepped out, but I wasn't going back for a hat or an umbrella. I ignored Parry and set such a furious walking pace that when I got to a corner and looked round, he was fifty yards behind. My hair was soaked and water had already penetrated my right shoe, whose sole had a long-neglected gash. My anger came off in a cold glow, childishly undirected. Parry, of course, was to blame for coming between Clarissa and me, but my fury was for them both — he was the affliction she had failed to support me against — and for everyone and everything, especially this seeping rain and the fact that I had no idea where I was going.

There was another thing too, like a skin, a soft shell around the meat of my anger, limiting it and so making it appear all the more theatrical. It was a quarter-memory, a niggle, a faint connection rooted in a forgotten bout of reading, irrelevant to my purposes at the time but lodged in me like an enduring fragment of a childhood dream. It was relevant now, I thought, it could help me. The key word was *curtain*, which I imagined in my own handwriting, and just as the rain on my lashes splintered and refracted the streetlight, so this word seemed to come apart, tugged this way and that by associations that lay just off the screen of recall. I saw a grand house in long perspective, reproduced in the smudged black and white of an old newspaper, and high railings and perhaps some kind of military presence, a security guard or sentry. But if this was the house where the significant curtain hung, it meant nothing to me.

I pushed on, past real houses, huge lit villas that rose above their high entryphone gates, behind which I glimpsed carelessly parked cars. Such was my mood that I could consciously and pleasurably forget our own half-million-pound apartment and indulge the fantasy that I was a poor down-and-out scurrying in the rain past the rich folks' houses. Some people had all the breaks, I'd wasted what few chances came my way, and I was nothing and there was no one out here to care for me now. I hadn't tricked my own feelings like this since I was an adolescent, and the discovery that I could still do it gave me almost as much pleasure as a five-minute mile. But then, when I felt for *curtain* again, there was no association at all, not even a shadow, and as I began to slow my pace, I thought how the brain was such a delicate, fine-filigreed thing that it could not even fake a change in its emotional state without transforming the condition of a million other unfelt circuits.

I sensed my tormentor closing on me just before I heard him half shout, half yodel my name. Then he called again. "Joe! Joe!" I realized he was sobbing. "It was you. You started this, you made this happen. You're playing games with me, all the time, and you're pretending . . ." He couldn't finish. I picked up speed again, and I was almost running when I crossed the next street. His crying wavered with each jarring footfall. I was disgusted and frightened. I reached the other side and looked back. He had followed me and now he was trapped in the center of the road, waiting for a gap in the traffic. There was just a chance he could have fallen forward under a passing set of wheels, and I wanted it, the desire was cool and intense, and I wasn't surprised at myself, or ashamed. When he saw my face turned toward him at last, he shouted a series of questions. "When are you going to leave me alone? You've got me. I can't do anything. Why don't you admit what you're doing? Why do you keep pretending that you don't know what I'm talking about? And then the signals, Joe. Why d'you keep on?"

Still trapped in the center, his figure and his words obliterated at irregular intervals by the passing traffic, he raised his voice to such a hoarse screaming that I couldn't look away. I should have been running on, for this was the perfect moment to lose him. But his rage was compelling and I was forced to look on, amazed, although I never quite lost faith in the redeeming possibility of a bus crushing him as he stood there, twenty-five feet away, pleading as he damned me.

He uttered his words at a screech, on a repetitive rising note, as though a forlorn zoo bird had become approximately human. "What do you want? You love me and you want to destroy me. You pretend it's not happening. Nothing happening! You fuck! You're playing . . . torturing me . . . giving me all your fucking little secret signals to keep me coming toward you. I know what you want, you fuck. You fuck! You think I don't? You want to take me away from . . ." I lost his words to a house-sized removal truck. ". . . and you think you can take me away from Him. But you'll come to me. In the end. You'll come to Him too, because you'll have to. You fuck, you'll beg for mercy, you'll crawl on your stomach . . ."

Parry's sobs got the better of him then. He took a step toward me, but a car surging up the middle of the road forced him back with an angry blaring klaxon whose receding Doppler effect inverted his own sorry sound. At some point while he was shouting I felt almost sorry for him again, despite my hostility and revulsion. But perhaps sorrow wasn't quite it. Seeing him stuck there, raving, I felt relieved it wasn't me, much as I do when I see a drunk or a schizophrenic conducting the traffic. I also thought that his condition was so extreme, his framing of reality so distorted, that he couldn't harm me. He needed help, though not from me. This in parallel with the abstract desire to see this nuisance guiltlessly obliterated on the asphalt.

I benefited from a third current of thought and feeling while I listened to him. It was prompted by a word he had used twice: *signals*. Both times it caused the curtain that had troubled me earlier to stir and twitch, and the two words mated to spawn an elementary syntax: a curtain used as a signal. Now I was closer than before. I almost had

150

it. A grand house, a famous residence in London, and the curtains in its windows used to communicate . . .

The struggle with these fragile associations brought to mind the curtains in my study, and then the study itself. Not its comfort, not the glow of its parchment lamps or the glowing reds and blues of the Bokhara or the submarine tones of my Chagall forgery (*Le Poète Allongé*, 1915), but the hundred feet or so of box files that filled five shelves, the whole of one wall, black labeled boxes jammed with clippings, and on the other side, by the south-facing window, the little skyscraper of a hard disk drive where three gigabytes of data waited to help me build a bridge between this mansion and these two words.

I thought of Clarissa with a sudden leap of cheerful love, and it seemed an easy matter to set right our row — not because I had behaved badly or was wrong, but because I was so obviously, incontrovertibly right, and she was simply mistaken. I had to get back there.

The rain was still coming down, but less heavily. The lights two hundred yards up the road had already changed, and I could see from the disposition of the advancing traffic that within seconds Parry would have his opportunity to cross the road. So I left him where he was, with his hands over his face, crying. He probably didn't see me as I turned and set off at a fast jog down a narrow residential road. And even if in his desolation he had had the heart to pursue me at this speed, I could have doubled round the block and lost him in a minute.

Eleven

Dear Joe,

I feel happiness running through me like an electrical current. I close my eyes and see you as you were last night in the rain, across the road from me, with the unspoken love between us as strong as steel cable. I close my eyes and thank God out loud for letting you exist, for letting me exist in the same time and place as you, and for letting this strange adventure between us begin. I thank Him for every little thing about us. This morning I woke and on the wall beside my bed was a perfect disk of sunlight and I thanked Him for that same sunlight falling on you! Just as last night the rain that drenched you drenched me too and bound us. I praise God that He has sent me to you. I know there is difficulty and pain ahead of us, but the path that He sets us on is hard for a purpose. His purpose! It tests us and strengthens us, and in the long run it will bring us to even greater joy.

I know I owe you an apology — and that word is too small. I stand before you naked, defenseless, dependent on your mercy, begging your forgiveness. For you knew our love from the very beginning. You recognized in that glance that passed between us, up there on the hill after he fell, all the charge and power and blessedness of love, while I was dull and stupid, denying it, trying to protect myself from it, trying to pretend that it wasn't happening, that it *couldn't* happen like this, and I ignored what you were telling me with your eyes and your every gesture. I thought it was enough to follow you down the hill and suggest that we pray together. You were right to be angry with me for not seeing what you had already seen. What had happened was so obvious. Why did I refuse to acknowledge it? You must have thought me so insensitive, such a moron. You were right to turn from me and walk away. Even now, when I bring to mind that moment when you started back up the hill and I remember the stoop of your shoulders, the heaviness in your stride that spoke of rejection, I groan aloud at my behavior. What an idiot! I could have lost us what we have. Joe, in the name of God, please forgive me.

Now at least you know that I have seen what you saw. And you, constrained as you are by your situation and by your sensitivity to Clarissa's feelings, have welcomed me in ways that no intrusive ears or eyes will intercept, by means that I alone can understand. You knew that I was bound to come to you. You were waiting for me. That's why I had to phone you late that night, as soon as I realized what you had been telling me with your eyes. When you picked up the phone I heard the relief in your voice. You accepted my message in silence, but don't think I wasn't aware of your gratitude. When I put the phone down I wept with joy, and I guessed that you were weeping too. Now at last life could begin. All the waiting and loneliness and praying had borne its fruit, and I got down on my knees and gave thanks, over and over again until it was dawn. Did you sleep that night? I don't think so. You lay awake in the dark, listening to Clarissa's breathing and wondering where all this was taking us.

Joe, you really have started something now!

We have so much to tell each other, there's a lot of catching up to do. Exploration of the ocean floor has begun, but the surface remains undisturbed. What I'm trying to say is, you've seen my soul (I'm certain of that), and you know how to reach deep into me, but you know next to nothing about the ordinary details of my life — how I live, where I live, my past, my *story*. It's only the outer clothing, I know, but our love has to include it all. I already know a lot about your life. I've made it my job, my mission. You've drawn me into your daily life and demanded that I understand it. The thing is, I can deny you nothing. If I ever sit an exam about you I'll come top, I won't get a single thing wrong. You'll be so proud of me!

So, my own outer clothing. I know you'll be here one day soon. It's a beautiful house, set back from a little kink in Frognal Lane, surrounded by lawns, with its own courtyard in the center which no one can see, even if they were to step beyond the front gates (hardly anyone does, apart from the postman) and come right up to the front door. It's a miniature version of some rather grand French place. It even has faded green louvered shutters and a cockerel weathervane on the roof. It belonged to my mother, who died from cancer four years ago, and she inherited it from her sister, who got it in a divorce settlement just weeks before she died in a car crash. I'm telling you this because I don't want you to get a false impression about our family. My aunt had a terrible marriage to a crook who got rich in a property boom, but the rest of our family scraped by with ordinary jobs. My father died when I was eight. I've got an older sister in Australia, but we weren't able to track her down when my mother died, and for some reason she wasn't mentioned in the will. I've got a handful of cousins I never see, and as far as I know, I'm the only one in our family to get an education past the age of sixteen. So here I am, the king of my castle, which God has granted to me for a purpose of His own.

I can feel your presence all around me. I don't think I'm going to phone you again. It's so awkward, with Clarissa, and writing to you brings you closer. I imagine you sitting here next to me, seeing what I am seeing. I'm sitting at a small wooden table on a covered balcony that extends from the study and looks out over the inner courtyard. The rain is falling on two flowering cherry trees. The branch of one grows through the railings, so that I am close enough to see how the water forms into oval beads tinged by the flowers' pale pink. Love has given me new eyes, I see with such clarity, in such detail. The grain of the old wooden posts, every separate blade of grass on the wet lawn below, the little tickly black legs of the lady bird walking across my hand a minute ago. Everything I see I want to touch and stroke. At last I'm awake. I feel so alive, so alert with love.

Speaking of touch and the wet grass reminds me. When you came out of your house yesterday evening and you brushed the top of the hedge with your hand, I didn't understand at first. I went down the path and put out my own hand and fingered the leaves that you had touched. I felt each one, and it was a shock when I realized they were different from the ones you hadn't touched. There was a glow, a kind of burning on my fingers along the edges of those wet leaves. Then I got it. You had touched them in a certain way, in a pattern that spelled a simple message. Did you really think I would miss it? Joe! So simple, so clever, so loving. What a fabulous way to hear of love, through rain and leaves and skin, the pattern woven through the skein of God's sensuous creation unfolding in a scorching sense of touch. I could have stood there for an hour in wonder, but I didn't want to be left behind. I wanted to know where you were leading me through the rain.

But let me go back to the ocean surface. I used to teach English as a foreign language in a place near Leicester Square. It was bearable, but I never really got on with the other teachers. There was a general lack of seriousness, which irritated me. I think they talked about me behind my back because I cared about my religion — not fashionable these days! As soon as I came into the money and the house, I gave up the job and moved in. I thought of myself as in retreat — waiting. I was always quite clear in my mind that this amazingly beautiful place had come to me for a purpose. One week, a shabby one-bedroom flat in Arnos Grove, the next a little chateau in Hampstead and a small fortune in the bank. There had to be a design in this, and my duty, I thought (and time has proved me right), was to be calm and attentive to the silence, and ready. I prayed, meditated, and sometimes took long walks in the country, and I knew that sooner or later His purpose would unfold. My responsibility was to be finely tuned, prepared for the first sign. And despite all that preparation, I missed it! I should have known it when our eyes met, up there on the hill. Not until I came back that evening, back into the silence and solitude here, did I begin to comprehend, so I phoned you . . . But now I'm going round in circles!

This house is waiting for you, Joe. The library, the snooker room, the sitting room with its beautiful fireplace and huge old sofas. We even have a miniature cinema (videos, of course) and an exercise room and a sauna. There are barriers ahead, of course. Mountain ranges! The biggest of which is your denial of God. But I've seen through that, and you know it. In fact, you probably planned it that way. It's a game you're playing with me, part seduction, part ordeal. You are trying to probe the limits of my faith. Does it horrify you that I can see through you so easily? I hope it thrills you, the way it thrills me when you guide me with your messages, these codes that tap straight into my soul. I know that you'll come to God, just as I know that it's my purpose to bring you there, through love. Or, to put it another way, I'm going to mend your rift with

God through the healing power of love.

Joe, Joe, Joe . . . I'll confess it, I covered five sheets of paper with your name. You can laugh at me — but not too hard. You can be cruel to me — but not too much. Behind the games we play lies a purpose that is neither yours nor mine to question. Everything we do together, everything we are, is in God's care, and our love takes its existence, form, and meaning from His love. There's so much to talk about, so many fine details. We have yet to discuss the whole matter of Clarissa. I think it's right that you take the lead in this and let me know what you think is best. Do you want me to talk to her? I'd be very happy to. I don't mean happy, of course; I mean prepared. Or should we sit down, the three of us together, and talk it through? I'm convinced there are ways of handling it that will make it far less painful for her. But this has to be your call, and I'll wait to hear what you have decided is best. While I've been writing I've felt your presence, right by my elbow. The rain has stopped, the birds have taken up their songs again, and the air is even brighter. Ending this letter is like a parting. I can't help feeling that every time I leave you I'm letting you down. I'll never forget that time at the bottom of the hill, the way you turned away from me, rejected, stunned by my refusal to recognize in that first instance our love. I'll never stop saying I'm sorry. Joe, will you ever forgive me?

Jed

Twelve

My sense of failure in science, of being parasitic and marginal, did not quite leave me. It never had, really. My old restlessness may have been brought on afresh by Logan's fall, or by the Parry situation, or by the fine crack of estrangement that had appeared between Clarissa and me. Obviously, sitting in my study and thinking hard was not going to bring me to the source of my unease or to a solution. Twenty years ago I might have hired a professional listener, but somewhere along the way I had lost faith in the talking cure. A genteel fraud, in my view. These days I preferred to drive my car. A couple of days after Parry's letter arrived — his first letter, that is — I drove to Oxford to see Logan's widow, Jean.

The motorway was unaccountably empty that morning, the light was even, gray, and clear, and I had a brisk tailwind. Along the high flat stretch before the escarpment I came close to doubling the speed limit. The mighty onward rush, the requirement to keep a quarter of my attention on the rear-view mirror (for police, for Parry), and the general demand on concentration was calming and granted the illusion of purification. As I dropped down through the chalk cutting three miles north of the scene of the accident, the Vale of Oxford opened before me like a foreign country. Sixteen miles across the flat green haze, confined within a large Victorian house, was the sorrow I was driving toward. I let my speed fall to seventy and allowed myself a little more time for reflection.

A trawl through the database for *curtain/signal* had brought nothing. I had opened a few box files of clippings at random, but with no clear heading to guide me, I gave up after half an hour. I had read something somewhere about a curtain used as a signal, and it had some relevance to Parry. I thought my best chance was to cease pursuing it actively and hope that stronger associations would break through, perhaps in my sleep.

I was not having much better luck with Clarissa. It was true, we were talking, we were affable, we had even made love, briefly, in the morning before work. At breakfast I had read Parry's letter, then passed it to her. She seemed to agree with me that he was mad and that I was right to feel harassed. "Seemed" because she was not quite wholehearted, and if she said I was right — and I thought she did — she never really acknowledged that she had been wrong. I sensed she was keeping her options open, though she denied it when I asked her. She read the letter through the medium of a frown, pausing to look up at me at a certain point and say, "His writing's rather like yours."

Then she questioned me about what it was exactly I had said to Parry.

"I told him to bugger off," I said, perhaps too hotly. And then, when she asked again, I raised my voice in exasperation. "Look at that stuff about a message in the hedge! He's mad, don't you see?"

"Yes," she said quietly, and went on reading. I thought I knew what was bothering her. It was Parry's artful technique of suggesting a past, a pact, a collusion, a secret life of glances and gestures, and I seemed to be denying it in just the way I would if it had happened to be true. What was I so desperate about if I had nothing to hide? The bit about "the whole matter of Clarissa" on the penultimate page made her stop and look not at me but to one side, and she took a slow deep breath. She put down the page she had been holding and touched her brow with her fingertips. It wasn't that she believed Parry, I told myself, it was that his letter was so steamily self-convinced, such an unfaked narrative of emotion — for he obviously had experienced the feelings he described — that it was bound to elicit certain appropriate automatic responses. Even a trashy movie can make you cry. There were deep emotional reactions that ducked the censure of the higher reasoning processes and forced us to enact, however vestigially, our roles: I, the indignant secret lover revealed; Clarissa, the woman cruelly betrayed. But when I tried to say something like this, she looked at me and shook her head slightly from side to side in wonderment at my stupidity. She barely glanced at the last few lines of the letter.

When she stood up suddenly, I said, "Where are you going?"

"I've got to get ready for work." She hurried out of the room, and I felt we had been denied a conclusion. There should have been a moment of consolation, of mutual reassurance; we should have been standing side by side or back to back, protecting each other against this attempt to violate our privacy. Instead it seemed we had already been violated. I was about to say this to her when

she came back, and this time she was cheerful and kissed me on the mouth. We em-
braced for a whole minute in the kitchen
and said loving things. We were together, I
didn't need to say my piece. Then she broke
away, snatched her coat, and was gone. I
thought that there remained between us an
unarticulated dispute, though I wasn't certain what it was.

I lingered in the kitchen, clearing the
plates, finishing my coffee, and gathering up
the pages of the letter, those small blue
sheets that for some reason I associated with
semiliteracy. Our easy ways with each other,
effortlessly maintained for years, suddenly
seemed to me an elaborate construct, a
finely balanced artifice, like an ancient car-
riage clock. We were losing the trick of
keeping it going, or of keeping it going without concentrating hard. Each time I had
spoken to Clarissa lately, I had been aware
of the possible consequences of what I was
saying. Was I giving her the impression that
I was secretly flattered by Parry's attention,
or that I was unconsciously leading him
on, or that without recognizing the fact, I
was enjoying my power over him or —
perhaps she thought this — my power over
her?

Self-consciousness is the destroyer of

erotic joy. In bed, only an hour and a half before, we had been unconvincing somehow, as though there lay between our mucous membranes a fine dust or grit, or its mental equivalent, but as tangible as beach sand. Sitting in the kitchen after Clarissa had left, I conjured a morose causal sequence shading from psyche to soma — bad thoughts, low arousal, minimal lubrication — and pain.

What were these bad thoughts? One was a suspicion that in those realms of feeling that defy the responsibility of logic, Clarissa considered Parry my fault. He was the kind of phantom that only I could have called up, a spirit of my dislocated, incomplete character, or of what she fondly called my innocence. I had brought him upon us, and I was keeping him there, even while I disowned him.

Clarissa said I was wrong or ridiculous to think this, but she did not say much else about her own attitude. She had spoken about my own as we got dressed that morning. I was disturbed, she said. I was pulling on my boots and did not interrupt. She said she hated to see me back with that old obsession about getting back into science when I had such an enjoyable working life and was so good at what I did. She was trying to help me, but I had become in the space of just a couple of days so manic, so feverish in my attention to Parry, so . . . She had paused a second to locate the word. She was standing in the doorway, hitching a silk-lined pleated skirt round her waist. In morning light her pallor made her eyes appear all the greener. She was beautiful. She seemed unattainable, an impression intensified by the word she chose. ". . . *Alone,* Joe. You're so alone in all this, even when you speak to me about it. I feel you're shutting me out. There's something you're not telling me. You're not speaking from the heart."

I simply looked at her. Either I've always spoken to her from the heart in times like this, or I never have and I don't know what it means. But that wasn't what I was thinking. My thought was one I used to have when I first knew her: how did such an oversized, average-looking lump as myself land this pale beauty? And a new bad thought: was she beginning to think she had a poor deal?

She was about to leave the room to go down the hallway, where, unknown to us, Parry's letter was waiting. She misread my expression. Pleading with me rather than accusing me, she said, "I mean, the way you're looking at me now. You're making

169

calculations that I'll never know about. Some inner double-entry bookkeeping that you think is the best way to the truth. But don't you see how it cuts you off?"

I knew it would not have convinced her to say, "I was only thinking how lovely you are and how I don't deserve you." The fact that it wouldn't made me think as I got to my feet that perhaps she was the one who didn't deserve me. There. Balance, double entry. She was right, and twice over, for I had said nothing, and she would never know. I smiled at her and said, "Let's talk about it over breakfast." But what we talked about was Parry's letter, and we didn't do that well.

After she had left, after I had cleared the table, I remained sitting in the kitchen with my lukewarm coffee, sliding Parry's pages back into their tight little envelope as though to contain the viral spores that were invading our home. More bad thoughts; it was a daydream, really, but I had to let it run. It occurred to me that Clarissa was using Parry as a front. It was strange, after all, her reaction in this case. She seemed to be aggravating the difficulties by implicating me with Parry. What was the explanation? Was she beginning to regret her life with me? Could she have met someone? If she wanted to leave me, she'd find it easier if she could convince herself that there was something between Parry and me. Had she met someone? At work? A colleague? A student? Could this be an exemplary case of unacknowledged self-persuasion?

I got to my feet. Self-persuasion was a concept much loved by evolutionary psychologists. I had written a piece about it for an Australian magazine. It was pure armchair science, and it went like this: if you lived in a group, as humans have always done, persuading others of your own needs and interests would be fundamental to your well-being. Sometimes you had to use cunning. Clearly you would be at your most convincing if you persuaded yourself first and did not even have to pretend to believe what you were saying. The kind of self-deluding individuals who tended to do this flourished, as did their genes. So it was we squabbled and scrapped, for our unique intelligence was always at the service of our special pleading and selective blindness to the weaknesses of our case.

As I crossed the kitchen, I could honestly have said that I had no idea where I was going. When I reached the door of Clarissa's study, I had a notion I was entering to retrieve my stapler. As I crossed the small room to her desk, I might have told myself I wanted to see if the rest of my morning's post was mixed up with hers, as sometimes happened. There was a moral barrier I needed to hoist myself over, and I suppose the means was the very self-persuasion I ascribed to her.

The study was not quite the serious place Clarissa had intended. She had an office at the university where her real business was done. The study was a transit point, a dump bin between home and work, where papers, books, and student essays were piled. It was a tracking station for godchildren. Their letters were answered here, their presents wrapped, their drawings and gifts untidily displayed. She came in here to pay bills and to write to friends. She could always be relied on for stamps and good-quality envelopes and art postcards from last year's major exhibitions.

When I arrived at her desk, I actually put myself through the motions of looking for the stapler, which I discovered under a newspaper. I even made a little sound of satisfaction. Was there a presence, a godly bystander in the room I was hoping to convince? Were these gestures the remnants — genetically or socially ingrained — of faith in a watchful deity? My performance, as well as my honesty and innocence and self-respect, fell apart the moment I slid the stapler into my pocket but did not leave the room and instead continued to sift the litter on the desk.

Of course, I could no longer deny what I was doing. I told myself that I was acting to untie knots, bring light and understanding to this mess of the unspoken. It was a painful necessity. I would save Clarissa from herself, and myself from Parry. I would renew the bonds, the love through which Clarissa and I had thrived for years. If my suspicions had no basis in fact, then it was vital to be able to set them aside. I pulled open the drawer in which she kept her recent correspondence. Each successive act, each moment of deeper penetration, was coarsening. I cared less by the second that I was behaving badly. Something tight and hard — a screen, a shell — was forming to protect myself from my conscience. My rationalizations crystalized around a partial concept of justice: I had a right to know what was distorting Clarissa's responses to Parry. What was stopping her from being on my side? Some hot little bearded fuck-goat of a postgraduate. I lifted an envelope clear. It had been postmarked three days before. The address was written in small, artfully disordered italic. I pulled a single sheet of paper clear. The salutation alone clutched my heart. *Dear Clarissa.* But it was nothing. An old woman friend from school days sending family news. I chose another — her godfather, the eminent Professor Kale, inviting us to lunch in a restaurant on her birthday. I already knew about that. I glanced at a third — a letter from Luke — then a fourth, a fifth, and their cumulative blamelessness began to sicken me. I looked at three more. Here is a life, they implied, the life of the woman you say you love, busy, intelligent, sympathetic, complex. What are you doing in here? Trying to stain us with your poison! Get out! I started to open one last letter, then I changed my mind. I was so loathsome that as I retreated from the room I touched my pocket to confirm, or give the impression of confirming, the presence of the stapler.

Now I was in a queue of traffic entering the cluttered ordinariness of Headington. A double-decker bus had broken down beyond the lights, where the road was already narrowed by a repair team. Cars were having to wait their turn to squeeze past. My intrusion was a landmark in our decline and in Parry's insidious success. When Clarissa came home that night she was friendly, even vivacious, but I was too ashamed of myself to relax. More self-consciousness. Now I really did have something to conceal from her. I had crossed and recrossed the line of my own innocence.

The following morning, when I sat in my study alone, it seemed a parallel development, the death of an innocent dream, when I opened a letter from my professor and learned that there could be no question of a place being found for me in the department. Not only were there the problems of admittance procedures and of diminishing funds for pure science, but my proposal for work on the virtual photon was redundant. "I should assure you that it is not because the answers have been found, rather that the questions have been radically reframed in the past five years. This redefinition appears to have passed you by. My advice to you, Joseph, would be to continue with the very successful career you already have."

I was getting nowhere. For twenty-five minutes I sat in Headington High Street, waiting for my turn to pass the bus, watching people go in and out of the bank, the chemist's, and the video store. In fifteen minutes or less I would arrive outside Mrs. Logan's house, and I did not know what I wanted to say. My motives in coming were no longer clear. Originally I had wanted to tell her of her husband's courage, in case nobody else did, but there had been coverage in the papers since. When I spoke to her on the phone, she sounded calm and said she was glad I was coming, and that seemed reason enough to make the visit. I had thought then that I would simply let it take its course, but now that I was almost there I was not so sure. First thing in the morning I had been happy enough at the prospect of being out of the house, in my car, out of the city. Now all that had worn off. I was keeping a rendezvous with real grief, and I was confused.

It was a semidetached house choking in fresh greenery, deep in the heart of the North Oxford garden suburb. My theory was that one day we would rediscover the true ugliness of Victorian domestic architecture, and that would be the day after we had defined for our own time what a well-designed house should look like. Until then we could think of nothing better, and a Victorian house was just fine. Getting out of the car may have entailed a slight reduction in blood supply to my head and a corresponding backward drift in my thoughts. *I don't trust myself* was what I thought. *Not since my attack on Clarissa's privacy.* I paused by the front gate. A brick path flanked by dandelions and bluebells ran to the front door. It would have been too easy to assume that the sadness coming off the house was mere projection, and I made myself find the signs: the neglected garden, closed curtains in two upstairs windows, and, below the steps by the door, broken glass — of a milk bottle, perhaps. I didn't trust myself. What I was thinking of again as I pressed the doorbell was that stapler, and how dishonestly we can hold things together for ourselves. I heard a stirring inside the house. I hadn't come to tell Mrs. Logan of her husband's courage; I had come to explain, to establish my guiltlessness, my innocence of his death.

Thirteen

The woman who came to the door was surprised to see me, and we looked at each other a full two seconds before I hurriedly reminded her of our arrangement. The eyes that held mine were small and dry, not reddened by grief but sunk, and glazed by weariness. She looked a long way off, out on her own in unspeakable weather, like a lone Arctic explorer. She brought to the door a warm, home-baked smell, and I thought she might have been sleeping in her clothes. She wore a long necklace of irregular chunks of amber, in which her left hand was awkwardly entwined. Throughout my visit she rolled and worried one piece, smaller than the rest, between forefinger and thumb. When I spoke she said, "Of course, of course," heroically animating her features and opening the door wider.

I knew this kind of North Oxford interior from visits I had made over the years to various professors of science. It was a vanishing type now that nonacademic money was buying up the suburb. The conversion had been made in the fifties or sixties. The books and a few pieces of furniture had been moved in, and since then, no change. No colors but brown and cream. No design or style, no comfort, and in winter, very little warmth. Even the light was brownish, at one with the smells of damp, coal dust, and soap. There would be no heating in the bedrooms, and it looked like there was just one telephone in the house, a dialer kept in the hall, far from any chair. There was lino, and grimy electrical piping on the walls, and from the kitchen the sour scent of gas, and a glimpse of laminated shelves on metal brackets supporting bottles of brown and red sauce. This was the austerity once thought appropriate to the intellectual life, unsensually aligned to the soul of English pragmatism — unfussy, honed to the essential, to the collegiate world beyond the shops. In its time it might have appeared to strike a blow at the Edwardian encumbrances of an older generation. Now it seemed a perfect setting for sorrow.

Jean Logan led me into a cramped back room that gave onto an enormous walled garden dominated by a cherry tree. She bent stiffly to gather up a blanket from the floor by a two-seater sofa whose cushions and covers were tangled and skewed. Bunching the blanket against her stomach with two hands, she asked me if I would like some tea. I guessed she had been asleep when I rang the doorbell, or lying inert beneath her cover. When I offered to help her in the kitchen, she laughed impatiently and told me to sit down.

The air was so thick that breathing was a conscious effort. There was a gas fire on, burning yellow and probably leaking carbon monoxide. That and the holed-up sorrow. While Jean Logan was out of the room, I tried to adjust the flame, and when that failed, I pushed open the french windows an inch or so, and then I straightened the cushions and sat down.

There was nothing in the room to suggest that children lived here. Jammed into an alcove, weighed down with books and heaps of magazines and academic periodicals, was an upright piano whose candleholders bore some sprays of dried twigs — last year's buds, perhaps. The books on either side of the chimney breast were uniform collected editions of Gibbon, Macaulay, Carlisle, Trevelyan, and Ruskin. Along one wall was a dark leather chaise longue with a gash in the side stuffed with yellowing newspapers. Layers of faded and thinning rugs covered the floor. Facing the poisonous fire, set opposite the sofa, were two chairs of what I thought were forties design, with high wooden armrests and low-slung boxy seats. Jean or John Logan had surely inherited the house unchanged from parents. I wondered whether the sense of sorrow in the place pre-dated John Logan's death.

Jean returned with two workman's mugs of tea. I had by now prepared a little opening speech, but as soon as she was seated on the edge of her uncomfortable low chair she started in on her own.

"I don't know why you've come," she said. "I hope it isn't to satisfy your curiosity. Since we don't know each other, I'd rather not hear condolences, consolations, that kind of thing, if you don't mind." The attempt to say this without emotion conveyed it all the more powerfully by way of brisk and breathy phrasing. She tried to soften the effect by smiling wonkily and adding, "I mean, I'm trying to save you the awkward bits."

I nodded and attempted to sip the scalding tea from the small china bucket in my hands. For her, suffering the way she was, a social encounter like this must have been like drunk driving — hard to gauge the right conversational speed, easy to overcompensate with reckless steering.

It was difficult to see her beyond the terms of her bereavement. Was the brown stain on her pale blue cashmere sweater, just below her right breast, anything other than the self-neglect of the grieving? Her hair was greasy and pulled back harshly across her scalp and held in a ragged bun by a red rubber band. Grief too, or was it a certain kind of academic style? I knew from the newspaper stories that she taught history at the university. If you knew nothing, you might guess by her face that she was a sedentary sort of person with a heavy cold. Her nose was sharpened and bloomed pink at the tip and at its base, around the nostrils, from the friction of sodden tissues. (I had seen the near-empty box on the floor at my feet.) But it was an attractive face, almost beautiful, almost plain, a long pale uncluttered oval, with thin lips and nearly invisible eyebrows and lashes. The eyes were an irresolute sandy color. She gave the impression of a stringy kind of independence, and of a temper easily lost.

I said to her, "I don't know if any of the others, the people who were there, have been to see you. My guess is they haven't. I know you don't need me to tell you that your husband was a very courageous man, but perhaps there are things you want to know about what happened. The coroner's court doesn't sit for another five weeks . . ."

I tailed off, uncertain why the coroner had come into my thoughts. Jean Logan still sat on the edge of her chair, hunched forward over her mug, breathing its heat into her face, perhaps to soothe her eyes. She said, "You thought I'd like to go over the details of how he lost his life."

Her sourness surprised me and made me meet her gaze. "There could be something you want to know," I said, speaking more slowly than before. I felt more at ease with her antagonism than with the embarrassment of her sadness.

"There are things I want to know," Jean Logan said, and the anger in her voice was suddenly there. "I've got lots of questions for all sorts of people. But I don't think they're going to give me the answers. They pretend they don't even understand the questions." She paused and swallowed hard. I had tapped into a repeating voice in her head, I was overhearing the thoughts that tormented her all night. Her sarcasm was too theatrical, too energetic, and I felt the weight of exhausted reiteration behind it. "I'm the mad one, of course. I'm irrelevant, I'm in the way. It's not convenient to answer

183

my questions, because they don't fit the story. There, there, Mrs. Logan! Don't go fretting about things that don't concern you and aren't important anyway. We know it's your husband, the father of your children, but we're in charge and please don't get in the way . . ."

Father and *children* were the words that undid her. She set down the mug, snatched a balled-up tissue from the sleeve of her sweater, and pressed it, screwed it, into the space between her eyes. She went to rise from her chair, but its lowness defeated her. I felt that empty, numbing neutrality that comes when one person in the room appears to monopolize all the available emotion. There was nothing for me to do for the moment but wait. I thought she was probably the kind of woman who hates to be seen crying. Lately she would have got used to it. I looked past her, into the garden, past the cherry blossom, and saw the first evidence of the children. Partly obscured by shrubbery was a tent, a brown igloo-style tent on a patch of lawn. The struts had collapsed on one side and it was teetering into a flower bed. It had a sodden, abandoned look. Had he put it up for them not long before he died, or had they erected it to make contact with the sporty outdoor spirit that had fled the house? Perhaps they needed somewhere to sit and be beyond the penumbra of their mother's pain.

Jean Logan was silent. Her hands were clasped tightly in front of her and she stared at the floor, still needing to be, as it were, alone. The skin between her nose and her thin upper lip was raw. My numbness disappeared with the simple thought that what I was seeing was love, and the slow agony of its destruction. Imagining what it would mean to lose Clarissa, through death or by my own stupidity, sent a hot pricking sensation up through the skin of my back, and I felt myself drowning in the small room's lack of decent air. It was urgent that I return to London and save our love. I had no course of action in mind, but I would have been glad to get to my feet and make an excuse. Jean Logan looked up and said, "I'm sorry. I'm glad that you came. It was kind of you to make the journey."

I said something conventionally polite. The muscles in my thighs and arms were tensed, as though ready to push me out of my chair, back toward Maida Vale. What I saw in Jean's grief reduced my own situation to uncomplicated elements, to a periodic table of simple good sense: when it's gone, you'll know what a gift love was. You'll suffer like this. So go back and fight to keep it. Everything else, Parry included, is irrelevant.

"You see, there are things I want to know . . ."

We heard the front door opening and closing and footsteps in the hall, but no sound of voices. She paused, as though waiting for a summons. Then the footsteps — three people, perhaps — went up the stairs and she relaxed. She was about to tell or ask me something important, and I knew I could not possibly leave. Nor could I make my legs relax. I wanted to suggest that we talk in the garden, under the blossom, in the fresh air.

She said, "There was someone with my husband. Did you notice?"

I shook my head. "There was my friend Clarissa, two farm laborers, a man called —"

"I know about them. There was someone in the car with John when he stopped. Someone got out when he did."

"He came from the other side of the field. I didn't see him until we were all running toward the balloon. There was no one else then, I'm sure of that."

Jean Logan was not satisfied. "You could see his car?"

"Yes."

"And you didn't see someone standing beside it, watching?"

"If there'd been someone there, I'd remember."

She looked away. These were not the answers she wanted. She assumed a let's-start-again voice. I didn't mind. I sincerely wanted to help.

"Do you remember the car door being open?"

"Yes."

"One door or two?"

I hesitated. The summoned image held both doors open, but I wasn't sure and I didn't want to mislead her. There was something at stake here, perhaps a powerful fantasy. I didn't want to feed it. But in the end I said reluctantly, "Two. I'm not absolutely sure, but I think two."

"And why do you think two doors would be open if he was on his own?"

I shrugged and waited for her to tell me. She rolled the amber of her necklace faster than before. A pained excitement had replaced the sorrow. Even I, knowing nothing, could tell that vindication in this was going to mean more distress. She had to hear what she didn't want to know. But first she had questions, roughly put, in the tone of an aggressive barrister. For the moment I had become the surrogate object of her bitterness.

"Tell me this. Which way is London from here?"

"East."

"Which way are the Chilterns?"

"East."

She looked at me as though a substantial proof had been concluded. I continued to look blank and helpful. She was having to lead me by the hand toward the self-evident center of her torment. She had lived so long in her head with it, she could barely keep the irritation out of her voice at having to say, "How far is London?"

"Fifty-five miles."

"And the Chilterns?"

"About twenty."

"Would you drive from Oxford to London by way of the Chilterns?"

"Well, the motorway cuts right through them."

"But would you go to London by way of Watlington and all the little lanes around there?"

"No."

Jean Logan stared at the threadbare Persian carpet at her feet, lost to her case, to the misery that could never be set free by a confrontation with her husband. I heard footsteps in the room above us, and a voice, a woman's or a child's. Two or three minutes passed, then I said, "He was supposed to be in London that day."

She closed her eyes tight and nodded. "At a weekend conference," she whispered. "A medical conference."

I cleared my throat softly. "There's probably a perfectly innocent explanation."

Her eyes were still closed and her voice dropped to a low monotone, as though she were speaking under hypnosis to recall the unspeakable day. "It was the police sergeant from the local station who brought the car back. It was on a breakdown lorry because they couldn't find the keys. They should have been in the car, or in John's pocket. That was why I looked inside. Then I said to the sergeant, 'Have you gone through the car? Did you look for fingerprints?' And he said they didn't look and they didn't take prints. Do you know why? Because there hadn't been a crime."

She opened her eyes to see if I had taken in the significance of this, the full impact of its absurdity. I didn't think I had. I parted my lips to echo the word, but she said it first, repeating it loudly.

"A crime! There hadn't been a crime!" She was suddenly on her feet and crossing the room and seizing a plastic bag from a corner where books were piled waist high. She returned and thrust it at me. "You look. Go on. Tell me what it is."

It was a heavily weighted white carrier bag printed with a crude picture of children dancing in and out of a supermarket's name. Whatever was in there sagged heavily to the bottom. As soon as it was in my hands I was aware of the smell that rose from it, the coarse, intimate whiff of rotting meat.

"Go on. It won't hurt you."

I held my breath and parted the top of the bag, and for a moment the contents made no sense. There were plastic wrappers buckled around a grayish paste, a sphere of tinfoil, a brown mess on a square of cardboard. Then I glimpsed dark red, curved in glass, mostly obscured by paper. It was a bottle of wine, the reason for the bag's heaviness. And then everything else fell into place. I saw two apples.

"It's a picnic," I said. The queasiness I felt was not entirely due to the smell.

"It was on the floor by the passenger seat. He was going to picnic with her. Somewhere in the woods."

"Her?" I felt I was being pedantic, but I thought I ought to continue to resist the suggestive power of her fantasy. She was

190

pulling something from the pocket of her skirt. She took the bag from me and put in my hand a small silk scarf with gray and black zebra markings in stylized form.

"Smell it," she commanded as she carefully stowed the bag in its corner.

It smelled salty, of tears or snot, or of the sweat of Jean's clenched hand.

"Take a deeper breath," she said. She was standing over me, rigid and fierce in her desire for my complicity.

I raised the scrap of silk to my face and sniffed again. "I'm sorry," I said. "It doesn't smell of anything much to me."

"It's rosewater. Can't you smell it?"

She took it from me. I no longer deserved to hold it. She said, "I've never used rosewater in my life. I found it on the passenger seat." She sat down and seemed to be waiting for me to speak. Did she feel that as a man I was somehow party to her husband's transgression, that I was the proxy who should come clean and confess? When I didn't speak, she said, "Look, if you saw something, please don't feel you have to protect me. I need to know."

"Mrs. Logan, I saw no one with your husband."

"I asked them to look for fingerprints in the car. I could trace this woman . . ."

"Only if she has a criminal record."

She didn't hear me. "I need to know how long it was going on and what it meant. You understand that, don't you?"

I nodded, and I thought I did. She had to have the measure of her loss, and to know what to grieve for. She would have to know everything and suffer for it before she could have any kind of peace. The alternative was tormented ignorance and a lifetime's suspicion, black guesses, worst-case thoughts.

"I'm sorry," I started to say, but she cut me off.

"I simply have to find her. I have to talk to her. She must have seen the whole thing. Then she would have run off. Distressed, demented. Who knows?"

I said, "I'd have thought there was a good chance of her making contact with you. It might be impossible to resist, coming to see you."

"If she comes near this house," Jean Logan said simply as the door behind us opened and two children came into the room, "I'll kill her. God help me, but I will."

Fourteen

It was with a touch of sadness that Clarissa sometimes told me that I would have made a wonderful father. She would tell me that I had a good way with children, that I leveled with them easily and without condescension. I've never looked after a child for any length of time, so I've never been tested in the true fires of parental self-denial, but I think I'm good enough at the listening and talking. I know all seven of her godchildren well. We've had them for weekends, we've taken some on holiday abroad, and we devotedly cared for two little girls for a week — Felicity and Grace, who both wet the bed — while their parents tore each other apart in a divorce hearing. I was of some use to Clarissa's eldest godchild, an inwardly stormy fifteen-year-old befuddled by pop culture and the oafish codes of street credibility. I took him drinking with me and talked him out of leaving school. Four years later he was reading medicine at Edinburgh and doing well.

For all that, there's an uneasiness I have to conceal when I meet a child. I see myself through that child's eyes and remember how I regarded adults when I was small. They seemed a gray crew to me, too fond of sitting down, too keen on small talk, too accustomed to having nothing to look forward to. My parents, their friends, my uncles and aunts, all seemed to have lives bent to the priorities of other, distant, more important people. For a child it was, of course, simply a matter of local definition. Later I discovered in certain adults dignity and flamboyance, and later still these qualities, or at least the first, stood revealed in my parents and most of their circle. But when I was an energetic, self-important ten-year-old and found myself in a roomful of grownups, I felt guilty, and thought it only polite to conceal the fun I was having elsewhere. When an aged figure addressed me — they were all aged — I worried that what showed in my face was pity.

So when I turned in my chair to meet the stare of the Logan children, I saw myself configured in their eyes — yet one more dull stranger in the procession lately filing through their home, a large man in a creased blue linen suit, the coin of baldness on his crown visible from where they stood. His purpose here would be unintelligible, beyond consideration. Above all, he was yet another man who was not their father. The girl was about ten, and the boy must have been two years younger. Standing behind them, just out of the room, was the nanny, a cheerful-looking young woman in a track suit. The children looked at me and I returned their stare while their mother uttered her death threat. They both wore jeans, trainers, and sweaters with Disney motifs. There was an appealing scruffiness about them, and they didn't look crushed to me.

The boy did not take his eyes off me as he said, "It's completely wrong to kill people." His sister smiled tolerantly, and since Jean Logan was now giving instructions to the nanny, I said to the boy, "It's just a way of speaking. It's what you say when you really don't like someone."

"If it's wrong to do it," the boy said, "it's wrong to say you're going to do it."

I said, "Have you ever heard someone say, 'I'm so hungry I could eat a horse'?"

He gave this honest consideration. "I've said that," he admitted.

"Isn't it wrong to eat horses?"

"It's wrong here," the girl said. "But it

isn't wrong in France. They eat them all the time."

"That's true," I said. "But if something's wrong, I don't see why crossing the Channel should make it right."

Still standing shoulder to shoulder, the children came closer. After what had gone before, a discussion of moral relativism was pure relief.

The girl said, "People in different countries have different ideas. In China it's polite to burp after a meal."

"It's true," I said. "When I was in Morocco I was told that I should never pat children on the head."

"I hate people who do that," the girl said, and her brother spoke over her excitedly. "My dad saw them cut off a goat's head in India."

"And they were *priests*," the girl added. The mention of the father brought no outward change, no remorse. He was still a living presence.

"So," I said. "Aren't there any rules the whole world can agree on?"

The boy was triumphant. "Killing people."

I looked at the girl and she nodded, and at the sound of the door closing we all turned to look at their mother, who had just finished with the nanny.

"This is Rachael and Leo. And this is Mr. —"

"Joe," I said.

Leo went and sat on his mother's lap. She locked her hands firmly around his waist. Rachael crossed to the window and stared out at the garden. "That tent," she said quietly to herself.

"I have to find her." Jean Logan resumed our conversation in a businesslike way. "If you didn't see her, that's too bad. But perhaps you can still help me. The police are completely useless. One of the others might have seen something. I can't speak to them myself, but if you wouldn't mind . . ."

"What are you talking about, Mummy?" Rachael asked from the window. I caught the anxious, protective tone of her hesitant question, and with it a glimpse of her ordeal. There must have been scenes whose repetition the girl dreaded and had to head off.

"Nothing, darling. Nothing that concerns you."

I could not think of a way of refusing, much as I wanted to. Was my life to be entirely subordinate to other people's obsessions?

"I've got the phone numbers of the farm people," she said. "That young man's number won't be difficult to find. I've got his address. His name is Parry. Three phone calls, that's all I'm asking."

It was too complicated to refuse. "All right," I said. "I'll do it." Even as I agreed, I realized that I would be in a position to censor the information and perhaps save the family some misery. Wouldn't Rachael and Leo agree, there were times when it was right to lie?

The boy slid from his mother's lap and went over to his sister. Jean Logan, having smiled her thanks, straightened her skirt with a smoothing movement of her palms, a gesture that suggested she was ready now for me to leave. "I'll write the phone numbers down for you."

I nodded and said, "Look, Mrs. Logan. Your husband was a very determined and courageous man. You mustn't lose sight of that." Rachael and Leo were fooling about by the window, and I was obliged to raise my voice. "He was determined to save that boy, and he hung on to the end. The power lines were a real danger. The kid could easily have died. Your husband just wouldn't let go of that rope, and he put the rest of us to shame."

"The rest of you are alive," she said, and then paused and frowned as Leo squealed from behind the long curtains that framed the french windows. His sister was tickling him through the fabric. Their mother seemed about to tell them to pipe down, but she changed her mind. Like me, she had to speak louder. "Don't think this isn't going round in my mind all the time. John was a mountaineer and a good sailor. But he was also a doctor. He was on rescue teams, and he was a very, very cautious man." On each *very* she clenched her fist tighter. "He never took stupid chances. They used to make fun of him on the climbs because he was always weighing up the possibilities of a change in weather, or loose rock or hazards that no one else would think about. He was the group's pessimist. Some people even thought he was timid. But he didn't care. He never took unnecessary risks. As soon as Rachael was born he gave up serious climbing. And that's why this story doesn't make sense." She half turned to speak to the children, who were making even more noise now, but she was intent on finishing what she had to tell me, and she had more privacy behind their din. She turned back. "This business of holding on to the rope . . . You see, I've thought about it, and I know what killed him."

At last we were at the center of the story.

I was about to be accused, and I had to interrupt her. I wanted my own account in first. There came to me, as encouragement, an image of something, someone, dropping away in the instant before I let go. But I also knew the old cautionary tag from my distant laboratory days: believing is seeing. "Mrs. Logan," I said, "you might have heard something from one of the others, I don't know. But I can honestly say —"

She was shaking her head as I spoke. "No, no. You've got to listen to me. You were there, but I know more about this than you. There was another side to John, you see. He always wanted to be the best, but he was no longer the all-round athlete he once was. He was forty-two. It hurt. He couldn't accept it. And when men start to feel like that . . . I knew nothing about this woman. I suspected nothing, it didn't occur to me, I don't even know if she was the first, but I know this. She was watching him, and he knew she was watching, and he had to show her, he had to prove himself to her. He had to run right into the middle of the scene, he had to be the first to take the rope and the last to let go, instead of doing what he usually would — hanging back and seeing what was best. That's what he would have done without her, and it's pathetic. He was showing off to a girl, Mr. Rose, and we're all suffering for it now."

This was a theory, a narrative that only grief, the dementia of pain, could devise. "But you can't know this," I protested. "It's so particular, so elaborate. It's just a hypothesis. You can't let yourself believe in it."

She gave me a pitying look before turning to the children. "This really is too much noise. We can't hear ourselves speak." Then she stood impatiently. Leo had wound himself up in the curtain until only his feet were visible. Rachael had been prancing around him, chanting something and poking him and eliciting in return a chanted response. Now she stood back as her mother unwound the boy. Jean Logan's tone was hardly scolding, more a gentle reminder. "You'll bring the curtain rail down again. I told you yesterday, and you promised me."

Leo emerged flushed and happy. He caught his sister's eye and she began to giggle. Then he remembered me and squared up to his mother for my benefit. "But this is our palace and I'm the king and she's the queen and I only come out when she gives the signal."

There was more from Leo, and the mildest of censure from his mother, but I heard none of it. It was as though delicate lace-work were repairing its own torn fabric by the power of its intricacy alone. It all came at once, and it seemed impossible that I could have forgotten. The palace was Buckingham Palace, the king was King George the Fifth, the woman outside the palace was French, and the time was shortly after the Great War. She had traveled to England on a number of occasions and wanted nothing more than to stand outside the palace gates in the hope of catching sight of the king, with whom she was in love. She had never met him and never would, but her every waking thought was of him.

I was on my feet and Rachael was saying something to me, which I did not hear, but I nodded all the same.

This woman was convinced that all of London society was talking of her affair with the king and that he was deeply perturbed. On one visit, when she could not find a hotel room, she felt the king had used his influence to prevent her from staying in London. The one thing she knew for certain was that the king loved her. She loved him in return, but she resented him bitterly. He turned her away, and yet he never stopped giving her hope. He sent her signals that she alone could read, and he let her know that however inconvenient it was, however embarrassing and inappropriate, he loved her and always would. He used the curtains in the windows of Buckingham Palace to communicate with her. She lived her life in the prison gloom of this delusion. Her forlorn and embittered love was identified as a syndrome by the French psychiatrist who treated her, and who gave his name to her morbid passion. De Clerambault.

When Jean Logan saw me stand up, she assumed I was about to leave. She had gone over to a desk and was scrawling names and numbers down.

The children approached again and Rachael said, "I've thought of another one."

"Really?" It was difficult to concentrate on her.

"Our teacher said that in most of the world they don't have hankies and it's okay to blow your nose like this." She pinched the bridge of her nose between forefinger and thumb, with the other fingers lifted clear of the nostrils, and blew a raspberry at me. Her brother yelped in glee. I took the folded piece of paper from Jean Logan, and together we left the room and went down the brown hall to the front door. Even before we reached it, I was back with de Clerambault. De Clerambault's syndrome. The name was like a fanfare, a clear trumpet sound recalling me to my own obsessions. There was research to follow through now, and I knew exactly where to start. A syndrome was a framework of prediction, and it offered a kind of comfort. I was almost happy as she opened the front door for me and the four of us crowded out onto the brick path to say our goodbyes. It was as if I had at last been offered that research post with my old professor.

Jean Logan thanked me for coming, and I told her I would phone as soon as I had made the calls. Now that I was leaving, the children hung back. I was a stranger again. I pinched my nose and made a politer version of Rachael's sound. They indulged me with forced smiles. I made them shake my hand. I couldn't help feeling as I went up the path that my leaving would return them to their father's absence. The family was grouped by the front door, the mother's hands resting on her children's shoulders. When I reached my car and unlocked the door, I turned to call out one last goodbye, but all three had gone back inside the house.

Fifteen

On the way home I turned south off the motorway where the Chilterns rise and drove to the field. I parked exactly where Logan had, with the car banked on the grass verge. Standing by the passenger door, she would have had a clear view of the whole drama, from the balloon and its basket dragging across the field to the struggle with the ropes and the fall. She wouldn't have been able to see where he landed. I imagined her, pretty, in her early twenties, frantic in distress, running back up the road to the nearest village. Or she might have gone the other way, down the hill toward Watlington. I stood there in her place and daydreamed of the secret phone calls or notes that might have preceded their picnic. Perhaps they were in love. Did he suffer tortures of guilt and indecision, the honorable family man? And what violent transformation for her, from the anticipated idyll with the man she adored to the nightmare, the moment round which the rest of her life would pivot. Even in her terror she would have remembered to snatch her things from the car — her coat and bag, perhaps, but not the picnic and her scarf — and she would have started running. It made sense to me that she did not come forward. She stayed at home and read the newspapers and lay whimpering on her bed.

With no particular aim, I set off across the field. Everything looked different. In less than two weeks the hedgerows and surrounding trees had thickened with the first spring growth, and the grass underfoot gave a hint of the extravagance to come. As though walking through a police reconstruction, I picked up the path Clarissa and I had taken and followed it to the patch where we had sheltered from the wind. It seemed like a half-remembered place from childhood. We were so happy in our reunion, so easy with each other, and now I could not quite imagine a route back into that innocence.

From here I walked slowly into the center of the field, along the direction of my sprint, to the point where our fates converged, and then along the route the wind had driven us, right to the edge of the escarpment. There, traversing the field, was the footpath that brought Parry into my life. Back there, where my car was now, was where Logan had stopped. This was where we stood and watched him fall from the sky; it was also where Parry caught my glance and became stricken with a love whose morbidity I was now impatient to research.

These were my stations of the cross. I went down the hill, into the field, and toward the next place. The sheep were gone, and the minor road beyond the hedge was closer than I remembered. I looked for an indentation in the ground, but there was only the beginning of a nettle patch that extended almost to the gate the policemen had climbed. This was where Parry had wanted to pray, and it was from here that I had walked away. I walked away now, trying to imagine how he could have read rejection in my posture.

It cost me more effort than last time to climb the hill. Then adrenaline had powered my limbs and accelerated every thought. Now my reluctance was deep in the muscles of my thighs, and I could feel my heart knocking in my ears. While I paused at the top to recover, I looked about me. A hundred acres or so of fields and one steep slope. Now I was here, it seemed as though I had never really left, for this was the stage, the green painted flats, of my preoccupations, and it would not have been such a surprise to have seen approaching me from different corners Clarissa, John and Jean Logan, the unnamed woman, Parry and de Clerambault. Imagining this, seeing them arrive to back me against the escarpment's edge in a horseshoe, I had no doubt they would come to accuse me collectively — but of what? Had I known immediately, I would not have been so indictable. A lack, a deficiency, a failed extension into mental space as difficult to describe as one's first encounter with the calculus. Clarissa I would listen to at any time, even though we didn't trust each other's judgment at present, but it was the Frenchman in the double-breasted suit who fascinated me now.

I began to return across the field toward my car. It was a simple idea, really, but a man who had a theory about pathological love and who had given his name to it, like a bridegroom at the altar, must surely reveal, even if unwittingly, the nature of love itself. For there to be a pathology, there had to be a lurking concept of health. De Clerambault's syndrome was a dark, distorting mirror that reflected and parodied a brighter world of lovers whose reckless abandon to their cause was sane. (I walked faster. The car was four hundred meters or so away, and seeing it now, I knew for certain the front doors had stood wide open, like wings.) Sickness and health. In other words, what could I learn about Parry that would restore me to Clarissa?

The traffic into London was heavy, and it was almost two hours before I parked outside our apartment building. I had thought about it on the way, and I expected him to be there, but seeing him waiting for me as I got out of the car gave me a jolt to the heart. I paused before I crossed the road. He had taken up a position by the entrance where I would have to walk by him. He looked dressed up — black suit, white shirt buttoned to the top, black patent shoes with white flashes. He was staring at me, but his expression told me nothing. I walked toward him quickly, hoping to brush right by him and get indoors, but he stood across my path and I had to stop or push him aside. He looked tense, possibly angry. There was an envelope in his hand.

"You're in my way," I said.

"Did you get my letter?"

I decided to try to squeeze past him by pushing into the low privet hedge that flanked the path, but he closed the gap and I didn't want to touch him.

"Let me through or I'll call the police."

He nodded eagerly, as though he had heard me inviting him up for a drink. "But I'd like you to read this first," he said. "It's very important?"

I took the envelope from him, hoping he would then stand aside for me. But it was not enough. There was something he wanted to tell me. First he glanced at the presence over his shoulder. When he spoke his voice was breathy, and I guessed his heart was racing. This was a moment he had prepared for.

He said, "I paid a researcher and he got me all your articles. I read them last night, thirty-five of them. I've got your books too."

I just looked at him and waited. Something had shifted in his manner. The yearning was there, but there was a hardness too, a change around the eyes. They looked smaller.

"I know what you're trying to do, but you'll never succeed. Not even if you wrote a million and I read them all, you'll never destroy what I have. It can't be taken away."

He seemed to expect to be contradicted, but I folded my arms and continued to wait, concentrating my attention on a shaving cut, a black hairline nick on his cheek. What he said next appeared at the time to refer to the ease of hiring a researcher, although I wasn't completely sure. Afterward I considered his words carefully and began to think that perhaps I was being threatened. But then, it was easy to feel threatened, and I ended up with no clear idea at all.

He said, "I'm pretty well off, you know. I can get people to do things for me. Anything I want. There's always someone who needs the money. What's surprising is how cheap it is, you know, for something you'd never do yourself?" He let this pseudo question hang, and watched me.

"I've got a phone in the car. If you don't let me through, I'm calling the police now."

I got the same warm look as before. The hardness dropped from Parry as he gratefully accepted the affection he had detected in my warning. "It's okay, Joe. It really is. It's difficult for me too. I understand you just as well as you understand me. You can be open with me. You don't have to wrap it up in code, really you don't."

As I stepped back and turned toward my car, I said, "There is no code. It would be better if you accepted that you need help."

Even before I had finished he laughed, or rather he whooped and slapped his thigh, cowboy style. He must have heard from me a rallying cry to love. He was almost shouting in his joy. "That's right. I've got every-one and everything on my side. It's going to go my way, Joe, and there's nothing you can do!"

Mad as this was, he also took the trouble to stand back and let me pass. Was there calculation here? I couldn't even trust his derangement, and for that reason alone I was glad to end the conversation and go indoors. Also, it was obvious the police wouldn't have helped. I did not even look back to see if he was going to wait around. I did not want to give him the satisfaction of knowing that it bothered me. I put his envelope in my back pocket and took the stairs two at a time. It was like a painkiller, the distance and height I opened between us in fifteen seconds. Studying Parry with reference to a syndrome I could tolerate, even relish, but meeting him yet again in the street, especially now that I had read his first letter, had frightened me. Fearing him would grant him great power. I could well imagine preferring not to come home. As I reached the landing outside the apart-ment door, I was wondering whether he had in fact threatened me; if a researcher was easy to hire, so too were a few goons to thrash me within an inch of my life. Perhaps I was overinterpreting. The ambiguity fed my fear. As threats went, it was perfectly nuanced.

These were my thoughts as I unlocked the door and stepped into the hall. I stood there a moment, recovering my breath, reading the silence and the quality of the air. Although her bag was not on the floor by the door, nor was her jacket draped across the chair, I sensed through my skin that Clarissa was back from work and something was wrong. I called her name and, hearing nothing, walked into the sitting room. It is L-shaped, and I had to go several paces in before I was certain she was not there. I thought I heard a sound in the hall I had just left, and I called her name again. Buildings have their own archives of creaks and clicks, mostly prompted by small changes in temperature, so I was not surprised to see no one when I went back, though I still did not doubt that Clarissa was somewhere in the apartment. I went into the bedroom, thinking she might be taking a nap. The shoes she wore to work were lying side by side, and the bedspread had an indent where she had lain. There was no sign she had used the bathroom. I made a quick search of the other rooms — the kitchen, her study, the children's bedroom — and I checked the bolt on the door that led out onto the roof. It was then that I changed my mind and devised a logical sequence: she had come home, kicked off her shoes, lain on the bed awhile, put on another pair of shoes, and gone out. In my anxiety following the encounter with Parry, I had simply misread the air.

I went into the kitchen to fill the kettle. Then I wandered into my study, and that was where I found her. It was so obvious, and it was such a shock. I saw her as if for the first time. She was barefoot, slumped in my swivel chair, with her back to the desk, facing the door. With all that had happened that day, I should have guessed it. I returned her stare as I came into the room and said, "Why didn't you answer?"

She said, "I thought this would be the first place you'd look." When I frowned she added, "Didn't you think I'd be going through your desk while you were out? Isn't that how it is with us these days?"

I sat wearily on the couch. Being so entirely in the wrong was a kind of liberation. No need to struggle, no point marshaling arguments.

She was calm, and very angry. "I've been sitting here half an hour, trying to tempt myself to open one of these drawers and take a look at your letters. And do you know, I couldn't raise the curiosity. Isn't that a terrible thing? I don't care about your secrets, and if you've got none, I don't care either. If you'd asked to see my letters I'd've said yes, go ahead. I've got nothing to hide from you." Her voice rose a little, and there was a tremor in it too. I had never seen such fury in her before. "You even left the drawer open so I'd know when I came in. It's a statement, a message, from you to me, it's a signal. The trouble is, I don't know what it means. Perhaps I'm being very stupid. So spell it out for me now, Joe. What is it you're trying to tell me?"

Sixteen

Dear Joe,

The student I hired rang my bell at four yesterday afternoon and I went out to meet him at the gate. I gave him five hundred pounds for his work and he handed the bundle through the bars. Thirty-five photocopied articles by you. He went off happy, but what about me? I had no idea then what kind of night lay ahead. Perhaps they were the worst few hours of my life. It was torture, Joe, coming face to face with your sad dry thoughts. To think of the fools who paid you good money for them, and the innocent readers who had their day polluted by them!

I sat in the room my mother used to call the library, though the shelves were always pretty bare, and I read every last word, and actually heard them, in my head, spoken by you straight to me. I read each article as a letter sent by you into the future that was going to contain us both. What were you trying to do to me, I kept thinking. Hurt me? Insult me? Test me? I hated you for it, but I never forgot that I loved you too, and that was why I kept going. *He needs my help*, I told myself whenever I came close to giving up, *he needs me to set him free from his little cage of reason.* I had moments when I wondered if I had truly understood what God wanted from me. Was I to deliver into His hands the author of these hateful pieces against Him? Perhaps I was intended for something simpler and purer. I mean, I knew you wrote about science, and I was prepared to be baffled or bored, but I didn't know you wrote out of contempt.

You've probably forgotten the article you wrote four years ago for the *New Scientist* about the latest technological aids to biblical scholarship. Well, who cares about the carbon dating of the Turin Shroud? Do you think people changed their minds about their beliefs when they heard that it was a medieval hoax? Do you think faith could depend upon a length of rotting cloth? But it was another piece that really shocked me, when you wrote about God Himself. Perhaps it was a joke, but that makes it even worse. You pretend to know what or who He is — a literary character, you say, like something out of a novel. You say the best minds in the field are prepared to take "an educated guess" at who invented Yahweh, that the evidence points to a woman who was living around 1000 B.C., Bathsheba, the Hittite who slept with David. A woman novelist dreamed up God! The best minds would rather die than presume to know so much. You're dealing in powers neither you nor any person on earth can have any grasp of. You go on to say that Jesus Christ was a character too, mostly made up by Saint Paul and "whoever" wrote the Gospel of Saint Mark. I prayed for you, I prayed for the strength to face you, to go on loving you without being dragged down. How is it possible to love God and love you at the same time? Through faith alone, Joe. Not through facts, or pretend facts, or intellectual arrogance, but by trusting in God's wisdom and love as a living presence in our lives, the kind of presence that no human, let alone a literary character, could ever have.

I suppose I was naive to think in that first rush of feeling I had for you that it could all come right simply because I wanted it so much. When the dawn came,

I still had ten more pieces to read. I took a taxi to your place. You were asleep, unaware of your own vulnerability, indifferent to the protection you enjoy from a source whose existence you deny. Life has been very good to you, and I suppose standing out there I began to think you were ungrateful. It probably never crosses your mind to give thanks for what you have. It all happened by blind chance? You made it all yourself? I worry for you, Joe. I worry for what your arrogance could bring down on you. I crossed the road and put my hand on the hedge. No message this time. Why should you speak to me when you don't have to? You think you have everything, you think that you can meet all your needs on your own. But without an awareness of God's love, you're living in a desert. If only you understood fully what it is I'm offering you. Wake up!

You might have got the impression that I hate science. I was never much good at school and I don't take a personal interest in the latest advances, but I know it is a wonderful thing. The study and measurement of nature is really nothing more than a form of extended prayer, a celebration of the glory of God's universe. The more we find out about the intricacies of His creation, the more we realize how little we know and how little we are. He gave us our minds, He granted us our wonderful cleverness. It seems so childish and sad that people use this gift to deny His reality. You write that we know enough about chemistry these days to speculate how life began on earth. Little mineral pools warmed by the sun, chemical bonding, protein chains, amino acids, etc. The primal soup. We've flushed God out of this particular story, you said, and now he's been driven to his last redoubt, among the molecules and particles of the quantum physicists. But it doesn't work, Joe. Describing how the soup is made isn't the same as knowing why it's made, or who the chef is. It's a puny rant against an infinite power. Somewhere in among your protestations about God is a plea to be rescued from the traps of your own logic. Your articles add up to a long cry of loneliness. There's no happiness in all this denial. What can it give you in the end?

I know you won't hear me — yet. Your mind is closed, your defenses are in place. It suits you and it protects you to tell yourself that I'm a madman. Help!

There's a man outside offering me love and the love of God! Call the police, call an ambulance! There's no problem with Joe Rose. His world is in place, everything fits, and all the problems are with Jed Parry, the patient idiot who stands in the street like a beggar, waiting to glimpse his loved one and to offer his love. What is it I have to do to make you begin to hear me? Only prayer can answer this question, and only love can carry it through. But my love for you is no longer of the beseeching sort. I don't sit by the phone waiting for kind words from you. You don't stand above me deciding my future, you don't have the power to command me to do whatever you like. My love for you is hard and fierce, it won't take no for an answer, and it's moving steadily toward you, coming to claim you and deliver you. In other words, my love — which is also God's love — is your fate. Your denials and refusals and all your articles and books are like the little foot stampings of a tired infant. It's only a matter of time, and you'll be grateful when the moment comes.

See? Reading you all night has strengthened me. That's what God's love does. If you're beginning to feel uncomfortable now, it's because the changes in you are already beginning to happen and one day you'll be glad to say, Deliver me from meaninglessness. There'll come a time when we'll look back fondly on these exchanges. We'll know then where they were leading, and it will make us smile to think how hard I had to push, and how hard you fought to keep me off. So whatever you're feeling now, please don't destroy these letters.

When I came in the early morning, I hated you for what you had written. I wanted to hurt you. Perhaps even more than that. Something more, and God will forgive me, I thought. On the way over in the taxi I imagined you telling me in your cold way that God and His Only Son were just characters, like James Bond or Hamlet. Or that you yourself could make life in a laboratory flask, given a handful of chemicals and a few million years. It's not only that you deny there's a God — you want to take His place. Pride like this can destroy you. There are mysteries we should not touch, and there's humility too we all must learn, and I hated you, Joe, for your arrogance. You want the final word on everything. After reading thirty-five of your articles, I should know. There's never a moment's doubt or hesitation or admission of ignorance. You're there with the up-to-the-minute truth on bacteria and particles and agriculture and insects and Saturn's rings and musical harmony and risk theory and bird migration . . . My brain was like a washing machine, churning and spinning, full of your dirty washing. Can you blame me for hating you for the things you allow to fill your mind — satellites, nanotechnologies, genetic engineering, biocomputers, hydrogen engines? It's all shopping. You buy it all, you're a cheerleader for it, an ad man hired to talk up other people's stuff. In four years' journalism, not a word about the real things, like love and faith.

Perhaps I'm angry because I'm impatient for our life together to begin. I remember I once went walking with my school in Switzerland in the summer holidays. One day we spent the whole morning climbing a boring rocky path. We all complained — it was so hot and pointless, but the teacher made us keep going. Just before lunch we arrived at a high alpine meadow, a huge sunny expanse of flowers and grasses, with electric green mosses around the banks of a stream. It was a miraculous place. We were a noisy bunch of kids, but we suddenly went very quiet. Someone said in a whisper that it was like arriving in Paradise. It was a great moment in my life. I think when our difficulties are over, when you come here and we're together, it will be like arriving at that meadow. No more rocky uphill! Peace, and time stretching out before us.

There's one last thing I have to say to you. I've exploded into your life, just as you have into mine. You're bound to wish it hadn't happened. Your life is about to be upended. You have to tell Clarissa, you have to move all your stuff, and you'll probably want to get rid of most of it anyway. You'll have to explain yourself to all your friends, not only your change of address but the revolution in your beliefs. Pain and bother, and you'll want none of it. There'll be times when you wished I had never troubled your ordered and satisfying life. You'll wish I didn't exist. It's understandable, and you shouldn't feel any guilt about it. You'll feel anger, and you'll want to try and drive me away because I represent upheaval and turmoil. All that is how it has to be. It's the steep rocky path! Everything you feel, you must find expression for. Curse me, throw stones at my head, take a swing at me —

if you dare. But there is one thing you must never do while we are still making our way to our meadow, and that is to ignore me, to pretend it's not happening, to deny the difficulty, or the pain or the love. Don't ever walk by me as if I weren't there. Neither of us can be fooled. Never deny my reality, because in the end you'll deny yourself. The despair I felt at your rejection of God had something to do with my sense that you were also rejecting me. Accept me, and you'll find yourself accepting God without a thought. So promise me. Show me your fury or bitterness. I won't mind. I'll never desert you. But never, never try to pretend to yourself that I do not exist.

Jed

Seventeen

I don't know what led to it, but we were lying face-to-face in bed, as though nothing were wrong. It may have been mere tiredness. It was late at night, long past midnight. The silence appeared so rich as to have a visual quality, a sparkle or hard gloss, and a thickness too, like fresh paint. This synesthesia must have been due to my disorientation, for this was so familiar, lying here in the green field of her stare, feeling her smooth thin arms. It was so unexpected too. We were hardly at war, but everything between us was stalled. We were like armies facing each other across a maze of trenches. We were immobilized. The only movement was that of silent accusations rippling over our heads like standards. To her I was manic, perversely obsessed, and, worst of all, the thieving invader of her private space. As far as I was concerned, she was disloyal, unsupportive in this time of crisis, and irrationally suspicious.

There were no rows, or even skirmishes,

as though we sensed that a confrontation might blow us apart. We remained on tight speaking terms; we small-talked about work and exchanged messages about shopping, cooking, and household repairs. Clarissa left the house every weekday to give seminars and lectures and do battle with the management. I wrote a long and dull review of five books on consciousness. When I started out in science writing, the word was more or less proscribed in scientific discourse. It wasn't a subject. Now it was up there with black holes and Darwin, almost bigger than dinosaurs.

We continued our daily round because little else seemed clear. We knew we had lost heart, we had lost our heart. We were loveless, or we had lost the trick of love, and we didn't know how to begin talking about it. We slept in the same bed, but we didn't embrace. We used the same bathroom, but we never saw each other naked. We were scrupulously casual because we knew that anything less — cold politeness, for example — would have exposed the charade and led us into the conflict we longed to avoid. What had once seemed natural, like lovemaking or long talks or silent companionship, now appeared as robustly contrived as Harrison's fourth sea clock, impossible as well as anachronistic to re-create. When I looked at her, brushing her hair or bending to retrieve a book from the floor, I remembered her beauty like some schoolbook fact got by heart. True, but not immediately relevant. And I could recon-struct myself in her own gaze as oafishly large and coarse, a biologically motivated bludgeon, a giant polyp of uninspired logic with which she was mistakenly associated. When I spoke to her, my voice rang dull and flat in my skull, and not just every sentence but every word was a lie. Muted anger, finely disseminated self-loathing — these were my elements, my colors. When our eyes met, it was as if our ghostly, meaner selves held up hands before our faces to block the possibility of under-standing. But our gazes rarely met, and when they did it was only a second or two before they shrank nervously away. Our for-mer loving selves would never have under-stood us or forgiven us, and that was it, right there: the dominant, unacknowledged emotion around our household in those days was shame.

Now here we were, somewhere between half past one and two in the morning, lying in bed, staring at each other by the low light of one lamp, I naked, she in a cotton nightdress, our arms and hands touching, but neutrally, without commitment. All the questions were heaped around us, and for a while neither of us dared speak. It was enough that we could look each other in the eye.

I've said we still managed to talk to each other about everyday matters, but one aspect of our lives had become absorbed into the daily routine and we could not bear to discuss it. People often remark on how quickly the extraordinary becomes commonplace. I think that every time I'm on a motorway at night, or on a plane as it rises through cloud cover into sunlight. We are highly adaptive creatures. The predictable becomes, by definition, background, leaving the attention uncluttered, the better to deal with the random or unexpected.

Parry was sending three or four letters a week. They were generally long and ardent, and written in an increasingly focused present tense. He often took as his subject the process by which the letter itself was written, the room he was in, the changing light and weather, his shifting mood, and the fact that by writing to me he had successfully conjured my presence, right there at his side. His signings-off were lengthy expressions of sorrow at parting. The religious references

229

would have seemed formulaic had they not been so fervent: his love was like God's, patient and all-embracing, and it was through Parry that God would bring me to Him. There was usually an element of accusation, either running as a strain throughout or concentrated in one pained passage: I had started this love affair and I should therefore face my responsibilities toward him. I was playing with him, leading him on, sending him messages of encouragement, then turning away from him. I was a tease, a coquette, I was the master of slow torture and my genius was never to admit what I was doing. I no longer seemed to be sending messages via curtain or privet. I spoke to him now in dreams. I appeared radiantly before him like a Bible prophet and assured him of my love and foretold the happier days to come.

I learned how to scan these letters. I lingered only on the accusations or expressions of frustration, always looking for a repeat of the threat I thought he had made outside the house. The anger was there, all right. There was a darkness in him, but he was too cunning to set it down. It had to be there, though, when he wrote that I was the source of all his pain, when he speculated that I might perhaps never come to live with him, when he hinted that it might "end in sorrow and more tears than we ever dreamed, Joe." I wanted more than that. I longed for it. *Please put the weapon in my hands, Jed.* One little threat would have given me enough to take to the police, but he denied me, he played with me and held back, just as he said I did. I needed him to reiterate his threat because I wanted the certainty of it, and the fact that he would not give me satisfaction kept my suspicion alive that sooner or later he would do me harm. My researches confirmed this. Well over half of all male de Clerambaults in one survey had attempted violence on the subjects of their obsessions.

Just as routine as the letters was Parry's presence outside the building. He came most days and took up a position across the street. He seemed to have found an equilibrium between the demands of time and the pressure of his needs. If he didn't catch sight of me, he would remain for about an hour before walking away. If he saw me come out of the building, he would follow me a little way, always remaining on his side, and then turn down a side street and stride away without looking back. He would have had enough contact then to keep his love alive, and as far as I could tell, he would go straight home to Hampstead to start a letter. One of them began, "I understood your glance this morning, Joe, but I think you're wrong . . ." But he never mentioned his decision not to talk to me again, and I was suddenly bereft, for if he would not threaten me by letter, I hoped he might oblige by letting me capture his words on tape. I kept a tiny dictating machine in my pocket and wore a microphone under my lapel. On one occasion, watched by Parry, I lingered by the privet and ran my hands along it to imprint it with a message, and then I turned his way and looked at him. But he wouldn't come; nor did he refer to that moment in the letter he wrote later the same day. The pattern of his love was not shaped by external influences, even if they originated with me. His was a world determined from the inside, driven by private necessity, and this way it could remain intact. Nothing could prove him wrong, nothing was needed to prove him right. If I had written him a letter declaring passionate love, it would have made no difference. He crouched in a cell of his own devising, teasing out meanings, imbuing nonexistent exchanges with their drama of hope or disappointment, always scrutinizing the physical world, its random placements and chaotic noise and colors, for the correlatives of his current emotional state — and always finding satisfaction. He illuminated the world with his feelings, and the world confirmed him at every turn his feelings took. When the despair rose, it was because he had read the darkness in the air or a variation in a bird's song that told him of my contempt. When it was joy, it came validated as an effect of some blissfully unexpected cause — a kind message from me in a dream, an intuition that had "come up" during a prayer or meditation.

This was love's prison of self-reference, but joy or despair, I could not get him to threaten me, or even to talk to me. Three times I crossed the street toward him with my hidden tape recorder turning, but he would not stay.

"Clear off, then!" I shouted at his retreating back. "Stop hanging around here. Stop bothering me with your stupid letters." *Come back and talk to me* was what I really meant. *Come back and face the hopelessness of your cause and issue your unveiled threats. Or phone them in. Leave them on my message machine.*

Naturally, what I shouted that day did not affect the tone of the letter I received the next day. It was all happiness and hope.

He was inviolable in his solipsism, and I was getting the jitters. The logic that might drive him from despair to hatred, or from love to destruction in one leap, would be private, unguessable, and if he came at me there'd be no warning. I was taking extra care locking up the flat at night. When I was out alone, especially at night, I kept track of who was behind me. I was taking taxis more frequently, and I always looked around me when I got out. With some difficulty I secured an appointment with an inspector at my local police station. I began to fantasize about what I might need for my own defense. Mace? A knuckle-duster? A knife? I daydreamed violent confrontations that always fell out in my favor, but I knew in my logical heart, that organ of dull common sense, that he was unlikely to come at me head on.

At least Clarissa seemed to have disappeared from Parry's thoughts. He made no reference to her in the letters now, and he never tried to talk to her. In fact, he actively avoided her. I watched from the living room window each time she left the flat. As soon as he saw her through the glass-fronted lobby coming down the stairs, and even before she had stepped out of the building, he hurried up the street. When she was gone, he returned to his position. Did he believe in his private narrative that he was sparing her feelings? Did he imagine that I had explained everything to her and that she was essentially out of the picture, or that he himself had somehow fixed it? Or did the story require no consistency at all?

We had been lying in silence now for ten minutes. She was on her left side, and I thought I heard the shuffling iambs of her pulse in my pillow. Perhaps it was my own rhythm. It was slow, and I was sure it was getting slower. There was no tension here in this silence. We looked in each other's eyes and our gaze moved regularly over each other's features, eyes to lips to eyes. It was like a long and slow remembering, and as each minute passed and we did not speak, our recovery gathered its own quiet strength. Surely the inertial power of love, the hours, weeks, and years harmoniously spent in each other's company, was greater than the circumstances of the mere present. Didn't love generate its own reserves? The last thing we should do now, I thought, was descend to a bout of patient explaining and listening. Too much was made in pop psychology, and too much expected, of talking things through. Conflicts, like living organisms, had a natural lifespan. The trick was to know when to let them die. At the wrong moment, words could act like so many fibrillating jolts. The creature could revive in pathogenic form, feverishly regenerated by an interesting new formulation or by this or that morbidly "fresh look" at things. I shifted my hand and faintly increased the pressure of my fingers on her arm. Her lips parted, a sensual ungluing marked by a soft plosive sound. All we had to do was look at each other and remember. Make love and the rest could take care of itself. Clarissa's lips framed my name, but there wasn't a sound, not even a breath. I couldn't move my eyes from her lips. So supple, so glossily rich in natural color. Lipstick was invented so that women could enjoy a poor version of lips like these. "Joe . . ." the lips said again. Another reason for not talking now of our problem was that we would be bound to let Parry into our bedroom, into our bed.

"Joe . . ." This time she blew my name through the half-pucker of her beautiful lips, and then she frowned and inhaled deeply and gave her words their rich low tone. "Joe, it's all over. It's best to admit it now. I think we're finished, don't you?"

When she said that, I did not find myself crossing a threshold of reconceptualization, nor did the ground, or the bed, drop away beneath me, though I certainly entered the lofty space in which I could observe these things not happening. Of course, I was in a state of denial. I felt nothing at all, not a thing. I didn't speak, not because I was speechless but because I felt nothing at all. Instead, my cold-blooded thoughts hopped, froglike, to Jean Logan, with whom Clarissa now shared a neural address, a category in my mind of women who believed themselves to be wronged and who expected something from me.

I try to be diligent. I had sat at my desk with Mrs. Logan's scrap of paper and made the phone calls. I called Toby Greene in Russell's Water first and got a vigorous old lady with a crackly voice who must have been his mother. I asked kindly after her son's broken ankle, but she cut me short.

"And what would you be wanting him for?"

"It's about the accident, the ballooning accident. I just wanted to ask him —"

"We've had enough reporters round here, so why don't you just bugger off."

It was neatly done, and she was quite calm about it. I left it a couple of hours before I tried again, and this time I got in quickly with my name and the fact that I was one of the fellows hanging on the ropes along with her son. When at last Toby Greene hobbled to the phone, he wasn't able to help me. He had seen John Logan's car on the far side of the field, but he had been busy with the hedging and then he was running toward the balloon and he had no idea whether Logan had been alone. It was hard to keep Greene on the subject. He wanted to talk about his ankle, or the sick pay he should have been receiving on its account. "We've been to the benefits people three times now . . ." I listened for twenty minutes to a tale of administrative bungle and condescension, until his mother called him away and he left the phone without a goodbye.

His friend in Watlington, Joseph Lacey, was not expected home for a day, so I phoned Reading and asked to speak to James Gadd, the balloonist. It was his wife who answered. Her voice was smooth and kindly.

"Tell him I'm one of the people who risked his life trying to stop his grandson being carried away."

"I'll have a jolly good try," she said. "But he doesn't like talking about it awfully much."

I heard the sound of the television news and Gadd's voice calling over it, "Everything I've got to say I'll say in the coroner's court." Mrs. Gadd came back and relayed the message in a tone of resignation and mild regret, as though she too were suffering from his failure to talk.

When I reached Lacey at last, he turned out to be a more focused spirit.

"What do they want? They can't need more witnesses."

"It's for his widow. She thinks there was someone with him."

"If that someone exists, they must have a good reason for not coming forward. Sleeping dogs, I'd say."

There was something a little too immediate and overdetermined about this, so I told him straight. "She thinks it was a woman. She found this picnic stuff in the car, and a silk scarf. She thinks he was having an affair. It's torturing her."

He made a clicking sound with his tongue, and there followed a long silence.

"Are you still there, Mr. Lacey?"

"I'm thinking."

"So you saw her?"

There was another silence, then he said, "I'm not talking about it on the phone. You come down here to Watlington, then we'll

239

see." He gave me the address, and we fixed a time.

When I asked her, Clarissa said she thought Logan's car had had two doors open, perhaps even three, but she had seen no one apart from Logan himself. That left Parry. As I remembered it, the footpath he had come along had taken him closer than any of us to the car. Could I have approached him with my hidden tape recorder, made my factual inquiries, then goaded him into threatening me? Apart from the absurdity of that, the idea of obtaining linear information from him seemed fantastic. His world was emotion, invention, and yearning. He was the stuff of bad dreams, to such an extent that it was difficult to imagine him carrying through mundane tasks like shaving or paying a bill. It was almost as if he didn't exist.

Because I hadn't said a thing, couldn't motivate myself to reply, Clarissa spoke again. We still held each other's gaze. "You're always thinking about him. It never stops. You were thinking about him just then, weren't you? Go on, tell me honestly. Tell me."

"I was, yes."

"I don't know what's happening with you, Joe. I'm losing you. It's frightening. You need help, but I don't think it can come from me."

"I'm seeing the police on Wednesday. They might be able to —"

"I'm talking about your mind."

I sat up. "There's nothing wrong with my mind. It's a good mind. Sweetheart, he's a real threat, he could be dangerous."

She was struggling to sit up too. "Oh God," she said. "You don't get it," and she started to cry.

"Listen, I'm researching this thoroughly." I put my hand on her shoulder, but she shrugged me away. I went on, though. "From what I've read, it seems that people with de Clerambault's syndrome fall into two groups . . ."

"You think you can read your way out of this." She was suddenly angry and no longer crying. "Don't you realize you've got a problem?"

"Of course I do," I said. "But just listen. It really helps to know. There are those whose symptoms are part of a general psychotic disorder. They're very easy to spot. And there are those with the pure form of the disease, who are completely obsessed by the object of their love, but they function perfectly well in all other parts of their lives."

"Joe!" she shouted. "You say he's outside, but when I go out there's no one. No one, Joe."

"When he sees you crossing the lobby, he goes a little way up the street and stands behind a tree. Don't ask me why."

"And the letters, the handwriting . . ." She looked at me, and her lower lip went slack. Something crossed her mind and made her hesitate.

I said, "What about the letters?"

She shook her head. She was out of bed now, gathering up the clothes she needed for tomorrow. She stood in the doorway with them. "I'm frightened," she said.

"I am too. He could get violent."

She was looking not at me but at a space above my head. Her voice was croaky. "I'm going to sleep in the children's room tonight."

"Please stay, Clarissa."

But she was gone, and the next day she moved her things into that room, and in the manner of these things, an impulsive decision became a settled arrangement. We continued to live side by side, but I knew that I was on my own.

Eighteen

Saturday was Clarissa's birthday. When I gave her a card, she kissed me full on the lips. Now it was settled in her mind I was unhinged, now she had told me we were finished, she appeared elated and generous. A new life was about to begin, and she had nothing to lose by being kind. A few days earlier her buoyancy might have made me suspicious, or jealous, but now it confirmed me in my reasoning: she had done neither the research nor the thinking. Parry's condition could not stand still. Given that fulfillment was not on hand, his love must turn to either indifference or hatred. Clarissa thought that her emotions were the appropriate guide, that she could feel her way to the truth, when what was needed was information, foresight, and careful calculation. It was therefore natural, though disastrous for us both, that she should think I was mad.

As soon as she had left for work, I went into my study and wrapped the present I was going to give her at the lunch we had planned that day with her godfather, Professor Kale. I gathered all Parry's letters together, arranged them chronologically, and fixed them in a clasp folder. I lay on the chaise longue turning the pages slowly from the beginning, looking out for and marking significant passages. These I typed out, with location references in brackets. By the end, I had four sheets of extracts, of which I made three copies, placing each in a plastic folder. This patient activity brought on in me a kind of organizational trance, the administrator's illusion that all the sorrow in the world can be brought to heel with touch typing, a decent laser printer, and a box of paper clips.

I was attempting to compile a dossier of threats, and while there were no single obvious examples, there were allusions and logical disjunctures whose cumulative effect would not be lost on the mind of a policeman. It needed the skill of a literary critic like Clarissa to read between the lines of protesting love, but I knew that she would not help me. After an hour or so I realized it was a mistake to concentrate on overt expressions of frustration and disappointment — that I had started it all, that I was leading him on, teasing him with false promises, reneging on my undertakings to live with him. These assertions had seemed intimidating at the time, but in retrospect they appeared merely pathetic. The real threats, I began to see, were elsewhere.

For example, he broke off an account of how lonely he was away from me to reflect on solitude, and how he remembered when he was fourteen going to stay in the country with his uncle. Parry used to borrow a .22 rifle and go out hunting rabbits. Going creeping along the hedgerows, all senses alert, completely concentrated on the task — this was the solitude he loved most. The description would have been harmless enough had he not given quite so much energy to reliving the pleasures of the kill: "power of death that leaped from my fingers, Joe, power at a distance. I can do this! I can do this! I used to think. Getting the creature on the run, seeing it do that little skipping somersault, and then hit the ground, writhing and twitching. Then it would go still, and I would come up to it, feeling like fate itself, and loving the little thing that I had just destroyed. The power of life and death, Joe. God has it, and we who are in His image have it too."

I copied out three sentences from another letter: "I wanted to hurt you. Perhaps even more than that. Something more, and God will forgive me, I thought." In another recent letter there was an echo of the remark he had made to me the day I came back from Oxford: "You started this, and you can't run from it. I can get people to do things for me — you already know that. Even as I'm writing this letter a couple of guys are redecorating the bathroom! In the old days I would have done it myself, money or not. But now I'm learning to delegate." I stared at this one a long time. What was the precise connection between my not being able to run and his being able to get things done by others? There was a missing step. In his very latest letter he wrote, apropos of nothing, "I went to the Mile End Road yesterday — you know, where the real villains live. Looking for more decorators!"

Elsewhere there were portentous invocations of God's darker side. "God's love," he wrote, "may take the form of wrath. It can show itself to us as calamity. This is the difficult lesson it's taken me a lifetime to learn." And related to this: "His love isn't always gentle. How can it be when it has to last, when you can never shake it off? It's a warmth, it's a heat, and it can burn you, Joe, it can consume you."

There were very few biblical references in Parry's correspondence. His religion was dreamily vague on the specifics of doctrine, and he gave no impression of being attached to any particular church. His belief was a self-made affair, generally aligned to the culture of personal growth and fulfillment. There was a lot of talk of destiny, of his "path" and how he would not be deterred from following it, and of fate — his and mine entwined. Often, God was a term interchangeable with self. God's love for mankind shaded into Parry's love for me. God was undeniably "within" rather than in his heaven, and believing in him was therefore a license to respond to the calls of feeling or intuition. It was the perfect loose structure for a disturbed mind. There were no constraints of theological nicety or religious observance, no social sanction or congregational calling to account, none of the moral framework that made religions viable, however failed their cosmologies. Parry listened only to the inner voice of his private God.

His one concession to a source beyond himself was a couple of references to the story of Job, and even here it was not obvious that he had read the primary material. "You looked uncomfortable," he wrote once about seeing me in the street. "You even looked as though you might have been in pain, but that shouldn't make you doubt us.

Remember how much pain Job was in, and all the time God loved him." Again, the unexamined assumption was that God and Parry were one, and between them they would settle the matter of our common fates. Another reference raised the possibility that I was God. "We're both suffering, Joe, we're both afflicted. The question is, which one of us is Job?"

When I left the flat in the late morning with a brown envelope containing my meticulously documented extracts, and with Clarissa's present in my pocket, Parry was not there. I paused to look around, half expecting him to appear from behind one of his trees. The change in routine made me uneasy. I hadn't seen him since the morning of the day before. Now that I had read the literature and knew the possibilities, I preferred him to be where I could see him. On my way to the police station I glanced back a few times to check if he was following me.

It was a quiet time of day, but I had to sit for over an hour in the waiting room. Where the human need for order meets the human tendency to mayhem, where civilization runs smack against its discontents, you find friction, and a great deal of general wear and tear. It was there in the stringy holes in the lino on the threshold of each door, in the snaky vertical crack up the frosted glass behind the reception officer's counter space, and in the hot, exhausted air that forced each visitor out of his jacket and each cop into shirtsleeves. It was in the slumped posture of two kids in bomber jackets who stared at their feet, too furious with each other to speak, and in the chiseled graffiti on the arm of the chair on which I sat: it was bland defiance or mounting anguish — *fuck fuck fuck*. And I saw it in the fluorescent pallor of Duty Inspector Linley's large round face as he wearily showed me at last into an interview room. It looked as if he rarely went outdoors. He had no need when all the trouble filed through here.

A journalist friend who had served three years on the crime desk of a tabloid had advised me that the only way to get the police even faintly interested in my case was to make an official complaint about the way it had been handled so far. This way I could get past the woman in glasses who guarded the reception desk. The complaint would have to be dealt with, at least, and I could explain my problem to someone a little further up the station hierarchy. The same friend warned me not to expect too much. My man would be looking at retirement and wanting a quiet life. His brief was to suppress complaints while appearing to address them.

Linley waved me into one of two metal stacking chairs. We faced each other across a Formica table patterned in coffee rings. At every point on its surface my cold chair was greasy to the touch. The ashtray was the sawn-off butt of a plastic Coke bottle. Near it squatted a used tea bag on a spoon. The squalor in here was laconic in its challenge: who was I going to report it to?

I had submitted my complaint, Linley had eventually phoned me, and I had given him the story. At the time I had trouble deciding whether he was slightly clever or very stupid. He had one of those strangulated voices with which comedians sometimes characterize officialdom. Linley's had suggested a degree of imbecility. On the other hand, he hadn't said much. Even now, as he opened the file, no good morning or where were we or hum and hah. Just the electronic whistle of breath through nasal hair. Into such silences, I guessed, suspects and witnesses said more than they intended, so I kept quiet too as I watched him turn the couple of pages of his slanting spiky handwriting in which he had recorded his notes.

Linley raised his eyes, but he didn't look

at me. He was staring into my chest. It was only when he drew breath to speak that the focus of his tiny gray eyes brushed past mine. "So. You're being harassed and threatened by this character. You've reported it, and got no satisfaction."

"That's it," I said.

"The harassment consists of . . . ?"

"As I told you before," I said, trying to read his writing upside down. Had he not been listening to me? "He sends three or four letters a week."

"Obscenities?"

"No."

"Lewd suggestions?"

"No."

"Insults?"

"Not really."

"Sexual sort of things, then."

"It doesn't seem to be about sex. It's an obsession. He's completely fixated on me. He doesn't think about anything else."

"Does he phone you?"

"Not anymore. It's just the letters."

"He's in love with you."

I said, "He's suffering from a condition known as de Clerambault's syndrome. It's a delusional state. He thinks I started it, he's convinced I'm encouraging him with secret signals —"

"Are you a psychiatrist, Mr. Rose?"

"No."

"But you are a homosexual."

"No."

"How did you meet?"

"I've already told you. The ballooning accident."

He twitched a page of his notes. "I don't seem to have a record of that."

I gave him a brief account while he rested his heavy symmetrical head on his hands, still untempted to write the story down. When I had done, he said, "How did it start?"

"He phoned late that night."

"He said he loved you and you hung up. You must have been upset."

"Disturbed."

"So you discussed it with your wife."

"The next morning."

"Why the delay?"

"We were very tired and stressed out from the accident."

"And what's her reaction to all this?"

"She's upset. It's put quite a strain on us."

Linley looked away and made a show of pursing his lips. "Does she ever get angry with you about this business? Or you with her?"

"It's put a lot of pressure on our relationship. We were very happy before."

"Any history of psychiatric illness, Mr. Rose?"

"None at all."

"Stress at work, that sort of thing?"

"Nothing like that."

"Pretty tough business, journalism, isn't it?"

I nodded. I was beginning to detest Linley and his curious globular face. I said into the pause that followed, "I've got good reasons to believe this guy will turn nasty. I came to the police for help."

"Quite right," said Linley. "I'd do the same myself. And it looks like the law on this sort of thing is about to be tightened up. So he stands outside the house and bothers you when you come out."

"He used to. These days he just stands there. If I try to talk to him, he walks away."

"So he's not actually . . ." He trailed off and looked, or pretended to look, through his notes. He was muttering to himself. "That's the harassment, um . . ." Then to me, brightly, "Now what about the threats?"

"I've copied out some passages. They're not right out front. You'll need to read carefully."

Duty Inspector Linley settled back to

read, and while his gaze was lowered I stared at his face. It wasn't the pallor that was repellent, it was the puffy, inhuman geometry of its roundness. A near-perfect circle was centered on his button nose and encompassed the white dome of his baldness and the curve of his fattened chin. This circle was inscribed on the surface of a barely misshapen sphere. His forehead bulged, his cheeks rolled out tightly from below his little gray eyes, and the curve was picked up again in the bluish undimpled bulge between his nose and his upper lip.

He dropped my pages onto the desk, clasped his hands behind his head, and contemplated the ceiling for a few seconds, then looked at me with a hint of pity. "As stalkers go, Mr. Rose, he's a pussycat. What do you want us to do? Arrest him?"

I said, "You've got to understand the intensity of this delusion and the frustration that's building up. He needs to know he can't just do anything —"

"There's nothing here that's threatening, abusive, or insulting as defined by Section Five of the Public Order Act." Linley was talking faster. He wanted me out of there. "Nothing in the Offenses Against the Person Act of 1861. We couldn't even caution him. He loves his God, he loves you, and I'm sorry about that, but he hasn't broken the law." He picked up the extracts and let them drop. "I mean, where's the threat, exactly?"

"If you read carefully and think logically, you'll see he's implying that he can get someone, hire someone, to beat me up."

"Too weak. You should see what we get in here. He hasn't trashed your car, has he, or waved a knife at you, or tipped the dustbin over your front path. He hasn't even sworn at you. I mean, have you and your wife considered asking him in for a cup of tea and a chat?"

I was doing well to keep so calm, I thought. "Look, he's a classic case. De Clerambault's, erotomania, stalking, call it what you want. I've gone into it in some depth. The literature shows that when he realizes that he's not going to get what he wants, there's a real danger of violence. You could at least send a couple of officers round to his place and let him know he's on your books."

Linley stood, but I remained obstinately sitting. He had his hand on the doorknob. His show of patience was a form of mockery. "In the kind of society we have, or want to have, not to mention our limited manpower, we can't send officers to Citizen A on account of Citizen B reading a few books and deciding there's violence in the air. Nor can my men be in two places at once, watching him, protecting you."

I was about to answer, but Linley opened the door and stepped out. He spoke to me from the corridor. "But I'll tell you what I will do. I'll send our home beat officer to your house sometime in the coming week. He's got ten years' experience in community problems, and I'm sure he'll be able to make some useful suggestions." Then he was gone and I heard him in the waiting room, saying in a loud voice, presumably to the lads in bomber jackets, "Complaint? You two? What a joke! Listen to me. You both kindly fuck off now and I just might see my way to losing that file."

I was late for lunch and I walked quickly up the street, away from the station, glancing over my shoulder for a taxi. I should have been angry or alarmed, but somehow the brush-off from Linley was clarifying. I had made two attempts to get the police interested. I needn't bother again. Perhaps it was the weight of Clarissa's present in my pocket that brought my thoughts to her instead, and all our unhappiness. I couldn't quite take seriously her insistence that we were finished. It had always seemed to me that our love was just the kind to endure.

Now, hurrying along the Harrow Road, prompted also by a phrase Inspector Linley had used, I found myself remembering her last birthday, when we had celebrated without a trace of complication in our lives.

The phrase was "in two places at once," and the memory was of early morning. I left her sleeping and went to make the tea. I probably gathered up the mail from the hallway floor and sorted the birthday cards from the rest and put them on a tray. While I was waiting for the kettle, I looked at a radio talk I was going to record that afternoon. I remember it well because I used the material later for the first chapter of a book. Might there be a genetic basis to religious belief, or was it merely refreshing to think so? If faith conferred selective advantage, there were any number of possible means, and nothing could be proven. Suppose religion gave status, especially to its priest caste? Plenty of social advantage in that. What if it bestowed strength in adversity, the power of consolation, the chance of surviving the disaster that might crush a godless man? Perhaps it gave believers passionate conviction, the brute strength of singlemindedness.

Possibly it worked on groups as well as on individuals, bringing cohesion and identity and a sense that you and your fellows were right, even — or especially — when you were wrong. With God on our side. Uplifted by a crazed unity, armed with horrible certainty, you descend on the neighboring tribe, beat and rape it senseless, and come away burning with righteousness and drunk with the very victory your gods had promised. Repeat fifty thousand times over the millennia, and the complex set of genes controlling for groundless conviction could get a strong distribution. I floated in and out of these preoccupations. The kettle boiled and I made the tea.

The night before, Clarissa had braided her hair into a single plait, which she had secured with a strip of black velvet. When I came in with the tea and birthday cards and morning paper, she was sitting up in bed, loosening her hair and shaking it out. Being in bed with your lover is a fine thing, but returning to her in its night-long warmth is sweet. I toasted her in tea, we read the cards and set about the birthday cuddle. Clarissa weighs eighty pounds less than me, and she sometimes likes to start out on top. She gathered the bedclothes around her like a bridal train and sat sleepily astride me. On this particular morning we had a game going. I lay on my back pretending to read the newspaper. While she drew me in and sighed and wriggled and shivered, I made a show of being unaware of her, of turning the pages and frowning at the piece before me. It gave her a little masochistic thrill to feel she was ignored; she wasn't noticed, she wasn't there. Annihilation! Then she took a controlling pleasure in destroying my attention, drawing me from the frantic public realm into the deep world that was entirely herself. Now I was the one who was to be obliterated, and along with me, everything that was not her.

However, on this particular occasion she did not quite succeed, for I briefly achieved what Linley had claimed to be impossible for his policemen. I was excited by Clarissa, but I was actually reading about the queen. She was off to visit a town called Yellowknife in the remote Northwest Territories of Canada, a region the size of Europe with a population of fifty-seven thousand, most of whom, apparently, were drunks and hoodlums. What caught my attention as Clarissa writhed above me was a paragraph about the territory's appalling weather, and these two desultory sentences: "Recently a blizzard engulfed a football match north of Yellowknife. Unable to find their way to safety, both teams froze to death." "Listen to this," I said to Clarissa. But then she looked at me, and that was as far as I got. I was hers.

The act of reading and understanding engages a number of separate but overlapping functions of the brain, while the region that controls sexual function operates at a lower level, more ancient in evolutionary terms and shared by countless organisms but still available to the intercession of higher functions — memory, emotion, fantasy. If I remembered that morning of Clarissa's birthday so well — cards and torn envelopes scattered across the bed, intrusive sunlight burning through the curtained gap — it's because one of our little playful episodes brought me for the first time in my life to a full and complete experience in two places at once. Aroused by Clarissa, fully sentient and appreciative, and yet gripped by the tragedy behind the newspaper tidbit, the two teams scattering midplay in the violent winds to die in their boots on the edge of the invisible field. All copulating creatures are vulnerable to attack, but selection over time must have proved that reproductive success was best served by undivided attention. Better to allow the occasional couple to be eaten midrapture than dilute by one jot a vigorous procreational urge. But for seconds on end I had wholesomely and simultaneously indulged two of life's central, antithetical pleasures, reading and fucking.

"Don't you think," I had asked Clarissa later in the bathroom, "that I'm some kind of evolutionary throw forward?"

Clarissa the Keats scholar was crouching naked on a cork stool, painting her toenails — a gesture toward birthday festivity. "No," she had said. "You're just getting old. And anyway" — and here she had mimicked a know-all radio voice — "evolutionary change, speciation, is an event that can only be known in retrospect."

Now, inwardly, I congratulated her on her grasp of the idiom, and as a taxi drew up for me I realized how sharply I missed our old life together, and I wondered how we would ever return to such love and fun and easy intimacy. Clarissa thought I was mad, the police thought I was a fool, and one thing was clear: the task of getting us back to where we had been was going to be mine alone.

Nineteen

I arrived twenty minutes late. The place was doing good lunchtime business; conversation was at a roar, and stepping in from the street was like walking into a storm. It was as if there were a single topic — and an hour later there would be. The professor was already seated, but Clarissa was on her feet, and even from across the room I could see that she was in that same elated mood. She was creating a little fuss around her. A waiter was on his knees at her feet, praying style, wedging a table leg; another was bringing her a different chair. When she saw me she came skipping through the din and took my hand and led me to the table as if I were blind. I put the skittishness down to celebratory mood, for we had some cause to raise a glass: it wasn't only a birthday. Professor Jocelyn Kale, Clarissa's godfather, had been appointed to an honorary position on the Human Genome Project.

Before I sat down, I kissed her. These days our tongues never touched, but this time they did. Jocelyn half rose from his seat and shook my hand. At the same moment champagne in an ice bucket was brought to the table and we pitched our voices in with the roar. The ice bucket sat within a rhombus of sunlight on a white tablecloth; the tall restaurant windows showed off rectangles of blue sky between the buildings. I had a hard-on from the kiss. In memory, it was all success, clarity, clatter. In memory, all the food they brought us first was red: the bresaola, the fat tongues of roasted pepper laid on goat cheese, the raddiccio, the white china bowl of radish coronets. When later I remembered how we had leaned in and shouted, I seemed to be remembering an underwater event.

Jocelyn took from his pocket a small parcel done up in blue tissue. We drew down an imaginary silence on our table while Clarissa unwrapped her present. Perhaps that was when I glanced to my left, at the table next to ours. A man whose name I learned afterward was Colin Tapp was with his daughter and his father. Perhaps I noticed them later. If I registered at the time the solitary diner who sat twenty feet away with his back to us, it left no trace in memory. Inside the tissue was a black box, and inside the box, on a cumulus of cotton wool, was a golden brooch. Still without speaking, she lifted it out, and we examined it on her palm.

Two gold bands were entwined in a double helix. Crossing between them were tiny silver rungs in groups of three representing the base pairs, the four-letter alphabet that coded all living things in permutating triplets. Engraved on the helical bands were spherical designs to suggest the twenty amino acids onto which the three-letter codons were mapped. In the full light gathered from the tabletop, it looked in Clarissa's hand more than a representation. It could have been the thing itself, ready to cook up chains of amino acids to be blended into protein molecules. It could have divided right there in her hand to make another gift. When Clarissa sighed Jocelyn's name, the sound of the restaurant surged back on us.

"Oh God, it's beautiful," she cried, and kissed him.

His weak yellow-blue eyes were moist. He said, "It was Gillian's, you know. She would have loved you to have it."

I was impatient to produce my own present, but we were still in the spell of Jocelyn's. Clarissa pinned the brooch on her gray silk blouse.

Would I remember the conversation now

if I did not know what it preceded?

We began by joking that the Genome Project gave out such jewelry free by the dozen. Then Jocelyn talked about the discovery of DNA. Perhaps that was when I turned in my seat to ask a waiter to bring us water and noticed the two men and the girl. We finished the champagne and the antipasto was cleared away. I don't remember what food we ordered after that. Jocelyn began to tell us about Johann Miescher, the Swiss chemist who identified DNA in 1869. This was supposed to be one of the great missed chances in the history of science. Miescher got himself a steady supply of pus-soaked bandages from a local hospital (rich in white blood cells, Jocelyn added for Clarissa's benefit). He was interested in the chemistry of the cell nucleus. In the nuclei he found phosphorous, an improbable substance that didn't sit with current ideas. An extraordinary find, but his paper was blocked by his teacher, who spent two years repeating and confirming his student's results.

It wasn't boredom that let my attention shift, though I knew the Miescher story; it was restlessness, an impatience that came from a sense of release after my interview. I would have liked to tell the story of my encounter with Inspector Linley, spice it up a little and squeeze some amusement from it, but I knew that to do so would lead me straight back to the divisions between Clarissa and me. At the next table the girl was being helped through the menu by her father, who had to slide his glasses down his nose to see the print. The girl leaned fondly against his arm.

Meanwhile Jocelyn, enjoying the triple privilege of age, eminence, and the bestower of gifts, told his story. Miescher pressed on. He assembled a team and set about working out the chemistry of what he called nucleic acid. Then he found them, the substances that made up the four-letter alphabet in whose language all life is written: adenine and cytosine, guanine and thymine. It meant nothing. And that was odd, especially as the years went by. Mendel's work on the laws of inheritance had been generally accepted, and chromosomes had been identified in the cell nucleus and were suspected of being the location of genetic information. It was known that DNA was in the chromosomes, and its chemistry had been described by Miescher, who in 1892 speculated in a letter to his uncle that DNA might code for life, just as an alphabet codes for language and concepts.

"It was staring them in the face," Jocelyn said. "But they couldn't see, they wouldn't see. The problem, of course, was the chemists . . ."

It was hard work, talking against the din. We waited while he drank his water. The story was for Clarissa, an embellishment on the present. While Jocelyn was resting his voice there was movement behind me, and I was obliged to pull in my chair to let the girl through. She went off in the direction of the lavatories. When I was next aware of her, she was back in her seat.

"The chemists, you see. Very powerful, rather grand. The nineteenth had been a good century for them. They had authority, but they were a crusty lot. Take Phoebus Levine, at the Rockefeller Institute. He was absolutely certain that DNA was a boring, irrelevant molecule containing random sequences of those four letters, ACGT. He dismissed it, and then, in that peculiar human way, it became a matter of faith with him, deep faith. What he knew, he knew, and the molecule was insignificant. None of the younger chaps could get round him. It had to wait for years, until Griffith's work on bacteria in the twenties. Which Oswald Avery picked up in Washington — Levine was gone by then, of course. Oswald's work took forever, right into the forties. Then Alexander Todd, working in London on the sugar phosphate links, then 'fifty-two and 'three, Maurice Wilkins and Rosalind Franklin, and then Crick and Watson. You know what poor Rosalind said when they showed her the model they had built of the DNA molecule? She said it was simply too beautiful not to be true . . ."

The accelerated roll call of names and his old chestnut, beauty in science, slowed Jocelyn into speechless reminiscence. He fumbled with his napkin. He was eighty-two. As student or colleague, he had known them all. And Gillian had worked with Crick after the first great breakthrough on adapter molecules. Gillian, like Franklin herself, had died of leukemia.

I was a second or two slow on the uptake, but Jocelyn had lobbed me an excellent cue. I reached into my jacket pocket and could not resist the chocolate-box lines. "Beauty is truth, truth beauty . . ." Clarissa smiled. She must have guessed long before that she might be getting Keats, but she could not have dreamed of what was now in her hands, in plain brown paper. Even before the wrapping was off, she recognized it and squealed. The girl at the next table turned in her seat to stare, until her father tapped her on the arm. Foolscap octavo in drab boards with back label. Condition: poor, foxed, slight water damage. A first edition of his first collection, *Poems* of 1817.

"What presents!" Clarissa said. She stood and put her arms around my neck. "It must have cost you thousands . . ." Then she put her lips to my ear and it was like the old days. "You're a bad boy to spend so much money. I'm going to make you fuck me all afternoon."

She couldn't have meant it, but I played along and said, "Oh, all right. If it'll make you feel better." It was the champagne, of course, and simple gratitude, but that didn't stop me feeling pleased.

A day or so later it became a temptation to invent or elaborate details about the table next to ours, to force memory to deliver what was never captured, but I did see the man, Colin Tapp, put his hand on his father's arm as he spoke, reassuring him, soothing him. It also became difficult to disentangle what I discovered later from what I sensed at the time. Tapp was in fact two years older than I, his daughter was fourteen, and his father seventy-three. I did nothing so deliberate as speculate about their ages — by now my attention was not wandering, our own table was absorbing,

269

we were having fun — but I must have assumed a good deal about the relationships of our neighbors, and done it barely consciously, out of the corner of my eye, wordlessly, in that preverbal language of instant thought linguists call mentalese. The girl I did take in, however glancingly. She had that straight-backed poise some teenagers adopt, self-possession attempting worldliness and disarmingly revealing its opposite. Her skin was dark, her black hair was cut in a bob, and the skin low on her neck was paler; the haircut was recent. Or were these details I observed later, in the chaos, or in the time after the chaos? Another example of the confusion hindsight can cause memory: I found myself inserting into my recollection of the scene an image of the man who sat eating alone, facing away from us. I didn't see him at the time, not until the very end, but I was unable to exclude him from later reconstructions.

At our table Clarissa had resumed her seat and the conversation concerned young men oppressed, put down, or otherwise blocked by older men — their fathers, teachers, mentors, or their idols. The starting point had been Johann Miescher and his teacher, Hoppe-Seyler, who had held up publication of his student's discovery of phosphorous in cell nuclei. Hoppe-Seyler also happened to be the editor of the journal to which Miescher's papers had been submitted. From there — and I had time later to trace our conversation backward — from Miescher and Hoppe-Seyler, we arrived at Keats and Wordsworth.

Clarissa was our source now, although outside his subject Jocelyn knew a little about most things, and he knew from the Gittings biography the famous story of the young Keats going to visit the poet he revered. I knew of the visit because Clarissa had told me about it. In late 1817 Keats had been staying at an inn, the Fox and Hounds by Box Hill on the North Downs, where he finished his long poem *Endymion*. He stayed on a week and walked the downs in a daze of creative excitement. He was twenty-one, he had written a long, serious, beautiful poem about being in love, and by the time he returned to London he was feeling high. There he heard the news and was overjoyed: his hero, William Wordsworth, was in town. Keats had sent his *Poems* with the inscription "To W. Wordsworth with the Author's sincere Reverence." (That would have been the one to give Clarissa. It was in the Princeton University Library, and according to her, there were many uncut pages.) Keats had grown up on Wordsworth's poetry. He had called *The Excursion* one of the "three things to rejoice at in this Age." He had taken from Wordsworth the idea of poetry as a sacred vocation, the noblest endeavor. Now he persuaded his painter friend Haydon to arrange a meeting, and they set out together from Haydon's studio at Lisson Grove to walk to Queen Anne Street to call on the great genius. In his journal, Haydon noted that Keats expressed "the greatest, the purest, the most unalloyed pleasure at the prospect."

Wordsworth was a notorious grouch at that stage of his life — he was forty-seven — but he was friendly enough to Keats, and after a few minutes of small talk asked him what he'd been working on. Haydon jumped in and answered for him, and begged Keats to repeat the ode to Pan from *Endymion*. So Keats walked up and down in front of the great man, reciting in "his usual half-chant (most touching) . . ." It was at this point in the story that Clarissa fought the restaurant clamor and quoted:

Be still the unimaginable lodge
For solitary thinkings; such as dodge
Conception to the very bourne of heaven,
Then leave the naked brain.

And when the passionate young man was done, Wordsworth, apparently unable to endure any longer this young man's adoration, delivered into the silence his shocking, dismissive verdict by saying drily, "A Very pretty piece of Paganism," which, according to Haydon, was "unfeeling and unworthy of his high Genius to a Worshipper like Keats — and Keats felt it *deeply*" — and never forgave him.

"But do we trust this story?" Jocelyn said. "Didn't I read in Gittings that we shouldn't?"

"We don't." Clarissa began to count off the reasons.

If I had stood up while she did so and turned toward the entrance, I would have seen across half an acre of talking heads two figures come in and speak to the maitre d'. One of the men was tall, but I don't think I took that in. I knew it later, but a trick of memory has given me the image as if I had stood then: the crowded room, the tall man, the maitre d' nodding and gesturing vaguely in our direction. And then what, in fantasy, could I have done to persuade Clarissa and Jocelyn and the strangers at the next table to leave their meals and run with me up the stairs to find by interconnecting doors a way down into the street? On a score of sleepless nights I've been back to plead with them to leave. *Look,* I say to our neighbors, *you don't know me, but I know what is about to happen. I'm from a tainted future. It was a mistake, it doesn't have to happen. We could choose another outcome. Put down your knives and forks and follow me, quick! No, really, please trust me. Just trust me. Let's go!*

But they do not see or hear me. They go on eating and talking. And so did I.

I said, "But the story lives on. The famous put-down."

"Yes," Jocelyn said eagerly. "It isn't true, but we need it. A kind of myth."

We looked to Clarissa. She was usually reticent about what she knew really well. Years ago, at a party, I had gone down on drunken knees to get her to recite from memory *La Belle Dame sans Merci*. But to-day we were celebrating and trying to forget, and it was best to keep talking.

"It isn't true, but it tells the truth. Wordsworth was arrogant to the point of being loathsome about other writers. Gittings has this good line about his being in the difficult second half of a man's forties. When he got to fifty he calmed down, brightened up, and everyone around him could breathe. By then Keats was dead.

There's always something delicious about young genius spurned by the powerful. You know, like The Man Who Turned Down the Beatles for Decca. We know that God in the form of history will have his revenge . . ."

The two men were probably making their way between the tables toward us by then. I'm not sure. I have excavated that last half-minute and I know two things for sure. One was that the waiter brought us sorbets. The other was that I slipped into a daydream. I often do. Almost by definition, daydreams leave no trace; they really do dodge conception to the very bourne of heaven, then leave the naked brain. But I've been back so many times, and I've retrieved it by remembering what triggered it: Clarissa's *By then Keats was dead.*

The words, the memento mori, floated me off. I was briefly gone. I saw them together, Wordsworth, Haydon, Keats, in a room in Monkton's house on Queen Anne Street, and imagined the sum of their every sensation and thought, and all the stuff — the feel of clothes, the creak of chairs and floorboards, the resonance in their chests of their own voices, the little heat of reputation, the fit of their toes in their shoes, and things in pockets, the separate assumptions

275

of recent pasts and what they would be doing next, the growing, tottering frame they carried of where they were in the story of their lives — all this as luminously self-evident as this clattering, roaring restaurant, and all *gone*, just like Logan was when he was sitting on the grass.

What takes a minute to describe took two seconds to experience. I returned, and compensated for my absence by telling Clarissa and Jocelyn a genius-spurned story of my own. A retired publisher, married to a physicist friend of mine, told me that back in the fifties he had turned down a novel called *Strangers from Within.* (By then the visitors must have been ten feet away, right behind our table. I don't think they even saw us.) The point about my friend was that he only discovered his error thirty years later, when an old file turned up at the place where he used to work. He hadn't remembered the name on the typescript — he was reading dozens every month — and he did not read the book when it finally appeared. Or at least, not at first. The author, William Golding, had renamed it *Lord of the Flies* and had excised the long boring first chapter that had put my friend off.

I think I was about to draw my resounding conclusion — that time protects us from our worst mistakes — but Clarissa and Jocelyn were not listening. I too had been aware of movement to one side. Now I followed their sight lines and turned. The two men who had stopped by the table next to ours seemed to have suffered burns to the face. Their skin was a lifeless prosthetic pink, the color of dolls or of Band-Aids, the color of no one's skin. They shared a robotic nullity of expression. Later we learned about the latex masks, but at the time these men were a shocking sight, even before they acted. The arrival of the waiter with our desserts in stainless steel bowls was temporarily soothing. Both men wore black coats that gave them a priestly look. There was ceremony in their stillness. The flavor of my sorbet was lime, just to the green side of white. I already had a spoon in my hand, but I hadn't used it. Our table was staring shamelessly.

The intruders simply stood and looked down at our neighbors, who in turn looked back, puzzled, waiting. The young girl looked at her father and back to the men. The older man put down his empty fork and seemed about to speak, but he said nothing. A variety of possibilities unspooled before me at speed: a student stunt; vendors; the man, Colin Tapp, was a doctor or lawyer and these were his patients or clients; some new version of the kissogram; crazy members of the family come to embarrass. Around us the lunchtime uproar, which had dipped locally, was back to level. When the taller man drew from his coat a black stick, a wand, I inclined to the kissogram. But who was his companion, who now slowly turned to survey the room? He missed our table, it was so close. His eyes, piglike in the artificial skin, never met mine. The tall man, ready to cast his spell, pointed his wand at Colin Tapp.

And Tapp himself was suddenly ahead of us all by a second. His face showed us what we didn't understand about the spell. His puzzlement, congealed in terror, could not find a word to tell us, because there was no time. The silenced bullet struck through his white shirt at his shoulder and lifted him from his chair and smacked him against the wall. The high-velocity impact forced a fine spray, a blood mist, across our tablecloth, our desserts, our hands, our sight. My first impulse was simple and self-protective: I did not believe what I was seeing. Clichés are rooted in truth: I did not believe my eyes. Tapp flopped forward across the table. His father did not move, not a muscle in his face moved. As for his daughter, she did the only possible thing: she passed out, her mind closed down on this atrocity. She slipped sideways in her chair toward Jocelyn, who put out a hand — the instincts of an old sportsman — and though he could not prevent her fall, he caught her upper arm and saved her head from a bang.

Even as she was falling, the man was raising his gun again and aiming at the top of Tapp's head, and would have killed him for sure. But that was when the man who had been eating alone jumped up with a shout, a doglike yelp, and just managed to cross the space in time to tilt the barrel with extended arm so that the second bullet sank high up on the wall. Even though his hair was cropped, how had I failed to recognize Parry?

At our table we could not move or speak. The two men moved away swiftly toward the entrance. The tall one tucked the gun and silencer into his coat as he went. I didn't see Parry leave, but he must have gone off in another direction and left by one of the fire exits. Only two tables witnessed the event. There may have been a scream; then, for seconds on end, paralysis. Further off, no one heard a thing. The chatter, the chink of cutlery against plates, went stupidly on.

I looked at Clarissa. Her face was rouged

on one side. I was about to say something to her when I got it, I understood completely, it came to me without effort, in that same neural flash of preverbal thought that comprehends relation and structure all at once, that knows the connection between things better than the things themselves. The unimaginable lodge. Our two tables — their composition, the numbers, the sexes, the relative ages. How had Parry known?

It was a mistake. Nothing personal. It was a contract, and it had been bungled. It should have been me.

But I felt nothing, not even a flicker of vindication. This was in the time before the invention of feeling, before the division of thought, before the panic and the guilt and all the choices. So we sat there, unmoving, hopeless in shock, while around us the lunchtime uproar subsided as understanding spread concentrically outward from our silence. Two waiters were hurrying toward us, their faces loopily amazed, and I knew it was only when they reached us that our story could continue.

Twenty

For the second time that afternoon, and the second time in my life, I sat in a police station — this time Bow Street — waiting to be interviewed. Statisticians call this kind of thing random clustering, a useful way of denying it significance. Along with Clarissa and Jocelyn, there were seven other witnesses in the room — four restaurant customers from two nearby tables, two waiters, and the maitre d'. Mr. Tapp was expected to be able to give a statement from his hospital bed the next day. The girl and the old man were still too shocked to talk.

It was only a few hours on and already we were headlines in the evening paper. One of the waiters went out for a copy and we gathered round, and found ourselves strangely exalted to read our experience assimilated to the common stock of "restaurant outrage," "lunchtime nightmare," and "bloodbath." The maitre d' pointed to a sentence that described me as "the well-known science writer" and Jocelyn as "the

eminent scientist," while Clarissa was simply "beauteous." The maitre d' inclined his
head toward us with professional respect.
We learned from the paper that Colin Tapp
was an undersecretary at the Department of
Trade and Industry. He was a businessman,
recently promoted from the back benches,
and was supposed to have "extensive connections as well as many enemies in the
Middle East." There was speculation about
"a fearless have-a-go diner" who had saved
Tapp's life and mysteriously vanished. Inside the paper were background pieces
about London as a "fanatics' playground"
and the availability of weapons, and an opinion piece on the fading of the "innocent,
unviolent way of life we used to know." The
coverage seemed so familiar, as well as eerily
instant. It was as if the subject had been
mapped out long ago, and the event we had
witnessed had been staged to give point to
the writing.

There were two detective constables dealing with witness statements, but it was taking them a while to set up. After the
excitement of the newspaper, we returned
to our seats and a thick silence settled over
us. There were frequent yawns, and weary
smiles in acknowledgment of how infectious
they were. At last the police were ready, and

Clarissa and Jocelyn were the first to go in. She came out twenty minutes later and sat by me to wait for her godfather. She took the Keats from its wrapping and opened it to smell the pages. Then she took my hand and squeezed it, and put her lips to my ear. "It's a wonderful present." Then, "Look, Joe, just tell them what you saw, okay? Don't go on about your usual stuff."

I already knew from something she had said earlier that she hadn't recognized Parry. I wasn't going to argue with her now. I was on my own. I just nodded and said, "Are you taking Jocelyn to his place?"

"Yes. I'll wait for you at home."

He came out, we shook hands, and they left. I settled down to wait and prepare what I wanted to say. The maitre d' came out, one of the diners went in, and later, one of the waiters. I was the second to last to be seen, and I was shown into the interview room by a polite young man who introduced himself as Detective Constable Wallace.

Before I sat down I said my piece. "I might as well tell you straightaway that I know what happened. The bullet that hit Mr. Tapp was meant for me. The man who was eating alone and who intervened is someone who's been bothering me. His name is Parry. I actually complained to the police about him earlier today. I'd like you to contact Inspector Linley at the Harrow Road station. I even told him that I thought Parry might hire someone to harm me."

While I said all this, Wallace was looking at me intently, though not, I thought, with any great surprise. When I finished he indicated a chair. "Okay. Let's go from the beginning," and he set about taking my name and address and my story from the time I arrived at the restaurant. The process was necessarily pedantic, and Wallace steered it from time to time toward irrelevancies: he wanted to know what we had talked about at our table, and at one point he asked me to characterize the moods of my companions; he also asked about the food and wanted me to comment on the service. He asked me twice if I had heard Parry or the men in coats shout out. When we were through he read my account back to me, intoning each sentence as though it were an item on a checklist. It was a prose I immediately wanted to disown. When he came to "There was a man eating lunch by himself at a table not far from our table where we were eating lunch and I recognized this man to be," I interrupted him. "Sorry. That's not what I said."

"You didn't notice him?"

"I saw him, but I didn't realize at first who he was."

Wallace frowned. "But you've seen him lots, standing outside your house and so on."

"He's cut his hair, and he was facing away from us."

Wallace made an alteration and read on to the end. As I was signing my name, he said, "If you don't mind staying on at the station, Mr. Rose, I'd like to have you back in just a little while."

"I don't mind waiting here," I said. "There's a man out there who wants to kill me." Wallace nodded and smiled, or rather, he stretched his lips without parting them.

All the restaurant witnesses had left, and I shared the waiting space now with a group of angry American tourists whose luggage, I overheard, had been stolen as it was being loaded onto their coach outside a hotel. There was also a young woman who sat apart, shaking her head in silent disbelief and trying, without success, to hold back tears.

I had decided while I was sitting with Clarissa not to press the police too hard. The disposition of events would do the work. My complaint earlier was on file; the scene in the restaurant was confirmation of an absolute kind. Parry had to be charged with attempted murder, and until he was, I needed protection. Now that I was the only one left from the restaurant, now the excitement was fading, I felt my isolation and vulnerability. Parry was all around me. I took care to sit facing the door, well away from the only window. Each time someone came in, I felt a cold drop in my stomach. Paranoia constructed an image of him for me, standing across the street from the police station, flanked by the men in coats. I went and stood in the station entrance and looked. I felt neither surprise nor relief that he wasn't there. Taxis and chauffeured cars were bringing the crowds in for the evening's opera. It was nearly seven-fifteen. Time had folded in on itself. The happy people who passed by me on their way home or to bars and cafés were blessed with a freedom they did not feel and I did not have: they were unencumbered, they had no one who wanted to kill them.

A friend who had been wrongly diagnosed with a terminal illness once told me of the loneliness she had felt as she left the doctor's office. The sympathy of friends simply marked her out with a different fate. She herself had known people who had died, and she knew well enough how life would go on without her. The waters would close over her head, her friends would feel sorrow and then recover, a little wiser, and the unrecorded workdays, parties, and dinners would tumble onward. That was how it was with me as I turned to go back into the police station. It was not quite self-pity, though there was an element of that; more a kind of shrinking into one's core, shrinking so deeply that everything else — the irritable tourists, the stricken girl — appeared as though on the other side of a thick glass panel. As I returned to the waiting room, my thoughts swam randomly in their little aquarium; nobody had what I had; if only I could exchange my arrangements for a ticket at the opera, or even a lost bag, or for whatever afflicted the girl.

I almost collided with Wallace, who had been looking for me. He was less polite and rather more animated than before. "It's this way," he said, and led me back along the corridor to the interview room. As I sat down, I was glad to see on the desk some faxed pages of Inspector Linley's notes.

Wallace was looking at me with new interest. This was no longer a routine transcription of a witness statement. "So. I had a little chat with Inspector Linley."

"Good. You got the picture."

He smiled. He was almost perky. "We think so. You won't like this, Mr. Rose. But I'm going to ask you to give it to me again."

"The statement? Why should I do that?"

"Can we start at the beginning? You were the last of your party to arrive. Take me through your movements that morning, let's say from nine o'clock."

Perhaps I've been a slow developer, but I was well into my forties before I realized that you don't have to comply with a request just because it's reasonable, or reasonably put. Age is the great disobliger. You can be yourself and say no. I folded my arms and smiled falsely. My refusal was friendly. "I'm sorry. I can't improve on it. I need to know what you're going to do."

"Ms. Mellon went off to work at about eight-thirty? Nine?"

"Have you sent a car round to Frognal Lane?"

"Let's stick with this, if you don't mind. What did you do then? Make phone calls? Write an article?"

It was an effort not to raise my voice. "I don't think you understand. This is a dangerous man."

Wallace was searching through the papers in front of him, through Linley's pages and his own, and muttering, "There's a note here somewhere."

"He's not going to stop at one attempt. I'd like to think you were doing something more than taking down a statement you've already heard."

"Here it is," Wallace said cheerfully, and he pulled out a sheet of paper torn in half.

I had my voice under control. "Unless you're going to tell me that it's a complete coincidence that the man I was on record complaining about at noon should be sitting a few feet away while —"

"Keats and Wordsworth?" Wallace asked.

I was momentarily thrown. On his lips, they sounded like suspects, two villains, drinking partners at the local pub.

"You were talking about them at lunch."

"Yes."

"One of them was putting down the other, right? Which was which?"

"Wordsworth putting down Keats — that's the story, anyway."

"And it wasn't true?"

I couldn't help myself. I'd been completely deflected. "Well, the only account we have is unreliable." I could see now that on Wallace's scrap of paper there was a numbered list.

He said, "That must be pretty unusual."

"Meaning?"

"Oh, you know, educated people like yourself, book writers and all that. Don't they all keep journals and stuff? You'd think that if anyone could get the record straight, they could."

I said nothing. I was being led somewhere. Best to let him get me there without resistance.

Wallace consulted his list. "Listen to this," he said. "It's quite interesting. Item number one: Mr. Tapp's party arrived half an hour after you." He raised a finger to forestall my denial. "That's from your Professor Kale. Item two, also from the professor: Mr. Tapp went to the toilet, not his daughter. Item three: Professor Kale says there was no one sitting alone near your table. And your Ms. Clarissa Mellon says there was someone sitting alone near your table but she'd never seen him before. She was very clear in her mind about that. Item four, Ms. Mellon: the gun was already on view when the two men came up to the Tapps' table. Number five is from all the witnesses except you: one of the men said something in a foreign language. Three think Arabic, one thinks French, the rest aren't sure. None of the three speaks Arabic.

The one who says French doesn't speak French or any other language. Six . . ."

Wallace changed his mind about item six. He folded the paper and put it in the top pocket of his jacket. He leaned forward with his elbows on the table and spoke in a confidential tone that had just a trace of pity. "I'll tell you something for free. There was an attempt on Mr. Tapp's life eighteen months ago in a hotel lobby in Addis Ababa."

There was a silence, during which I thought how unfair it was that the man shot in error had once been shot in earnest. All I needed at a time like this was a meaningless coincidence.

Wallace cleared his throat softly. "We needn't go right through the whole thing. Let's talk about the ice creams. Your waiter says he was bringing them to the table at the time of the shooting."

"That's not how I remember it. We started to eat them, then they were covered in blood."

"The waiter says the blood reached as far as him. The ice creams were bloodied when he set them down."

I said, "But I remember eating a couple of spoonfuls."

I felt a familiar disappointment. No one

could agree on anything. We lived in a mist of half-shared, unreliable perception, and our sense data came warped by a prism of desire and belief, which tilted our memories too. We saw and remembered in our own favor, and we persuaded ourselves along the way. Pitiless objectivity, especially about ourselves, was always a doomed social strategy. We're descended from the indignant, passionate tellers of half-truths, who, in order to convince others, simultaneously convinced themselves. Over generations success had winnowed us out, and with success came our defect, carved deep in the genes like ruts in a cart track: when it didn't suit us, we couldn't agree on what was in front of us. Believing is seeing. That's why there are divorces, border disputes, and wars, and why this statue of the Virgin Mary weeps blood and that one of Ganesh drinks milk. And that was why metaphysics and science were such courageous enterprises, such startling inventions, bigger than the wheel, bigger than agriculture, human artifacts set right against the grain of human nature. Disinterested truth. But it couldn't save us from ourselves, the ruts were too deep. There could be no private redemption in objectivity.

But exactly what interests of mine were

served by my own account of the restaurant lunch?

Wallace was patiently repeating a question. "What flavor was the ice cream?"

"Apple. If the guy says it was anything else, then we're talking about two different waiters."

"Your professor friend says vanilla."

I said, "Just tell me this. Why aren't you talking to Parry?"

Something rippled under the skin along Wallace's jawline, and his nostrils dilated fractionally. He was stifling a yawn. "He's on our list. We'll get to him. Our priority for now is finding the armed men. But if you don't mind, Mr. Rose, let's stay on the ice cream. Apple or vanilla?"

"Will it help you find the gunmen to know?"

"What helps is knowing that our witnesses are doing their best. It's the details, Mr. Rose."

"Apple, then."

"Which of the men was taller?"

"The one with the gun."

"Was he thinner?"

"I'd say they were both of medium build."

"Can you remember anything about their hands?"

I couldn't, but I went through the motions, frowning, turning my head, closing my eyes. Neuroscientists report that subjects asked to recall a scene while under a magnetic resonance imaging scanner show intense activity in the visual cortex, but what a sorry picture memory offers, barely a shadow, barely in the realm of sight, the echo of a whisper. You can't examine it for fresh information. It folds under scrutiny. I saw the sleeves of the long black coats, as dim as blurred daguerreotypes, and at the end of the sleeves . . . nothing. Or rather, anything. Hands, gloves, paws, hooves. I said, "I don't remember a thing about their hands."

"Just keep trying for me. Was there a ring, for example?"

I conjured a hand much like my own and gave it the ring Clarissa had given me, banded silver and gold, tastefully understated, deliberately undersized. She buttered my knuckle to get it on. That I couldn't remove it easily once gave us both pleasure. I said, "I can't remember." Then I added, "I think I'll leave," and I stood up.

Wallace stood up too. "I'd like you to stay and help us."

"I'd like you to help me."

He came round the desk. "Parry isn't behind this, believe me. Although I'm not saying you don't need help." As he spoke, he was fishing in his jacket pocket. He pulled out a silver blister pack and waved it right in front of my face. "You know what they are? Me, I take two before breakfast. Forty milligrams. A double dose, Mr. Rose."

As I hurried away down the corridor, I felt again that shrinking, isolated feeling. Perhaps it was self-pity after all: a maniac was trying to kill me, and all the law could suggest was Prozac.

It was already dark when I left my taxi at the bottom of my road and began walking toward our apartment building, using the line of plane trees for cover. He wasn't in his usual place, or further along, where he sometimes went when Clarissa came out. Nor was he behind me, or up one of the side streets, or behind the privet hedge, or round the side of the building. I let myself in and stood in the lobby listening. From one of the downstairs apartments came a muffled symphonic climax, banal and over-stated, Bruckner perhaps, and from some-where above me, in the ceiling space, the rush of water in a pipe. I took the stairs slowly and kept to the outside of the turns. I didn't really think he would have found a way into the building, but the rituals of caution were comforting. I let myself in and secured the front door with the dead-lock key. I knew immediately from the stillness in the air that Clarissa was asleep in the children's room, and sure enough, there was her note on the kitchen table. "Dead tired. Talk to you in the morning, Love, Clarissa." I looked at the *Love,* trying to extract meaning, or hope, from the upper-case *L.* I checked the locks on the skylights and went from room to room, turning on lamps and securing the windows. Then I poured myself a large grappa and went into my study.

I've always kept two address books. The pocket-size hardcover notebook is the one I use daily and is also the one I travel with. Two or three times now in the past twenty years I've left it in hotel rooms or, once, in a phone box in Hamburg and have had to replace it. The other is a scuffed, foolscap-size ledger book, which I've had since my twenties and which never leaves my study. Obviously, it serves as a backup or reservoir should I lose the little book, but over the years it has matured into a personal and social history. It tracks the blossoming complexity of the phone numbers themselves; the three-letter London codes of the earliest entries have an Edwardian quaintness. Abandoned addresses track the restlessness or social rise of many friends. There are names that would be pointless to transcribe; people die, or move out of my life, or fall out with me, or lose their identity altogether. There are dozens of names that mean nothing at all to me now.

I turned on the lamp by the chaise longue and settled there with the grappa and the ledger book open to the first page, and began to turn the overwritten pages, searching the palimpsests in the hope of finding a criminal connection. Perhaps I had, after all, led a narrow life, for I knew no one bad, no one bad in an organized way. Under H I found an acquaintance who sold dodgy secondhand cars. He had died of cancer. Under K, an old school friend who tended to depression and who worked in a casino for a stretch. He sank from sight into a rancorous marriage, and it was his psychiatrist wife who arranged for his electric shock treatment. Then they settled in Belgium.

I went on turning the friends, half-friends, quarter-friends, and strangers of a lifetime, most of them perfectly pleasant. One or two liars, perhaps, and a sloth, a boaster, and a self-deluder, but no one with a grip on illegality, no one functionally illicit. Here by the Ns was an English rose I had known back in the autumn of 1968, when we had shared a sleeping bag in Kabul and Mazar-i-Sharif. Back in England a few years later, she had interested herself in systematic shoplifting. Now she was a headmistress in Cheltenham. No tenacity. Also born under the sign of N was John Nolan, convicted twenty years ago of murder. At a drunken party he had thrown a cat from a second-floor balcony, skewering it on a park railing. He was righteously prosecuted by the RSPCA and fined fifty pounds. But still he kept his job with the Inland Revenue.

This Domesday Book of human exchange and fleeting possession that I had been extending and revising for more than a quarter of a century told one particular story of modern badness. The cast was too finely sifted, too entwined with the slants and sleights of character defect to have appealed to the criminal justice system. The alphabet of my society described a limited degree of failure and a fair amount of success, and all of it occurred within a narrow band of education and money. Not great wealth mostly, but reasonable sufficiency. There was simply no need to take other people's cash. Perhaps middle-class crime is mostly in the head, or in and around the bed. Battery, assault, abduction, rape, and murder were dourly fantasized when appropriate. But it's something less than morals — more like taste, *politesse* — that holds us back. Clarissa had taught me Stendhal's remark: "Le mauvais goût mène aux crimes."

Disappointment rising, I continued to rifle my Domesday, ignoring jolts of curiosity or the vague guilt prompted by certain names, until I entered at last the scrub desert of the final reaches, the U, V, X, Y, and Z that aridly encompass the oasis of last chances — the W. Sheltering here among the bucolic Woods, Wheatfields, Waters, and Warrens, written in faint, spidery pencil not of my own hand, was the name of Johnny B. Well, no criminal in my book but in my mind as extensively connected as a neuron.

His name was John Well, the B. having been borrowed by him, or for him, from Chuck Berry's kid hero who played the guitar like ringing a bell. As I remembered it, nothing ever came as easily to our Johnny as he roamed by public transport the suburbs of North and South London, bringing marijuana and hashish to the apartments of those too fastidious to descend to street level. By any definition he was a drug dealer, but the term was too harsh, too opprobrious, for Johnny B. Well was cast more in the type of a shopkeeper, the earnestly committed purveyor of fine wines or the busy proprietor of a delicatessen. He was careful with his prices, dealt only in the highest quality, and knew about his product to the point of tedium. He was also honest to the same degree — fussy and exact when he counted out the fivers in the change, showily punctilious when he returned the float on an unsuccessful deal. He was harmless and discreet, and acceptable everywhere. On his endless bleary rounds — for all fresh sales were sealed, or preceded, by a smoke — he might drift from tea with a consultant ophthalmologist to a bath at the home of a barrister friend, supper in a rock star's ménage, and on down to an overnight bed in a nest of nurses.

He had his own place too, a plumbed-in broom cupboard in Streatham. One evening Johnny opened the door to four grinning Jimmy Carter masks — it was as long ago as that — and in each pair of hands a crowbar. They didn't speak and they didn't touch him. They shouldered past and wrecked his flat — it must have taken all of five seconds — and then they left. Organized crime was closing down the hippies.

It was an early case of market rationalization. Before that, import and distribution had been the province of venture capitalists, lone dharma bums staking all on a bulging, fragrant backpack. The suits and crowbars streamlined and democratized, narrowing the product to third-grade Pakistani hashish and pushing out into pubs, football terraces, and prisons.

For a few months it looked as though Johnny B. Well was going to have to find another job, until he was offered protection by the very outfit that had wrecked his home. A small basic wage and commission on sales. This was the time he had been obliged to extend the range of his contacts, and why I thought he might be able to help me now. An ambitious bunch of lads who occupied a *chambre séparée* in the rear of The Dog at Tulse Hill became his employers. They had many friends and they sent Johnny on many errands. The thugs took him for the honest shopkeeper he was, and he moved among them unmocked and unscathed. At the same time he managed to keep open for his old, exacting clientele his line in connoisseur produce — stitched-leaf cornets from Nigeria, woven sticks from Natal and Thailand, new seedless varieties from Orange County, weightless golden sheets from the Lebanon. Under the new regime, a typical dreamy day might require a lunchtime experiment in lager with the modernizers and afternoon tea with the silks who sent them down.

It was a lonely life, and hard, a lot harder than ringing a bell. And Johnny B. Well never got rich. He was too earnest, too honest, too stoned. He never took taxis. What other dealer in the world would wait thirty-five minutes for a bus in his trodden-out shoes? He kept simple, heady faith in himself as a philanthropist, convinced that resin or fruity, flowering leaves, ignited and inhaled, were steadily easing humankind into a good mood, and that public and private battles would cease as sweet tempers prevailed and souls opened to the light. Meanwhile, as the 1980s got cracking, the suits and crowbars, along with the barristers, consultants, and rock stars, concentrated on the money.

In my study the circle of light in which I sat appeared to have brightened and shrunk about me. The grappa had been drained, though I did not remember finishing it. I stared at Johnny's spidery name and the seven digits beside it. Who better to help me? Why hadn't I thought of him before? Why hadn't I thought of him instantly? The answer was that I had not seen him in eleven years.

Like many before me, I had come to the

slow acknowledgment that the mind-altering substance of choice in a pressured, successful middle life is alcohol. Licit, social, with one's mild addiction easily concealed among everyone else's, and in all its infinite, ingenious manifestations, so colorful, so *tasty*, the drink in your hand triumphs by its very form; its liquidity is at one with the everyday, with milk, tea, coffee, with water, and therefore with life itself. Drinking is natural, whereas inhaling a smoldering vegetable is at some remove from breathing, as is the ingestion of pills from eating, and there is no penetration in nature that resembles that of the needle, except an insect's sting. A single malt and spring water, a cool glass of Chablis, may improve your outlook by only a modest degree but will leave unruffled the glassy continuum of your selfhood. Of course, there is drunkenness to consider, its boorishness, vomiting, and violence, and then craven addiction, physical and mental dereliction, and degrading, agonizing death. But these are the consequences of simple abuse, which flows, as surely as claret from a bottle, out of human weakness, defect of character. You can hardly blame the substance. Even chocolate biscuits have their victims, and I have one elderly friend who has led a fulfilling and useful life on thirty years' supply of pure heroin.

I stood in the semidark of the hallway and listened; only the creak and click of contracting wood and metal, and, deep in the pipework, the trickle of retreating water. From the kitchen, the susurration of the refrigerator, and beyond, the soothing rumble of the nighttime city. Back in my study, I sat with the phone in my lap, considering the moment, this turning point. I was about to step outside the illuminated envelope of fear and meticulous daydreaming into a hard-edged world of consequences. I knew that one action, one event, would entail another, until the train was beyond my control, and that if I had doubts, this was the moment to withdraw.

Johnny picked up on the fourth ring, and I said my name. It took him less than a second.

"Joe! Joe Rose. Hey! How you doing?"

"Well, I need some help."

"Oh yeah? I got some really interesting —"

"No, Johnny. Not that. I need your help. I need a gun."

Twenty-one

The next morning I drove Johnny out to
house on the North Downs. In my bac
pocket was a seven-hundred-and-fifty
pound wad, mostly in twenties. Fifties, ap
parently, were unacceptable.

As we crawled through the choking dull-
ness of Tooting, he was still messing with
the electric seat controls and muttering to
himself as he pressed the switches of the
map light and the trip computer, "So you've
done all right . . . Yeah, I always knew you'd
be okay."

From a near horizontal position he gave
me a lesson in gun etiquette. "It's like in
banks. You never say money. Or in funeral
parlors, no one says dead. With guns, no
one ever says gun. Only pricks who watch
TV say shooter or piece. If you can, you
avoid naming it at all. Otherwise it's the
item, or the wherewithal, or the necessary."

"They'll provide the bullets?"

"Yeah, yeah, but the word is *rounds*."

"And someone'll show me how it works."

"Christ, no. That wouldn't be cool. You can take it to the woods and work it out for yourself. They hand it over, you put it in your pocket." Johnny brought himself into a sitting position. "You sure you should be walking around with a gun?"

I said nothing. I was paying Johnny well for his help. Not explaining the background was protection for us both. We were still stuck in traffic. On the radio the jazz had been dishonestly succeeded by a program of atonal music, an earnest whooping and banging that was getting on my nerves. I turned it off and said, "Tell me more about these people." I already knew they were ex-hippies who had made it rich in coke. They had gone legal in the mid-eighties and dealt in property. Now things were not so good, which was why they were happy to sell me a gun for an inflated price.

"Relative to the scene," Johnny said, "these people are intellectuals."

"Meaning what?"

"They got books all over the walls. They like to talk about the big questions. They think they're Bertrand Russell or something. You'll probably hate them."

I already did.

By the time we reached the motorway, Johnny was horizontal again and asleep. He

wasn't usually up before noon. The road was quiet and straight and I had time to take a look at him. He still wore his mustache American frontier style, with the hairs, now whitened at the ends, curling over his upper lip, almost into his mouth. Was it flinty manhood women tasted, kissing a setup like that, or yesterday's vindaloo? Thirty-five years of grinning and squinting through the smoke had drawn crow's feet halfway to his ears. From his nostrils to the corners of his mouth, the smile lines ran deep with disappointment. I knew from my recent Streatham trip that apart from the shifting clientele and a new girlfriend, not much had changed for Johnny. But the marginal life was no longer original, the shortage of desirable possessions no longer a kind of lightness, and here came the universal message from the bones and sinews; the writing was on the skin, it was in the mirror. Johnny kept going in his trodden-out shoes, living like a student, like a charity worker, worrying that this newfangled Amsterdam skunk was too strong and bad for the heart.

A shift in key of the road surface rumble brought Johnny awake as we left the motorway. Still flat on his back, he fished a thin joint from his top pocket and lit up. Two lungfuls later he pressed the seat control and came looming and fuming into my field of vision with a whir. He didn't pass it. This was a private thing, the first of the day, the one he took with his tea and toast.

He inhaled and spoke at the top of his breath in the old style. What a saint. "Take a left. Follow the signs to Abinger." Soon we were dropping down past twisted boughs and trunks, through gloomy tunnels of greenery on a high-banked single-track road. I put on the headlights. We pulled into passing places to edge round the oncoming traffic. There was much grim-faced smiling and nodding among us car owners, pretending to be untouched by the insult of narrow spaces. We were deep in a countryside that was itself deep in a suburb. Every two or three hundred yards we passed a gateway in twenties brick and ironwork, or five-barred wooden gates with coach lanterns. There was a sudden clearing in the wood, a confluence of roads, a half-timbered pub, and a hundred cars parked outside, baking their colors in the heat. An empty snack packet jumped dreamily into the sunshine to touch our windscreen. Two Alsatian dogs were staring into the ground. Then we were back in the tunnel and the smoke was thick in the car.

"It's good to get out of the city," Johnny

said. I lowered my window. I thought I might be passively stoned. The wad was pressing hard into my buttock, and everything looked too emphatic, as though invisibly italicized. Perhaps it was fear.

Ten minutes later we turned down a rutted driveway whose crumbling asphalt was pierced by weeds.

"Amazing how life does that," Johnny said. "You know, just pushes through anyway?" This was a big question, surely a rehearsal for the company we were about to keep. I would have taken a shot at an answer to steady my nerves. But just then we came into view of an ugly mock Tudor house, and the words died in my throat.

The curving driveway took us to a double garage built of cement blocks and painted an unevenly faded purple. Its rusting up-and-over door was padlocked. In front, poking through the long grass and the nettles, were the skeletons and entrails of half a dozen motorbikes. It looked to me like a place where crimes could be safely committed. Running from an iron ring in the garage wall was a long chain with no dog on the end of it. This was where we stopped and got out. The nettles went right up to the Georgian front door. From the house came the sound of a bass guitar, a three-note figure fumblingly repeated.

"So where are the intellectuals?"

Johnny winced and made a downward-pressing movement with his hand, as though to stuff my words back into a bottle. He spoke in a near whisper as we approached the door. "I'll give you some advice you might be grateful for. Don't make fun of these people. They haven't had your advantages, and they're, uh, not too stable."

"You should have said. Let's go." I pulled at Johnny's sleeve, but with his free hand he was ringing the bell.

"It's cool," he said. "Just watch your step."

I took a pace back and had half turned away, thinking I might walk off down the drive, when the door snapped open and habitual politeness constrained me. A powerful odor of burned food and ammonia rolled, or blared, out of the house, momentarily silhouetting the figure who stood in the doorway.

"Johnny B. Well!" the man said. He had a shaved head and a small waxed mustache dyed with henna. "What are you doing here?"

"I phoned last night, remember?"

"Yeah, right, we said Saturday."

"It *is* Saturday, Steve."

"Uh-uh. It's Friday, Johnny."

Both men looked to me. I had been reading up on the restaurant attack and the newspapers were in my car, all over the back seat. "Actually, it's Sunday."

Johnny shook his head. He looked betrayed. Steve was staring at me with loathing. I guessed it wasn't his two lost days, it was my *actually*. He was right, it didn't sound good here, but I met his look full on. He spat something white into the nettles and said, "You're the guy who wants to buy a gun and some bullets."

Johnny had located an object of interest in the sky. He said, "You inviting us in or what?"

Steve hesitated. "If it's Sunday, we got people coming to lunch."

"Yeah. Us."

"That was yesterday, Johnny."

We laughed with effort. Steve stood aside so we could step into his stinking hall.

When the front door closed we were in virtual darkness. By way of explanation, Steve said, "We're making toast and the dog's crapped all over the kitchen floor." We followed his outline deeper into the house. Somehow the news about the dog made the gun seem pricey at seven-fifty.

We emerged into a large kitchen. A blue stratum of bread smoke hung at shoulder height, illuminated by french windows at the far end. A man in dungarees and gumboots was mopping the floor with undiluted bleach from a zinc bucket. He called out Johnny's name and nodded at me. There was no sign of a dog. At the stove was a woman stirring a pot. Her hair was combed straight and grew to her waist. She came toward us with a slow, floating movement, and I thought I recognized her type. In England, hippiedom had been largely a boys' affair. A certain kind of quiet girl sat cross-legged at the edges, got stoned, and brought the tea. And then, just as the Great War had emptied the stately homes of servants, so these girls disappeared overnight at the first trump from the women's movement. Suddenly they were nowhere to be found. But Daisy had stayed on. She came over and told me her name. Of course she knew Johnny and said his name as she touched his arm.

I guessed her to be about fifty. The long straight hair was a last rope to the bollard of her youth. Failure had written in lines on Johnny's face, but with Daisy it was all in the downward curve of her mouth. Lately I've noticed these mouths in some women of my age. A lifetime of putting out, as they saw it, and getting nothing back. The men were bastards, the social contract unjust, and biology itself an affliction. The weight of all disappointment bent and locked these mouths into their downturn, a Cupid's bow of loss. At a glance it looked like disapproval, but the mouths told a deeper tale of regret, though their owners never guessed what was being said about them.

I told Daisy my name. She kept her hand on Johnny's arm, but she spoke to me. "We're having a late breakfast. We've had to start again."

Minutes later we were sitting round the long kitchen table, each with a bowl of porridge and a slab of cold toast. Right across from me was the floor mopper, whose name was Xan. His huge forearms were hairless and meaty, and I felt he didn't like the look of me.

When Steve sat down at the head of the table, he pressed his palms together, raised his head, and closed his eyes. At the same time he inhaled deeply through his nose. Far back in some nasal cave, chance had fashioned out of mucus two-note panpipes, and we were forced to listen. He held his breath for many uncomfortable seconds, then released it at length. This was con-

313

trolled breathing, or a meditation, or a prayer of thanksgiving.

It was impossible not to look at his mustache. It couldn't have been less like Johnny's. It was dyed a fierce burnt orange and was ramrod straight, waxed to prissy Prussian points. I brought a hand to my face to conceal a smile. I felt weightless and shivery. The shock of yesterday's shooting, this plan of reckless acquisition, the background fear, all combined to make me feel that I wasn't really here, and I worried that I might do or say something stupid. My stomach kept plunging, and I felt skittish and giggly, feelings intensified by my sense of being trapped at this table. It must have been the passive smoking I had done in the car. I could not stop the similes accumulating around Steve's mustache. Two rusty nails hammered outward from his gums. The pointy masts of a schooner I built as a kid. Something to hang tea towels on.

Don't make fun of these people . . . they're not too stable. As soon as I remembered Johnny's warnings, as soon as it occurred to me that I must not laugh, I knew I was lost. The first minor explosion of breath through my nose I disguised as a reverse sniff. For cover I lifted my porridge spoon. But no one was eating yet. No one was talking. We were waiting for Steve. When his lungs were about to burst, he lowered his shaved head and exhaled, and the mustache tips quivered with rodent eagerness. From where I sat, human meaning appeared to be deserting the sinking ship of his face. Dancing in and out of my spiral of anxiety and hilarity was a train of yet more unbidden images from childhood. I tried to turn them away, but the evocative power of the ludicrous mustache swept all before it: a Victorian weightlifter on a biscuit tin lid, the bolt in the neck of Frankenstein's monster, a novelty alarm clock with a painted face telling a quarter to three, the dormouse at the Mad Hatter's tea party, Ratty in a school production of *Toad of Toad Hall.*

This was the man who was selling me a gun.

There was nothing I could do. The spoon in my hand was shaking. I put it down carefully and clenched my jaw and felt the sweat pricking my upper lip. I was beginning to rock. I was right in the line of Xan's suspicious scrutiny. The squeaking noise was my chair, the muffled clucking sound was me. So much air had vacated my lungs I knew the intake was going to be a noisy affair, but my choices had narrowed now to embarrassment or death. Time slowed as I yielded to the inevitable. I spun in my chair, sank my face in my hands, and made a screeching inhalation. As my lungs filled, I knew there was still more laughter to come. I hid it behind a yodeling, shouting sneeze. Now I was on my feet, and so was everyone else. Someone's chair hit the floor with a snap.

"It's the bleach," I heard Johnny say.

He was a true friend. I had my story. But stumbling through the commotion, I had yet to defeat the image of Steve's mustache. I snorted and coughed my way across the room, half blinded by tears, toward the french windows, which seemed to billow open at my approach, and stumbled down some wooden steps out onto a lawn of baked earth and dandelions.

Watched by them all, I turned my back to the house and spat and breathed deeply. When I was calm at last, I straightened and saw right in front of me, tied to a rusting bed frame by a length of electrical cord, a dog, presumably the one that had fouled the kitchen floor. It scrambled to its feet and cocked its head at me and gave a most tentative, apologetic half-swipe with its tail. What other animal, apart from ourselves and other primates, is capable of experiencing in duration the emotion of abject shame? The dog looked at me, and I looked at the dog, and it seemed to want to engage me in some form of cross-species complicity. But I wasn't going to be drawn. I turned and strode toward the house, calling out, "Sorry! Ammonia! Allergy!" And the dog, bereft of a generative grammar and the resources of deceit available to me, sank back onto its bare patch of earth to await forgiveness.

Soon we were back round the kitchen table, with windows and doors opened wide, and the subject was allergies. Xan gave his judgments the ring of fundamental truth by adorning them with *basically*.

"Basically," he said, looking at me, "your allergy is a form of imbalance."

When I said this was unfalsifiable, he looked pleased. I began to think he might not detest me after all. He had the same hostile regard for his porridge as he had for me. What I had thought was an expression was actually his face at rest. I had been misled by the curl of his upper lip, which some genetic hiatus had boiled into a snarl.

"Basically," he went on, "there has to be a reason for an allergy, and research has shown that in over seventy percent of cases, the roots can be traced back basically to frustrated needs in early childhood."

It was a while since I had heard this device, the percentages snatched from the air, the unprovenanced research, the measurements of the immeasurable. It had a peculiarly boyish ring.

I said, "I'm in the less than thirty percent."

Daisy was on her feet, ladling out more porridge. She spoke in the quiet voice of one who knows the truth but can't be fished to fight for it. "There's an overriding planetary aspect, with particular reference to earth signs and the tenth house."

At this point Johnny perked up. He had been tense since we had sat down again, probably worried that I was about to misbehave. "It was the Industrial Revolution. Like, before eighteen hundred no one had allergies, no one had *heard* of hay fever. Then when we started throwing up all this chemical shit into the air, and then into the food and water, people's immune systems started to jack it in. We weren't built to take all this crap —"

Johnny was warming up when Steve spoke over him. "Excuse me, Johnny. But that's really a tissue of horseshit. The Industrial

Revolution gave us a whole state of *mind*, and that's where we get our illnesses." He turned to me abruptly. "What's your opinion?"

My opinion was that someone should fetch the gun. I said, "My thing is definitely a state of mind. When I'm feeling good, ammonia doesn't bother me at all."

"You are unhappy," Daisy said. She pursed her own unhappy, downturned mouth. "I can see a lot of dirty yellow in your aura." If the table had been narrower, she might have reached for my hand.

"It's true," I said, and saw my opening. "That's why I'm here." I looked at Steve, and he looked away. There was a silence that tightened as I waited. Johnny was taking this in with that helpless air of his, and I wondered if he had made a mistake.

The silence was all about who was going to speak first. It was Xan. "We're not basically the sort of people who would have a gun."

He trailed away, and it was Daisy who helped him out. "In the twelve years we've had it, it's never been fired."

Steve spoke quickly, telling her what she must already know. "It's been oiled and cleaned regularly, though."

And she said to him, also for my benefit, "Yeah, but not because we expected to be firing it."

There was a confused pause. No one knew where we were. Xan started again. "The thing is, we don't approve of this gun . . ."

"Or any guns," Daisy said.

Steve clarified. "It's a Stoller thirty-two, made before the factory was sold by the Norwegians back to the Dutch and German conglomerate that developed it originally. It's got a carbide twin-action release that —"

"Steve," Xan said patiently. "Basically, this thing, like, came into our possession in a whole other time, when everything was crazy and different and who knows we might have needed it."

"Self-defense," Steve said.

"We've been talking about this a lot before you came," Daisy said. "We don't really like the idea of it being just, like, taken away by someone and, you know . . ."

She couldn't finish this, so I said, "Are you selling it or not?"

Xan folded his mighty forearms. "It's not like that. And it's not the money."

"Well, wait a minute," said Steve. "That's not true either."

"Jesus!" Xan was a touch irritable. He couldn't hitch his words round his thoughts; it was difficult, and people kept interrupting. His attitude was lining up behind his snarl. "Look," he said. "There was a time when it was all about money. Only the money. You could almost say it was simple. I'm not saying it was wrong, but look what happened. Nothing turned out the way people wanted. You can't think about it on its own. You can't think about anything on its own. Everything's connected, we know that now, it's been shown, it's a society. It's basically holistic."

Steve leaned in toward Daisy and said theatrically behind his hand, "What's he on about?"

Daisy spoke to me. Perhaps she was still thinking about my unhappiness. "It's simple. We're not against selling, but we'd like to know what you'd be wanting with a gun."

I said, "You get the money, I take the gun."

Johnny stirred again. The deal he had brokered might be slipping away. "Look, Joe has to be discreet. For our sake as well as his."

I didn't like the repetition of my name. It could hang in the air of this kitchen for weeks, along with everything else, and get used.

"But listen . . ." Johnny was touching my arm. "You could say something to put people's minds at rest."

They were all looking at me. Through the open french windows we heard the mongrel whine, a squeezed-out sound it seemed to be trying to suppress. All I could think about was leaving, gun or not. I made a show of looking at my watch and said, "I'll tell you in four words and nothing more. Someone wants to kill me."

In the silence everyone, including me, totted up the words.

"So it is self-defense," Xan said, with hope in his voice.

I shrugged a kind of yes. There was dither in these faces. They wanted the money and they wanted absolution. These coke dealers, these property crooks impoverished by negative equity and their dim beliefs, were making a stab at being moral, and they wanted me to help them out. I was beginning to feel better. So I was the bad person. Suddenly I was set free. I took the wad and tossed it on the table. What was the point of bargaining?

I said, "Why don't you count it?"

No one moved at first. Then there was a

flash, and Steve's hand got there just ahead of Xan's. Daisy stared hard. It looked serious. Perhaps they were living on toast and porridge.

Steve counted the notes in bank-clerk style, at high speed, and when he was done he put them in his pocket and said to me, "Right. So now you can fuck off, Joe!"

To keep face, I included myself in the nervous laughter.

Then I noticed that Xan wasn't laughing. He sat waiting, his arms folded, his snarl giving nothing away. In his right forearm, a muscle — it was one I didn't have myself — twitched rhythmically to an unseen movement of his hand. When the laughter died he spoke up, but not in the voice that had made the case for holism. It was pitched higher and it was husky, and his tongue clicked drily against the roof of his mouth. He was still, but I could see the turmoil beneath the skin, in the pulse at the base of his throat. That was when my own blood began to run a little harder. Xan said, "Steve, put the money back on the table and get the gun."

Steve was getting to his feet, holding Xan's stare all the while. "Fine," he said quietly, and began to cross the room.

Xan was out of his chair. "That money

isn't going in the tin box."

Without turning, Steve replied with equal certainty, "I'm owed," and continued on his way.

The nearest object to Xan was his empty porridge bowl. He seized it between thumb and forefinger and skimmed it hard, frisbee fashion, with left hand extended and splayed for balance. It missed Steve's neck by an inch and shattered on the door frame.

"No!" Daisy shouted. There was something of the weary impatient mother in this call. Then she walked out of the room without a word. We saw her retreating back and her hair swinging about her waist. She was gone and we heard her footsteps on the stairs. Johnny looked at me. I knew what he was thinking. Now the responsibility for the fight was all ours. In fact, it was all mine, for Johnny had sat down to roll himself a cigarette and was shaking his head and sighing at his trembling fingers.

Steve had turned and was coming back to the kitchen table. Xan went toward him and took him by his shirtfront and tried to push him against the wall. "Don't start this," he said breathily. "Put it on the table." But Steve was not so easy to push. His body was tight and hard, and he looked cruel. The two men leaned into each other in the center of the room. Their biggest effort, it seemed, was to breathe. They were so close, there hovered between their faces a gestalt candlestick.

Steve said quickly, "The household owes me, you both owe me. Now get your fucking hand off." But he did not wait for compliance. His left hand flew to Xan's throat and gripped. Xan swung back his free arm in a wide arc, then whiplashed his open hand against Steve's face. The crack of the blow sounded like a burst balloon, and the force of it thrust the men apart. For an instant they froze, then they charged and went into a clinch. The four-legged beast swayed and edged sideways across the kitchen floor back toward the table. Johnny and I heard only bottled grunts. Heads down, eyes closed, lips stretched across their teeth, they groped and clambered and wound over and under each other like lovers.

Something had to give. Xan got his hand under Steve's chin and began to force back his head. No neck muscles could be a match for that hideous impacted arm, but still, it was a mighty trembling effort, because Steve had hooked a thumb into Xan's nostril and was groping for his eyes and Xan, forced to lean away, was at full stretch. Steve's head was going back, and Xan's next move was

325

to slip a headlock on him, right arm around Steve's neck, left hand pulling on his own wrist to tighten the squeeze. I started toward them. Steve was going slowly to his knees. He was moaning and his hands were flailing, then beating weakly against Xan's legs.

I tapped Xan's face with the back of my hand and crouched down to speak in his ear. "You're going to kill him. Is that what you want?"

"Keep out of this. It's been coming a long time."

I tried pulling on his ear to get him to turn and look at me. "If he dies, you'll be inside for the rest of your life."

"Small fucking price!"

"Johnny," I shouted, "you've got to help!"

I saw Daisy come back in the room. She held a shoebox in two hands, and her expression was of weariness. Her downturned mouth asked us to see what she had had to put up with — the men in her life struggling for the mechanical advantage, for the leverage that would permit one to break the other's neck.

"Take it," she was whispering. "Take it, take it!"

I got to my feet and took the box from Daisy. It was heavy, and I needed two hands to support the flimsy cardboard. Steve moaned again, and I looked at Johnny. He made a pleading look and jerked his head toward the door.

"That's right," Daisy said firmly. "Better go."

The exhaustion in her manner made me wonder if this were not some kind of domestic ritual, or an overrehearsed prelude to a complicated sexual alliance. On the other hand, I thought we ought to be saving Steve's life.

Johnny pulled on my sleeve. I went with him a couple of paces across the room. He muttered into my ear, "If something happens, I don't want to be a witness."

I saw what he meant, so we nodded at Daisy, and with one last glance at Steve's head in the trembling vise of Xan's forearm, we hurried along the dark hallway to the front door.

As soon as we were in the car, Johnny pulled out a joint and lit it. It was the last drug I would have wanted just then. Far better to stop for a Scotch somewhere and calm down. I started the car and drove hard back up the drive.

"It's funny, you know," Johnny said through the smoke. "I've been there other times and we've had these really interesting discussions."

I swung out onto the road and was about to reply when the phone rang. I had left it plugged into the cigarette lighter.

It was Parry. "Joe, is that you?"

"Yes."

"I'm at your place, sitting here with Clarissa. I'm putting her on, okay? Are you there? Joe? Are you there?"

Twenty-two

I had the impression of having passed out for a second or two. The roar in my ears, I realized, was the car's engine. We were doing almost sixty and I had forgotten to change gears. I shifted from second to fourth and dropped my speed.

"I'm here," I said.

"Listen carefully, now," Parry said. "Here she is."

"Joe?" I knew immediately she was frightened. Her voice was pitched high. She was trying to keep control.

"Clarissa. Are you all right?"

"You have to come straight back. Don't talk to anyone. Don't talk to the police." The monotone was to let me know that the words weren't hers.

"I'm in Surrey," I said. "It's going to take me a couple of hours."

I heard her repeat this to Parry, but I didn't catch what he told her.

"Just come straight back," she said.

"Tell me what's happening there.

Are you okay?"

She was like a speaking clock. "Come straight here. Don't bring anyone. He'll be watching out the window."

"I'll do exactly as he says, don't worry." Then I added, "I love you."

I heard the phone changing hands. "You got all that? You won't let me down now, will you?"

"Listen, Parry," I said. "I'll do whatever you want. I'll be there in two hours. I won't talk to anyone. But don't hurt her. Please don't hurt her."

"It's all down to you, Joe," he said, and the line went dead.

Johnny was looking at me. "Trouble at home," he murmured sympathetically.

I opened my window and took some lung-fuls of fresh air. We were passing the pub and entering the woods. I turned off the road down a track and followed it for about a mile until it ran out into a small clearing by a ruined house. There were signs of reno-vation work — a cement mixer, a pile of scaffolding and bricks — but no one was around. I switched off the engine and reached for the shoebox on the back seat. "Let's take a look at that wherewithal."

I lifted the lid and we peered in. I had never fired a handgun before, or even seen one, but the object that lay partially concealed within the folds of a torn-up old white shirt looked familiar enough from the movies. Only the feel of it was a surprise. It was lighter than I expected, and drier, warmer to the touch. Oily, cold, and heavy was what I had imagined. Nor, as I lifted it up and aimed it through the windscreen, did it radiate the mystique of deadly potential. It was just another of those inert devices you unwrap at home after shopping — mobile phone, VCR, microwave — and wonder how difficult it's going to be to bring it to life. The absence of a sixty-page instruction manual seemed like a head start. I turned the gun over, looking for a way in. Johnny put his hand in the shirt cloth and pulled out a compact box of red cardboard, which he picked open.

"It's a ten-shot," he said, and took the weapon from me, slipped a catch at the base of the stock, and slid the magazine home. With a yellow forefinger he pointed out the safety lever. "Push it right forward till it clicks." He looked along the sights. "It's a nice one. Steve was just bullshitting. It's a Browning nine-millimeter. I like this polyamide grip. Better than walnut, really."

We got out of the car and Johnny gave me back the gun.

"I didn't think you'd know about this stuff," I said. We were walking behind the roofless house, into the woods.

"I was into guns for a while," he said dreamily. "It was the way the business was going then. When I was in the States, I went on a course in Tennessee. Cougar Ranch. I think some of the people there might have been Nazis. I'm not sure. But anyway, they kept on about their two tactical rules. Number one, always win, and number two, always cheat."

At another time I might have been drawn to elaborate the evolutionary perspective, drawn from game theory, that for any social animal, always cheating was a sure route to extinction. But now I felt sick. My legs were weak, and my bowels had gone watery. It was a constant and conscious effort as I walked on the crackling dry leaves beneath the beeches to keep my anal sphincter tight. I knew I shouldn't be wasting time. I should be racing toward London. But I had to be certain I knew what to do with the gun. "This'll do right here," I said. If I had walked another step, I might have crapped in my pants.

"Use both hands," Johnny said. "It's quite a kick if you're not used to it. Set your feet apart and distribute your weight evenly.

Breathe out slowly as you squeeze the trigger." I was doing all this when the gun went off and reared upward in my hands. We walked to the beech tree and took some moments to find the entry hole. The bullet was barely visible, sunk two inches into the smooth bark. As we walked back to the car, Johnny said, "A tree's one thing, but it's a big deal when you point a gun at someone. Basically, you're giving them permission to kill you."

I left him waiting in the front seat while I took some paper and went back into the trees and used my heel to scrape a shallow trench. While I crouched there with my pants around my ankles, I tried to soothe myself by parting the crackly old leaves and scooping up a handful of soil. Some people find their long perspectives in the stars and galaxies; I prefer the earthbound scale of the biological. I brought my palm close to my face and peered. In the rich black crumbly mulch I saw two black ants, a springtail, and a dark red wormlike creature with a score of pale brown legs. These were the rumbling giants of this lower world, for not far below the threshold of visibility was the seething world of the roundworms, the scavengers and the predators who fed on them; and even these were giants relative to the inhabitants of the microscopic realm, the parasitic fungi and the bacteria — perhaps ten million of them in this handful of soil. The blind compulsion of these organisms to consume and excrete made possible the richness of the soil and therefore the plants, the trees, and the creatures that lived among them, whose number had once included ourselves. What I thought might calm me was the reminder that for all our concerns, we were still part of this natural dependency, for the animals that we ate grazed the plants which, like our vegetables and fruits, were nourished by the soil formed by these organisms. But even as I squatted to enrich the forest floor, I could not believe in the primary significance of these grand cycles. Just beyond the oxygen-exhaling trees stood my poison-exuding vehicle, inside which was my gun, and thirty-five miles down teeming roads was the enormous city on whose northern side was my apartment, where a madman was waiting, a de Clerambault, my de Clerambault, and my threatened loved one. What, in this description, was necessary to the carbon cycle, or the fixing of nitrogen? We were no longer in the great chain. It was our own complexity that had expelled us from the Garden. We were in a mess of our own unmaking.

I stood and buckled my belt and then, with the diligence of a household cat, kicked the soil back into my trench.

Wrapped as I was in my own affairs, I was amazed to find Johnny asleep again. I woke him and explained that I was going to have to drive home fast. If he wanted, I could drop him near a railway station. He said he didn't mind. "But listen, Joe. If you get into a collision and the cops are involved, the Browning's nothing to do with me, okay?" I patted the right-hand pocket of my jacket and started the engine.

With the headlights full on, I raced up the single-track road and made no compromises with the oncoming traffic. Drivers reversed in front of me and scowled from the passing places. Once we were on the motorway, Johnny lit up his third of the day. I kept to a steady one hundred and fifteen, all the while watching the rearview mirror for patrol cars. I tried phoning the apartment but got no reply. I thought about calling the police. Fine — if I could find someone to dispatch an elite squad to rappel in on Parry and overpower him before he could do harm. What I'd get, though, if I was lucky enough to reach their level with a phone call, would be Linley or Wallace, or some other weary bureaucrat.

I stopped in Streatham High Street to give Johnny his money and drop him off. He leaned in the open passenger door to say goodbye. "When you've finished with the gun, don't keep it or sell it. Chuck it in the river."

"Thanks for everything, Johnny."

"I'm worried for you, Joe, but I'm glad I'm getting out."

The midafternoon traffic in central London was surprisingly light, and I reached my road an hour and a half after the phone call. I turned off before the apartment building and parked behind it. Round the back, where the dustbins were kept, was a locked fire escape for which only the residents had the key. I let myself through and went up quietly onto the roof. I hadn't been out here since the morning after Logan's accident, after Parry's first phone call. There was a stain on the table from my breakfast coffee. It was bright up here, and to see through the skylight I had to get down on my knees and cup my hands over the glass. My view was across the hallway and into a portion of the kitchen. I could see Clarissa's bag, but nothing else.

The second skylight gave me a reverse sight line along the hall, into the sitting room. Fortunately, the door was wide open.

Clarissa was sitting on the sofa, facing in my direction, though I could not make out the expression on her face. Parry was seated directly in front of her on a wooden kitchen chair. His back was to me, and I guessed he was doing the talking. He was thirty feet away at most, and I indulged a daydream of taking a shot at him right then, even though he was too close to Clarissa and I didn't trust my aim, or understand enough about guns to know how the glass of the skylight might deflect the bullet from its course.

This fantasy had little to do with the actual gun, which was beginning to weigh in my pocket. I went back to the car and parked round the front and sounded the horn as I got out. Parry came to the window and stood partly concealed by the curtain. He looked down and we exchanged a glance, inverting our usual perspective. As I went up the stairs, I felt for the gun and located the safety catch and practiced releasing it. I rang the doorbell and let myself in. I could hear my heart under my shirt, and the pressure of my pulse made my field of vision throb. When I called out Clarissa's name, my thickened tongue glued itself between the *c* and the *l*.

"We're in here," she replied, and then she

added on a rising pitch of caution, "Joe —" and was cut off by a shushing sound from Parry. I went slowly toward the sitting room and stopped in the doorway. My dread was of provoking sudden action. He had moved the kitchen chair to one side and was sitting on the sofa, with Clarissa close by him on his left. We looked at each other, and she closed her eyes for half a second, which I took to mean it was bad, he was bad, watch out. He looked young and gawky with his hair cut. His hands were shaking.

Since I had appeared before them there had been complete silence. To fill it I said, "I preferred the ponytail."

He glanced away to his right, to the invisible presence on his shoulder, before meeting my eye. "You know why I'm here."

"Well . . ." I said, and took a couple of paces into the room.

His voice cracked on a higher note. "Don't come any closer. I've told Clarissa not to move."

I was looking at his clothes, wondering about the weapon. He had to have one. He hadn't come to kill me with his bare hands. He could easily have borrowed or bought from the men he had hired. There was no obvious bulge in the beige cotton jacket he was wearing, though its cut was loose and it was hard to tell. An edge of something black, a comb perhaps, protruded from his top pocket. He wore tight-fitting jeans over gray leather boots, so whatever he had was in the jacket. He sat right up against Clarissa, with his left leg touching her right, almost squashing her into the arm of the sofa. She was perfectly still, her hands palm downward on her knees, her body radiating disgust and terror at his touch. Her head was turned a little toward him, ready for whatever he might do. She was still, but ripples of muscle and tendon at the base of her neck suggested that she was coiled, ready to spring away.

"Now you've got me here," I said, "you don't need Clarissa."

"I need you both," he said quickly. The tremor in his hands was so bad he clasped them. Sweat was beading on his forehead, and I thought I could smell the sweet grassy tang. Whatever he had in mind was about to happen. Even so, now that he was right in front of me, the idea of pointing a gun at him seemed ludicrous. And I wanted to sit down, I was suddenly so tired. I wanted to lie somewhere and rest. I felt let down by the adrenaline that was meant to bestow alertness. I couldn't help myself yawning, and he must have thought I was being very cool.

"You forced your way in here," I said.

"I love you, Joe," he said simply, "and it's wrecked my life." He glanced at Clarissa as though acknowledging a repetition. "I didn't want any of it — you knew that, didn't you? But you wouldn't leave me alone, and I thought there must be a point to it. You had to be leading me on for a reason. You were called to God and you were fighting it and you seemed to be asking me to help you . . ." He paused, looking across his shoulder for his next thought. I suffered no failure of attention, but my anxiety about his closeness to Clarissa continued to grow. Why wouldn't he let her move? I remembered a moment during my visit to the Logans when I had grasped what it might mean to lose her. Should I be doing something now? I also remembered Johnny's warning. As soon as I took out the gun, I would be giving Parry permission to kill. Perhaps the danger could be dissipated in talk. My one certainty was that I should not contradict him.

Clarissa's voice was very quiet and small. She was taking a risk, trying to reason with him. "I'm sure Joe didn't mean you any harm."

The sweat was fairly rolling off Parry now. There was something he was about to do. He forced a laugh. "That's debatable!"

"He was actually very frightened of you, you know, standing outside the house, and all the letters. He didn't know anything about you, then suddenly there you were . . ."

Parry tossed his head from side to side. It was an involuntary spasm, an intensification of his nervous sideways glance, and I had the feeling we were catching a glimpse of the core of his condition; he had to block out the facts that didn't fit. He said, "You don't understand. Neither of you do, but you especially." He turned toward her.

I put my right hand in my jacket pocket and felt for the safety catch, but I was fumbling too hard and couldn't find it.

"You've no idea what this has been about. How could you? But I haven't come here to talk about it. It's all in the past. It's not worth discussing, is it, Joe? We're finished, aren't we? All of us." He trailed a finger through the sweat along the line of his eyebrows and sighed loudly. We waited. When he raised his head, he was looking at me. "I'm not going to go on about it. That's not why I'm here. I've come to ask you something. I think you know what it is."

"Perhaps I do," I lied.

He took a deep breath. We were coming to it. "Forgiveness?" He said on a rising interrogative note. "Please forgive me, Joe, for what I did yesterday, for what I tried to do."

I was so surprised I could not speak immediately. I took my hand out of my pocket and said, "You tried to kill me." I wanted to hear him say it. I wanted Clarissa to hear.

"I planned it, I paid for it. If you wouldn't return my love, I thought I'd rather have you dead. It was insanity, Joe. I want you to forgive me."

I was going to ask him again to let Clarissa move away when he turned toward her, thrust his hand in his top pocket, and pulled out a short-bladed knife, which he drew through the air in a wide semicircular motion. I had no time to move. She raised both hands to her throat, but he wasn't aiming for that. He brought the tapering point of the blade right up under his own earlobe and held it there. The hand on the knife was shaking, and pressing hard. He turned right round to show her, and then he showed me.

He pleaded in a kind of rising wail, an unbearable sound. "You've never given me a thing. Please let me have this. I'm going to do it anyway. Let me have this one thing from you. Forgiveness, Joe. If you forgive me, God will too."

Surprise was making me stupid, and relief was confusing my responses. It was so extraordinary, such a reverse, that he was not about to attack Clarissa or me that the fact he was about to slit his throat in front of us presented itself with numbing slowness. I managed to say, "Drop the knife and we'll talk."

He shook his head and seemed to press harder. A plumb line of blood ran down from the knife's tip.

Clarissa too seemed paralyzed. Then she was stretching a hand toward his wrist, as though she might bring him back with the touch of a finger.

"Now," he said. "Please, Joe. Now."

"How can I forgive you when you're mad?"

I aimed at his right side, away from Clarissa. In the enclosed space the explosion seemed to wipe out all other senses, and the room flashed like a blank screen. Next I saw the knife on the floor and Parry slumped back with his hand to his shattered elbow, his face white and his mouth open in shock.

In a world in which logic was the engine of feeling, this should have been the moment when Clarissa stood, when we moved toward each other and folded into each other's arms with kisses and tears and conciliatory murmurs and words of forgiveness and love. We should have been able to turn our backs on Parry, whose thoughts must have shrunk to a brilliant point of pain, to his ruined ulna and radial (six months later I came across a chip of bone under the sofa); we should have been able to leave him behind, and when the police and ambulance men had carried him away, when we had talked and caressed and emptied the teapot twice over, we might have retreated to our bedroom to lie face to face and allow ourselves to be carried back to the pure familiar space. Then we could have set about rebuilding our lives, right there.

But such logic would have been inhuman. There were immediate and background reasons why the climax of the afternoon could not have been in this particular happiness. The narrative compression of storytelling, especially in the movies, beguiles us with happy endings into forgetting that sustained stress is corrosive of feeling. It's the great deadener. Those moments of joyful release from terror are not so easily had. Within the past twenty-four hours Clarissa and I had witnessed a bungled murder and an attempted suicide. Clarissa had spent the afternoon under the threat of Parry's knife. When she had spoken to me on the phone, he had held the blade against her cheek. For my part, aside from the stress, the accumulation of horrible certainties borne out by events brought no immediate comfort in vindication. Instead I felt cramped by a flat and narrow sense of grievance. It was a passionless anger, all the harder to bear or express because I intuited that being right in this case was also to be contaminated by the truth.

Besides, there isn't ever only one system of logic. For example, the police, as always, saw things differently. Whatever they might have had in store for Parry, they were quite clear in their minds, when they came to the flat twenty minutes after the shooting, about their business with me. Possession of an illicit firearm and malicious wounding with intent. Parry went his way on a stretcher while a police constable and a sergeant formally, and even a little apologetically, arrested me. An exception was made to the usual procedure where guns were involved, and I was permitted to walk downstairs unhandcuffed. On our way we passed the police photographer and forensic specialist going up. A routine, I was assured, in case one of us changed his story. My third visit to a police station in twenty-four hours, the third in my life. More random clustering. Clarissa was asked to come too, as a witness. Inspector Linley was off duty, but my file was brought out and read and I was treated pleasantly enough. All the same, I was held in custody overnight in a cell next door to a bawling drunk, and the following morning, after a long interview, I was bailed to return in six weeks. As it turned out, following a letter from Linley to the director of public prosecution, no charges were ever brought against me.

No caresses, then, that night, none of the kitchen table talk and bed that had held us together in the evening after John Logan's death. Worse, though, at the time, was an image that afflicted me during my sleepless night in the cell and lingered for days afterward. I saw the knife on the floor, I saw Parry slumped back on the sofa clutching his arm — and then I saw the expression on Clarissa's face. She was on her feet and she was staring at the gun in my hand with an expression of such repulsion and surprise that I thought we would never get past this moment. Lately my worst suspicions had tended to be confirmed. I was getting things right in the worst possible way. My score was depressingly high. Perhaps we really were finished.

Twenty-three

Dear Joe,

I'm sorry about our row. I'm not being sardonic — I really mean it, I genuinely regret it. We always prided ourselves on being able to get by without the occasional fights that other couples told us were necessary and therapeutic. I hated it last night. I hated being angry, and I was scared by your anger. But it's there now, it can't be unsaid. You said again and again that I owe you a profound apology for not standing with you "shoulder to shoulder" against Jed Parry, for doubting your sanity, for not having faith in your powers of rationality and deduction and your dedicated research into his condition. I think I gave you that apology several times last night and I'm giving it again now. I thought Parry was a pathetic and harmless crank. At worst, I thought of him as a creature of your imagining. I never guessed he would become so violent. I was completely wrong and I'm sorry, really sorry.

But what I was also trying to say last night was this: your being right is not a simple matter. I can't quite get rid of the idea that there might have been a less frightening outcome if you had behaved differently. That apart, there's no question that the whole experience has cost us dearly, however right you were. Shoulder to shoulder? You went it alone, Joe. Right from the start, before you knew anything about Parry, you became so intense and strange and worked up about him. Do you remember his first phone call? You waited two days to tell me about it. Then you were off on your old track about getting back into "real science," when we'd agreed that there was no point. Are you really saying this had nothing to do with Parry? That same evening you stormed out of the flat, slamming the door on me. Nothing like that had ever happened between us. You became more and more agitated and obsessed. You didn't want to talk to me about anything else. Our sex life dwindled to almost nothing. I don't want to go on about it, but your ransacking my desk was a terrible betrayal. What reason had I given you to be jealous? As the Parry thing grew, I watched you go deeper into yourself and further and further away from me. You were manic, and driven, and very lonely. You were on a case, a mission. Perhaps it became a substitute for the science you wanted to be doing. You did the research, you made the logical inferences, and you got a lot of things right, but in the process you forgot to take me along with you, you forgot how to confide.

There was another thing I tried to say to you last night, but you shouted me down. That evening after the accident — it was quite clear from the things you were saying then that you were very troubled by the thought that it might have been you who let go of the rope first. It was obvious you needed to confront that idea, dismiss it, make your peace with it, whatever. I thought we would be talking about it again. I thought I could help you. As far as I was concerned, you had nothing to be ashamed of. Quite the contrary, I think you were very courageous that day. But your feelings after the accident were real enough. Isn't it possible that Parry presented you with an escape from your guilt? You seemed to be carrying your agitation over into this new situation, running from your anxieties with your hands over your ears, when you should have been turning on yourself those powers of rational analysis you take such pride in.

I accept that Parry is mad in ways I could never have guessed at. All the same, I can understand how he might have formed the impression that you were leading him on. He brought out something in you. From day one you saw him as an opponent and you set about defeating him, and you — we — paid a high price. Perhaps if you had shared more with me, he might not have got to the stage he did. Do you remember my suggesting to you early on — the night you walked out on me in fury — that we ask him in and talk to him? You just stared at me in disbelief, but I'm absolutely certain that at that time Parry didn't know that one day he would want you dead. Together we might have deflected him from the course he took.

You went your own way, you denied him everything, and that allowed his fantasies, and ultimately his hatred, to flourish. You asked me last night if I realized that you had saved my life. In the immediate sense, of course, that's true. I'll always be grateful. You were brave and resourceful. In fact, you were brilliant.

But I don't accept that it was always inevitable that Parry was going to hire killers or that I should end up being threatened with a knife. My guess was that he was always more likely to do himself harm. How wrong and how right I was! You saved my life, but perhaps you put my life in jeopardy — by drawing Parry in, by overreacting all along the way, by guessing his every next move as if you were pushing him toward it.

A stranger invaded our lives, and the first thing that happened was that you became a stranger to me. You worked out that he had de Clerambault's syndrome (if that really is a disease) and you guessed that he might become violent. You were right; you acted decisively and you're right to take pride in that. But what about the rest? Why it happened, how it changed you, how it might have been otherwise, what it did to us — that's what we've got now, and that's what we have to think about.

I think we need some time apart. Or at least I do. Luke has offered me his old Camden Square place until he finds new tenants. I don't know where this takes us. We've been so happy together. We've loved each other passionately and loyally.

I always thought our love was the kind that was meant to go on and on. Perhaps it will. I just don't know.

Clarissa

Twenty-four

Two weeks after the shooting I drove to Watlington to keep my appointment with Joseph Lacey. The following day I spent the morning in my study making arrangements on the phone, and in the afternoon I walked to our local Italian food shop to collect ingredients for our picnic. It was much the same as before — a mozzarella globe, ciabatta, olives, tomatoes, anchovies, and for the children a no-frills pizza margarita. The next morning I packed the food into a backpack along with two bottles of Chianti, mineral water, and a six-pack of Cokes. The day was cloudy and cool, but there was a thin band of blue spreading from the west, and the confident forecast was a heatwave that would last over a week. I drove to Camden Town to collect Clarissa. When I had told her Lacey's story the day before, she had insisted on coming with me to Oxford. We had come this far together in the story, had been her argument, and whatever it had done to us, she

354

wanted to be there at its conclusion.

She must have been looking out for my car, for as soon as I parked she appeared at the top of the steps outside her brother's flat. I got out and watched as she approached, and wondered how we were going to greet each other. We hadn't met since the evening I had refused to help carry her suitcases of clothes and books down to her taxi. Leaning by the open car door now in the brightening air, I experienced a sudden ache — part desolation, part panic — at observing the speed with which this mate, this familiar, was transforming herself into a separate person. The print dress was new, and so were the green espadrilles. Even her skin looked different, paler, smoother. We said hi and fumbled a squeeze of hands — better than hypocritical pecks on the cheek. The familiarity of the perfume didn't reassure me. It made the new touches seem all the more poignant.

Perhaps she was having similar feelings, for as I started the car she said too cheerfully, "I like the new jacket."

I thanked her and said something pleasant about her dress. I had worried how we were going to pass the journey together. I didn't want another confrontation, nor could I ignore our differences. But in fact our week apart had granted us a supply of neutral topics. First, my interview with Joseph Lacey in his garden, and then the arrangements I had made for the day — that much took us as far as the outer western suburbs. Next we talked about work. There was a new lead in the search for Keats's last letters. She had been in touch with a Japanese scholar who claimed he had read unpublished correspondence twelve years ago in the British Library written by a distant relation of Keats's friend Severn. There was a reference to a letter addressed to Fanny but never meant to be posted, a "cry of undying love not touched by despair." Clarissa had spent every spare hour trying, without success, to track down the Severn connection. The library's transfer to King's Cross was complicating the search, and now she was considering flying to Tokyo to read the scholar's notes.

For my part, I had been to Birmingham to test-drive an electric car for a Sunday newspaper. I was due to fly to Miami to cover a conference about the exploration of Mars. When I described, with a degree of comic exaggeration, the horror of the public relations people when the electric prototype failed to move, Clarissa did not smile. Perhaps she was thinking of the centrifugal geography — Maida Vale and Camden Town, Miami and Tokyo — that was whirling our lives apart. There was a silence as we descended into the Vale of Oxford from the Chilterns, so I talked about the colonization of Mars. Apparently it might be possible to plant simple life forms like lichen, and then, later, hardy trees, and over the course of thousands of years an oxygen-based atmosphere could develop. The temperature would rise, and in time it could be a beautiful place. Clarissa stared through the windscreen at the road rolling under our feet and, to left and right, the thickening fields and the cow parsley just out along the hedgerows. "What's the point? It's beautiful here and we're still unhappy."

I didn't ask her who *we* were. I dreaded more personal talk in such an enclosed space. Our row had been a long and grisly affair, and though I came nowhere near shouting, as she suggested in her letter, I raised my voice — we both did — and paced the sitting room in a state of dreamlike agitation. This, in addition to the bloodstain on the carpet, was Parry's legacy — an orgy of mutual accusation, an autopsy that sent us weary and bitter to our separate beds at three in the morning. Clarissa's letter simply drove us further apart. Fifteen years ago I might have taken it seriously, suspecting that it embodied a wisdom, a delicacy that I failed in my bullish way to grasp. I might have thought it my duty, part of my sentimental education, to feel rebuked. But the years harden us into what we are, and her letter appeared to me simply unreasonable. I disliked its wounded, self-righteous tone, its clammy emotional logic, its knowingness that hid behind a highly selective memory. A madman paid to have me slaughtered in a restaurant? What was "sharing" one's feelings compared to that? And driven, obsessed, undersexed? Who wouldn't be? Here was a diseased consciousness clamoring to batten itself to mine. I didn't ask to be lonely. No one would listen to me. She and the police forced my isolation.

I had said all this on the phone the morning her letter came, and of course it got us nowhere. Now here we were in six feet of space — shoulder to shoulder, in fact — but the matter of our differences was unbroachable. I glanced at her and thought she looked beautiful and sad. Or was the sadness all mine?

We small-talked our way through Headington and the center of Oxford. I parked outside the Logans' house in exactly the same space as before. The trees lining the tranquil street made a tunnel of green light broken by brilliant points of sunshine, and as I got out of the car I wondered about the kind of life, boring and productive, one might have here. I took the backpack and we walked up the brick path to the front door like a married couple invited to lunch. Clarissa even murmured an approving remark about the front garden. This spell of intensified ordinariness was broken when the front door opened and little Leo stood before us, naked but for face paint done in clumsy tiger stripes across his chest and the bridge of his nose. He looked at me without recognition and said, "I'm not a tiger, I'm a wolf."

"You are a wolf," I said. "But where's your mum?"

She appeared behind Leo in the gloomy recesses by the kitchen and came toward us. Time had done nothing in the way of healing. The same thin nose, the same rawness over her upper lip. Perhaps her face was harder, perhaps her anger was setting into the bone. She had a handkerchief balled up in her right hand, which she transferred to her left to take Clarissa's hand, then mine. She asked us if we would like to wait in the back garden while she got Leo cleaned up and dressed, and this was where we found

Rachael, in shorts, on her front on the grass, working at a tan. When she heard us she flopped over, belly up, and pretended to be asleep, or in a trance. Clarissa knelt down and tickled the girl under the chin with a stalk.

With her eyes shut against the brightness, Rachael called out on a rising squeal, "I know just who you are, so don't think you can make me laugh!" When she could stand it no more she sat up, and found herself looking into Clarissa's face, not mine.

"You don't know who I am, so I can make you laugh," Clarissa said, "and I won't stop until you've guessed my name." The tickling continued until Rachael shouted, "Rumpelstiltskin" and begged for mercy. When I turned to go back indoors, she was taking Clarissa by the hand on a tour of the garden. I noticed that the collapsed tent had been trodden into the lawn.

I found Jean Logan on her knees in the hallway, buckling Leo's sandal. "You're old enough to be doing this yourself," she was saying. He was smoothing her head with the palm of her hand. "But I like you doing it," he said, looking at me with a smile of triumphant possession.

I said to her, "I want you to hear this

story at first hand. So I need to know where we're going to take our picnic."

She stood and sighed, and described a stretch of the Thames on Port Meadow. Then she pointed me to the phone at the foot of the stairs. I waited for her and Leo to go out to the garden before I dialed the college and asked to speak to the Euler Professor of Logic.

The meadow was barely five minutes' walk. Leo, jealous of his sister's new friend, was hanging on Clarissa's free arm and singing scraps of every Beatles song he could think of — anything to close off the conversation. Rachael simply talked louder. Jean Logan and I walked several paces behind this noisy trio. She said, "She's very good with them. You both are." I described the various children in our lives and the room we kept for them at the flat. Clarissa's bedroom, and now not even that.

As we were crossing a railway bridge, the meadow and its vast spread of buttercups was suddenly before us. Jean Logan said, "I know I've asked to hear this, but I'm not sure I can go through with it, especially with Rachael and Leo here."

"You can," I said, "and anyway, you have to now."

Followed by a curious band of young heifers, we walked straight across the field through the buttercups to the river, which we followed upstream for a few hundred yards. Where the bank was worn away by drinking cattle and ponies into a small beach, we stopped and made our camp. Jean spread a large army-surplus groundsheet, and as I was setting out the food I realized it must have belonged to John Logan and been with him on expeditions we would never know of. I poured wine for the women. Leo and Rachael were wading in the river, calling to me, daring me to join them. I took off my shoes and socks and rolled up my trousers and went after them. A whole lifetime since I had stood like this, feeling the ooze between my toes and breathing in the rich earth-and-water smell of a river. While Clarissa and Jean talked we fed the ducks, skimmed stones, and built a moated mud mound. During a lull, Rachael sidled up to me and said, "I remember when you came and we had this talk."

"I remember it too," I said.

"Let's have another talk, then."

"Okay," I said. "What about?"

"You start."

I thought for a moment, then I indicated the river. "Imagine the smallest possible bit of water that can exist. So tiny no one could ever see it . . ."

She was screwing up her eyes the way she had on the lawn. "Like the weeniest droplet," she said.

"Much smaller. Even a microscope wouldn't help you. It's almost nothing. Two atoms of hydrogen, one of oxygen, bound together by a mysterious powerful force."

"I can see it," she cried. "It's made of glass."

"So," I said. "Now think of billions, trillions of them, piled on top of each other in all directions, stretching almost to infinity. And now think of the riverbed as a long shallow slide, like a winding muddy chute, that's a hundred miles long, stretching to the sea."

We got no further. Leo had been busy on the bank, but now he was aware that something was happening without him. He came pushing in, ready to drench me if I did not include him.

"I hate you," Rachael shouted. "Go away!"

Just then we were called to eat, but before we reached the shore, Rachael pinched my arm, to let me know we were not finished yet.

The food prompted talk of Italy and holidays. The children joined in with evidently confused memories of a beach where parrots lived, and fir trees growing by a volcano, and, from Rachael alone, a glass-bottomed boat. Leo disputed that such a thing could exist. Because the boat had been hired for a day, the volcano climbed by means of a six-hour hike, and Leo carried much of the way, we inferred the energetic presence of John Logan, though even the boy did not refer to him directly now.

By the time we had finished lunch, wine and sunshine were making the adults lazy. Bored with us, the children took pieces of apple to feed to the ponies. Jean began to explain how Rachael was missing her father but refused to talk about it. "I saw her talking to you in the river. She attaches herself to any man who comes into the house. She seems to feel there's something she can get from them she can never have from me. She's so trusting. I wish I knew what it is she's looking for. Perhaps it's just the sound of a man's voice."

We were watching the children as she spoke. They were wandering further upriver. At a certain distance from his mother, Leo glanced back, then slipped his hand into his sister's. Jean was starting to tell us how well the children looked out for each other when

364

she suddenly broke off and said, "Oh God! There she is. That must be her."

We sat up and turned to look. I got to my feet.

"I know I asked you to do this," Jean said quickly. "But I don't think I can meet her. It's too soon for me. And she's brought someone with her. Her father. Or perhaps he's her lawyer. I don't want to talk to her. I thought I did . . ."

Clarissa put her hand on Jean's arm. "It's all right," she said.

The couple had stopped a dozen yards away and stood side by side, waiting for me. The girl looked away as I approached. I knew she was a student. She looked about twenty, and she was very pretty, the incarnation of Jean Logan's worst fears. The man was James Reid, Euler Professor of Logic at the girl's college. We shook hands and said our names. The professor was hardly older than me, fifty perhaps, and rather plump. He introduced the student as Bonnie Deedes, and as I took her hand I could imagine how an older man might risk everything. It was the kind of prettiness I would have dismissed as a cliché if I'd heard it described — that blond, blue-eyed peachiness that drew a line of descent from Marilyn Monroe. She wore cutoff jeans and a ragged pink shirt. The professor, by contrast, was in a linen suit and tie.

"Well," he said through a sigh, "shall we get this over with?" He was looking at his student, who looked down at her sandaled feet (the nails were painted red) and nodded miserably.

I led them across to the picnic and made the introductions. Jean would not look at Bonnie, and she in turn kept her eyes on her professor. I invited them to sit. Bonnie diplomatically arranged herself cross-legged on the grass, just at the edge of the groundsheet. Reid compromised between dignity and politeness by half kneeling. He looked at me and I nodded.

He placed his hands on his knee and stared at the ground a moment, focusing his thoughts, the habit of a lifetime's lecturing. "We've come," he said at last, "to explain and apologize." He addressed his words to Jean, but she kept her gaze on the vivid remains of the pizza. "You're living through this tragedy, this terrible loss, and heaven knows, the last thing you need is this extra pain. That scarf left behind in your husband's car was Bonnie's — there's no doubt about that."

Jean interrupted. Her ferocious gaze was suddenly on the girl. "Then perhaps I ought to hear it from her."

But Bonnie simply wilted in the heat of that gaze. She could not speak, nor did she dare look up.

Reid continued. "She was there, all right. But I was too, you see. We were together." He looked at Jean and let this sink in. Then he said, "I'll put it at its simplest. Bonnie and I are in love. Thirty years between us, all very foolish, but there it is, we're in love. We've kept it secret, and we know that soon we're going to have to face all kinds of complication and upset. We never imagined that our clumsy attempts at concealment would cause such distress, and I hope that when I've explained what happened, you'll find a way to forgive us."

Far away along the riverbank we heard the children calling to each other. Jean sat quietly. Her left hand was across her mouth, as if to restrain herself from speech.

"My position at the college and with the university is about to become impossible. It'll be a relief to resign. But that needn't concern you." He was looking at the girl, trying to catch her eye, but she wasn't playing along.

"Until recently, Bonnie and I had a rule never to be seen together in Oxford. Now we're throwing it all to the winds. On the day this happened, we'd planned a picnic in the Chilterns. I picked Bonnie up from a bus stop on the edge of town. We'd gone less than a mile together when my car broke down. We pushed it into a lay-by, and that's when she persuaded me that we shouldn't give up on the day. The car could be sorted out later. We should try and hitch a lift. So I cowered behind Bonnie, feeling terribly self-conscious and wondering if someone would recognize me. After a couple of minutes a car stopped, and it was your husband, on his way to London. He was very friendly and kind. If he guessed about us, he didn't show any disapproval. Quite the contrary. He offered to make a detour from the motorway and drop us up by Christmas Common. We were almost at the place when we saw the man and boy having trouble with their balloon in the strong wind. I didn't really take it in fully — I was sitting in the back, you see. Your husband pulled over sharply and without a word went running over to help. We got out to watch. I'm not a very physically active person, and there seemed to be quite a few people going in to sort it out, so at first, at least, it seemed sensible to stay put. I don't think I would have been much use. Then the whole ghastly thing started to get out of hand, and we realized that we should try and get over and help them hold the balloon down, and we started to run. Then it was too late, the balloon was up in the air — and you know the rest."

Reid hesitated over his choice of words. His voice dropped, and I had to lean forward to hear.

"After he fell, we were in a terrible state. It was panic, really. We went off down a footpath, trying to calm ourselves and think what to do. We left the car far behind and forgot that our picnic was in it, as well as Bonnie's scarf. We walked for hours. I'm ashamed to say that one of my worries was that if we came forward as witnesses, I would have to explain what I was doing in the middle of the countryside with one of my students. We just didn't know what to do.

"A few hours later we found ourselves walking into Watlington. We went into a pub to find out about buses or taxis. Standing at the bar was a man telling the barman and a group of regulars what had happened that afternoon. It was obvious he was one of the men who had been hanging on the ropes. We couldn't help ourselves letting him know that we had been there too. These things bind you together, you know, and you have to talk. The people who hadn't been there seemed like outsiders. We ended up going home with this fellow, Joseph Lacey, to talk more, and that was when I told him of my problem. Later on, he drove us back to Oxford, and on the way he gave us this advice. He thought there were enough witnesses to the accident. There was no need for us to add our accounts. But he also said that if it turned out there were disagreements, or conflicting stories, then he would get in touch with me, and I could think again. So. We never came forward. I know it's caused you distress, and I'm deeply, deeply sorry."

At these words I became aware once more of the meadow, the golden swaths of buttercups, a pack of horses and ponies galloping toward the village at the far end, the distant drone of the ring road, and close by, on the river, a sailing race proceeding with silent intensity. The children were walking slowly toward us, deep in conversation. Clarissa was unobtrusively packing the picnic away.

"Oh God," Jean sighed.

"He was a terribly brave man," the professor offered her, just as I had once. "It's the kind of courage the rest of us can only dream about. But can you ever forgive us for being so selfish, so careless?"

"Of course I can," she said angrily. There were tears in her eyes. "But who's going to forgive me? The only person who can is dead."

Reid was speaking over her, telling her she must not think that way. Jean raised her voice again to castigate herself. The professor's reassurances tangled with her words. This breathless scrambling for forgiveness seemed to me almost mad, Mad Hatterish, here on the riverbank where Lewis Carroll, the dean of Christ Church, had once entertained the darling objects of his own obsessions. I caught Clarissa's eye and we exchanged a half-smile, and it was as if we were pitching our own requests for mutual forgiveness, or at least tolerance, in there with Jean's and Reid's frantic counterpoint. I shrugged as though to say that, like her in her letter, I just did not know.

At last we were all standing. The picnic was stowed, the groundsheet folded up. Bonnie, who had still not spoken, had wandered a few steps away, and by her restless movements indicated she was impatient to go. She was either dim, a genuine dumb blonde, or contemptuous of us all. Reid was hovering helplessly, anxious to oblige her but constrained by politeness to make a proper farewell. I slung the backpack over my shoulder and was about to go and say goodbye and put him out of his misery when Rachael and Leo appeared on either side of me.

I've never outgrown that feeling of mild pride, of acceptance, when children take your hand. They drew me away with them toward the little muddy beach, where we stood and faced the slow brown expanse of water.

"So now," Rachael said, "tell Leo as well. Say it again slowly, that thing about the river."

Appendix I

Reprinted from *The British Review of Psychiatry*

Robert Wenn, MB Bch. MRCPsych, &
Antonio Camia, MA, MB, DRCOG,
MRCPsych

A homoerotic obsession, with religious overtones: a clinical variant of de Clerambault's syndrome

The case of a pure (primary) form of de Clerambault's syndrome is described in a man whose religious convictions are central to his delusions. Dangerousness and suicidal tendencies are also present. The case adds to recent literature supporting the view that the syndrome is a nosological entity.

Introduction

"Erotic delusions," "erotomania," and the associated pathologies of love have produced a rich and varied literature which describes, at one extreme, unusual behavior or acceptable occurrences without psycho-pathological implications, and at the other, strange variants encompassed by a schizo-phrenic psychosis. The earliest references are to be found in Plutarch, Galen, and Cicero, and as a review of the literature by Enoch & Trethowan (1979) makes clear, the term "erotomania" has suffered from the very beginning from a lack of clear defi-nition.

In 1942 de Clerambault carefully deline-ated the paradigm that bears his name, a syndrome he termed *les psychoses passionelles,* or "pure erotomania," to distinguish it from more generally accepted erotic paranoid states. The patient, or "subject," usually a woman, has the intense delusional belief that a man, the "object," often of higher social standing, is in love with her. The patient may have had little or no contact with the object of her delusion. The fact that the object is already married is likely to be regarded by the patient as irrelevant. His protestations of indifference or even ha-tred are seen as paradoxical or contradic-tory; her conviction that he "really" loves her remains fixed. Other derived themes in-clude beliefs that the object will never find true happiness without her, and also that the relationship is universally acknowledged and approved. De Clerambault was emphatic that in the pure form of the condition onset was precise and sudden, even explosive, and that this was an important differentiating factor; paranoid erotic states, he believed, probably erroneously (Enoch & Trethowan 1979), developed gradually.

Central to de Clerambault's paradigm was what he termed a "fundamental postulate" of the patient having "a conviction of being in amorous communication with a person of much higher rank, who has been the first to fall in love and was the first to make advances." Such communication may take the form of secret signals, direct contact, and the deployment of "phenomenal resources" to meet the patient's needs. She feels she is watching over and protecting the object of her delusion.

In one of his earliest and most celebrated cases, de Clerambault described a fifty-three-year-old Frenchwoman who believed King George V was in love with her. She persistently pursued him from 1918 onward, paying several visits to England:

She frequently waited for him outside Buckingham Palace. She once saw a curtain move in one of the palace windows and interpreted this as a signal from the king. She claimed that all Londoners knew of his love for her, but alleged that he had prevented her from finding lodgings in London, made her miss her hotel bookings, and was responsible for the loss of her baggage containing money and portraits of him . . . She vividly summarized her passion for him. "The king might hate me, but he can never forget. I could never be indifferent to him, nor he to me . . . It is in vain that he hurts me . . . I was attracted to him from the depths of my heart . . ."

Over the years, as more cases are described, there has been a tendency both to broaden and to clarify the defining criteria: not only women suffer, not only heterosexual attraction is involved. At least one of de Clerambault's patients was male, and more male sufferers have been identified since. In their survey of mostly male patients, Mullen and Pathe (1994) conclude that in intrusiveness and dangerousness, men predominate. Homosexual cases have been reported by Mullen & Pathe, by Lovett Doust & Christie (1978), by Enoch and his coworkers, by Raskin & Sullivan (1974), and by Wenn & Camia (1990).

Thus the diagnostic criteria for the primary syndrome (i.e., de Clerambault's syndrome) as suggested by Enoch & Trethowan would be likely to find general acceptance among those who accept the clinical entity: "a delusional conviction of being in amorous communication with another person, this person is of much higher rank, has been the first to fall in love, and the first to make advances, the onset is sudden, the object of the amorous delusion remains unchanged, the patient gives an explanation for the object's paradoxical behavior, the course is chronic, hallucinations are absent, and there are no cognitive defects."

Mullen and Pathe cite Peres (1993), who observes that an increasing awareness of the threat presented by de Clerambault sufferers is bringing about an "explosion" of legislation to protect their victims. Mullen and Pathe highlight the tragedy for patients and victims alike: for the patients, love becomes an "isolating and autistic mode of being, in which any possibility of unity with another is lost. The tragedy for those on whom they fix their unwanted attentions is that, at the very least, they suffer harassment and embarrassment, or the disintegration of their closest relationships, and at the worst they may fall victim to the violent expression of resentment, jealousy, or sexual desire."

Case History

A twenty-eight-year-old unmarried man, P, was referred from the courts following charges arising out of an attempted murder.

P was the second child of an elderly father who died when P was eight and of an unsupportive mother who remarried when P was thirteen. By his own account, P was an intense and lonely child, prone to daydreaming, who did not easily make friends. When his mother remarried he was sent to boarding school, where he was above average academically, but not dramatically so. While he was there, his older sister moved abroad, and he never saw her again. He did not remember being teased or bullied, but he formed no close friendships and thought the other boys looked down on him because he had "no father to boast about, the way they did." He gained entrance to university, where the pattern of isolation continued. P felt the students were frivolous. He joined the Student Christian Movement, and though he did not remain a member for long, he began to take comfort in his faith about this time. He left university with a poor degree in history and for the next four years drifted between low-skilled jobs. By now he had virtually no contact with his mother, who had divorced her second husband and had inherited a large house in North London and a sum of money from her sister.

P trained to become a teacher of English to foreigners and was one year into his first job when his mother died and he became the sole beneficiary of her estate, his sister being untraceable. He gave up his job and moved into the house, where both his isolation and his religious beliefs intensified. He meditated "on God's glory" for long periods of time and went for walks in the country. During this time he became convinced that God was preparing for him a challenge, which he must not fail.

It was while he was on one of his rambles that P assisted at the scene of an accident involving a helium balloon. He exchanged a glance with R, another passerby who was also helping, who appeared to P to fall in love with him at that moment. Late that night P made the first of many phone calls to R to let him know that the love was mutual. P realized that the task set him by God was to return R's love and to "bring him to God." This certainty grew when he discovered that R was a well-known science writer who wrote from an atheistic point of view. In P's various apprehensions of God's will, he experienced no hallucinations.

There now began the barrage of letters, doorstep confrontations, and street vigils so familiar in the sad literature of this condition. In an interesting echo of de Clerambault's famous case, P perceived messages from R in the changing arrangement of the curtains in R's apartment. P also received information by touching the leaves of a privet hedge and from published articles by R that had appeared in print long before their first meeting. R had been living contentedly with his common-law wife, M, and within days this relationship was under strain from P's determined onslaught. Later they separated. P was mostly euphoric, certain that despite R's outward hostility, he would come to accept his fate and live with P in his large house. He believed R was "playing with him" and testing his commitment.

Soon the euphoria turned to resentment. Early on, P had managed to steal M's appointment diary from her place of work. Using the information he had that R was to be at a certain restaurant, P hired contract killers to shoot R. The attempt ended with a diner at a nearby table being shot in the shoulder. P was overcome with remorse and intended to stab himself to death in front of R. This plan failed too, and P was arrested and charged not only with the restaurant shooting but also for having held M at knifepoint. The court ordered a full psychiatric report.

On interview, the patient presented well, with a normal affect commensurate with having been held on remand in an overcrowded prison. Because an initial examination at the behest of his solicitor had produced a diagnosis of schizophrenia, cognitive, physical, and laboratory examinations were instigated, but proved normal, as was the EEG. There was no disorder of form of thought, and hallucinations were absent. There was no evidence of other Schneiderian front-rank symptoms for schizophrenia (Schneider 1959). P showed above-average visuo-spatial abilities, abstraction, and concentration. His WAIS scores were: verbal 130, performance 110, full-scale 120. In the Benton test he showed no cognitive impairment. On the Weschler Memory Scale his short-term memory was intact for simple and complex material.

P stated that he knew R still loved him, as was evidenced by his having intervened to save P from killing himself. Also, at a procedural hearing in court, P had received a "message of love" from R. P regretted his attempt on R's life and felt that whatever lay ahead of him was a test, both of his faith in God and of his love for R. The patient was articulate and coherent in these assertions. The impression formed was of a well-encapsulated delusional system. Chemotherapy (5mg pimozide daily) and gently challenging insight-directed therapy were prescribed, but over a six-month period were observed to have no impact. Eventually the court ruled that P should be held indefinitely at a secure mental hospital. P was seen six months after admission, and despite a change of chemotherapy, the delusions appeared unremitted, P asserting as confidently as before his belief that R's love for him was undiminished and that through his suffering he would one day bring R to God. P writes daily to R from hospital. His letters are collected by the nursing staff but are not forwarded, in order to protect R from further distress. The patient will continue to be followed.

Discussion

Ellis & Mellsop (1985) concluded that de Clerambault's syndrome is an etiologically heterogeneous disorder. Theories of etiology have encompassed alcoholism, abortion, postamphetamine depression, epilepsy, head trauma, and neurological disorders. None of these is relevant in this case. Reviewing various descriptions of the premorbid personality in pure cases, Mullen & Pathe summarize by invoking "a socially inept individual isolated from others, be it by sensitivity, suspiciousness, or assumed superiority. These people tend to be described as living socially empty lives . . . the desire for a relationship is balanced by a fear of rejection or a fear of intimacy, both sexual and emotional."

The important change in this patient's life was the inheritance of his mother's house; a lifetime's failure to form close relationships culminated in a new arrangement whereby P, freed from the necessity of earning his living, was able to sever his remaining contacts with colleagues at the language school and his landlady and withdraw. It was at this time of increased loneliness that he became aware that he faced a test. On a country walk he was initiated into a makeshift community of passersby struggling to tether a balloon caught in strong winds. Such a transformation, from a "socially empty" life to intense teamwork, may have been the dominating factor in precipitating the syndrome, for it was when the drama was over that he became "aware" of R's love; the inception of a delusional relationship ensured that P would not have to return to his former isolation. Arieti & Meth (1959) have suggested that erotomania may act as a defense against depression and loneliness by creating a full intrapsychic world.

Also relevant to Mullen & Pathe's profile is the patient's fear of sexual intimacy. Questioned in interview about his erotic ambitions with regard to R, P was evasive and even offended. Although many male patients have specific and intrusive sexual designs on their subjects, others, as well as many female patients, have self-protectively vague notions of what they actually want from the love-object. Enoch & Trethowan quote Esquirol (1845), who observed that "the subjects of erotomania never pass the limits of propriety, they remain chaste." And Bucknell & Tuke, writing in the mid-nineteenth century, associated "erotomania proper" with a "sentimental form."

This case confirms the reports of some commentators (Trethowan 1967; Seeman 1978; Mullen & Pathe) on the relevance of absent or missing fathers. It must remain a matter for conjecture at this stage whether R, aged forty-seven, represented a father figure to P, or whether, as a successful, socially integrated individual, he represented an ideal to which P aspired.

Strong associations have been made, especially in recent work, between male erotomania and dangerousness (Gagne & Desparois 1995; Harmon, Rosner, & Owens 1995; Menzies, Fedoroff, Green, & Isaacson 1995). Hospitalization may be necessary in order to protect the love-object from assault by the patient (Enoch & Trethowan; Mullen & Pathe). In this case, where criminal charges had been brought, the issue of dangerousness, particularly in regard to outcome, was central. P stationed himself in a restaurant to watch the contract killing of R. When the attack went wrong, he tried to intervene. Later he showed remorse and redirected the violence against himself in the presence of R and M. As long as P's delusion continued unremitted, his potential for violence remained, and admission to a secure hospital was appropriate.

Lovett Doust & Christie, in their review of eight cases, suggest that "a close relationship may be posited between some pathological aspects of love and the tenets of the church for religious believers." It is reasonable to assume that the inhibitions placed on sexual expression by certain sects could be implicated in some pathologies. Further-more, celibate priests, by reason of their unavailability, may be favored subjects for de Clerambault sufferers. Other ministers of the church have been subjects of erotic delusions due to the status they enjoy within congregations (Enoch & Trethowan). However, P belonged to no particular denomination or sect, and the object of his delusion was an atheist. P's religious beliefs pre-dated the psychopathology, but those beliefs intensified once he had moved into his mother's house and his isolation was complete. His relationship with God was personal, and served as a substitute for other intimate relationships. The mission to "bring R to God" may be seen as an attempt to achieve a fully integrated intrapsychic world in which internalized religious sentiment and delusional love became one. In interview, P insisted that he had never heard the voice of God, nor seen any manifestations of his presence. He became "aware" of God's will or purpose in the generalized fashion of many people of intense religious persuasion. A search of the literature did not reveal another case of pure erotomania in which religious feeling or a love of God is similarly implicated.

Conclusion

P's condition satisfies all but one of the diagnostic criteria for the primary form of de Clerambault's syndrome suggested by Enoch & Trethowan and referred to above: P experiences a delusional conviction of being in amorous communication with another person, R, who was the first to fall in love and make advances. The onset was sudden. The object of P's delusion remains unchanged. He is able to rationalize R's paradoxical behavior, and the course looks set to be chronic. P suffers no hallucinations or cognitive defects. (However, although it could be said that R is of "higher rank," P could not have known this at their first meeting.) This degree of diagnostic concurrence, and the fact that P shares a number of premorbid characteristics with other patients, lend weight to the view that the syndrome is a nosological entity.

With regard to outcome, most commentators have leaned toward pessimism. De Clerambault described cases of pure erotomania that lasted without significant change for between seven and thirty-seven years. A review of the literature since suggests that this is indeed a most lasting form of love, often terminated only by the death of the patient.

The victims of de Clerambault patients may endure harassment, stress, physical and sexual assault, and even death. While in this case R and M were reconciled and later successfully adopted a child, some victims have had to divorce or emigrate, and others have needed psychiatric treatment because of the distress the patients have caused them. It is therefore important to continue to refine the diagnostic criteria and that these become broadly known by professionals. Patients with delusional disorders are unlikely to seek help, since they do not regard themselves as ill. Their friends and family may also be reluctant to see them in these terms, for as Mullen & Pathe observe, "the pathological extensions of love not only touch upon but overlap with normal experience, and it is not always easy to accept that one of our most valued experiences may merge into psychopathology."

References

Arieti, S. and Meth, M. (eds.) 1959. *American Handbook of Psychiatry*, Vol. 1. Basic Books, New York, pp. 525, 551.

Bucknell, J. C. and Tuke, D. H. 1882. *A Manual of Psychological Medicine*. 2d ed. Churchill, London.

de Clérambault, C. G. 1942. Les Psychoses passionelles. In *Oeuvres Psychiatriques*, pp. 315–22. Presses Universitaires, Paris.

El-Assra, A. 1989. "Erotomania in a Saudi Woman." *British Journal of Psychiatry* 153: 830–33.

Ellis, P. and Mellsop, G. 1985. *British Journal of Psychiatry* 146: 90.

Enoch, M. D. and Trethowan, W. H. 1979. *Uncommon Psychiatric Syndromes*. John Wright, Bristol.

Esquirol, J.E.D. 1845. *Mental Maladies: A Treatise on Insanity*, trans. R. de Saussure, 1965. Hafner, New York.

Gagne, P. and Desparois, L. 1995. L'erotomanie male: un type de harcelement sexuel dangereux. *Revue Canadienne de Psychiatrie* 40: 136–41.

Harmon, R. B., Rosner, R. and Owens, H. 1995. Obsessional harassment in a criminal court population. *Journal of Forensic Sciences* 42: 188–96.

Hollander, M. H. and Callahan, A. S. 1975. *Archives of General Psychiatry* 32: 1574.

Lovett Doust, J. W. and Christie, H. 1978. The pathology of love: some clinical variants of de Clerambault's syndrome. *Social Science and Medicine* 12: 99–106.

Menzies, R. P., Federoff, J. P., Green,

C. M. and Isaacson, K. 1995. Prediction of dangerous behaviour in male erotomania. *British Journal of Psychiatry* 166: 529–36.

Mullen, P. E. and Pathe, M. 1994. The pathological extensions of love. *British Journal of Psychiatry* 165: 614–23.

Perez, C. 1993. Stalking: when does obsession become a crime? *American Journal of Criminal Law* 20: 263–80.

Raskin, D. and Sullivan, K. E. 1974. Erotomania. *American Journal of Psychiatry* 131: 1033–35.

Schneider, K. 1959. *Clinical Psychopathology*, trans. M. W. Hamilton. Grune & Stratton, New York.

Seeman, M. V. 1978. Delusional loving. *Archives of General Psychiatry* 35: 1265–67.

Signer, J. G. and Cummings, J. L. 1987. De Clérambault's syndrome in organic affective disorder. *British Journal of Psychiatry* 151: 404–7.

Trethowan, W. H. 1967. Erotomania — an old disorder reconsidered. *Alta* 2: 79–86.

Wenn, R. and Camia, A. 1990. Homosexual erotomania. *Acta Psychiatrica Scandinavica* 85: 78–82.

Appendix II

Letter collected from Mr. J. Parry, written toward end of third year after admittance. Original filed with patient's notes. Photocopy forwarded to Dr. R. Wenn at his request.

Tuesday

Dear Joe,

I was awake at dawn. I slipped out of bed, put on my dressing gown, and without disturbing the night staff went and stood by the east window. See how willing I can be when you're kind to me! You're right, when the sun comes up behind the trees they turn black. The twigs at the very top are tangled against the sky, like the insides of some machine with wires. But I wasn't thinking about that, because it was a cloudless day and what rose up above the treetops ten minutes later was nothing less than the resplendence of God's glory and love. Our love! First bathing me, then warming me through the pane. I stood there, shoulders back, my arms hanging loosely at my sides, taking deep breaths. The old tears streaming. But the joy! The thousandth day, my thousandth letter, and you telling me that what I'm doing is right! At first you didn't see the sense of it, and you cursed our separation. Now you know that every day I spend here brings you one tiny step closer to that glorious light, His love, and the reason you know it now when you didn't before is because you are close enough to feel yourself turning helplessly and joyfully toward His warmth. No going back now, Joe! When you are His, you also become mine. This happiness is almost an embarrassment to me. I'm meant to be a prisoner. The bars are on the windows, the ward is locked at night, I spend my days and nights in the company of the shuffling, muttering, dribbling idiots, and the ones who aren't shuffling have to be restrained. The nurses, especially the men, are brutes who really ought to be inmates and have somehow scraped through to the other side. Cigarette smoke, windows that won't open, urine, TV ads. That's the world I've described to you a thousand times. I ought to be going under. Instead I feel more purpose than I've ever known in my life. I've never felt so free. I'm soaring, I'm so happy, Joe! If they'd known how happy I was going to be here, they would have let me out. I have to stop writing to hug myself. I'm earning our happiness day by day and I don't care if it takes me a lifetime. A thousand days — this is my birthday letter to you. You know it already, but I need to tell you again that I adore you. I live for you. I love you. Thank you for loving me, thank you for accepting me, thank you for recognizing what I am doing for our love. Send me a new message soon, and remember — faith is joy.

Jed

Acknowledgments

Above all I would like to thank Ray Dolan, friend and hiking companion, for many years of stimulating discussion. I would also like to thank Galen Strawson, Craig Raine, Tim Garton Ash, and Chief Inspector Eamonn McAfee. I am indebted to the following authors and books: E. O. Wilson, *On Human Nature*, *The Diversity of Life*, *Biophilia*; Steven Weinberg, *Dreams of a Final Theory*; Steven Pinker, *The Language Instinct*; Antonio Damasio, *Descartes' Error*; Robert Wright, *The Moral Animal*; Walter Bodmer and Robert McKie, *The Book of Man*; Robert Gittings, *John Keats*; Stephen Gill, *William Wordsworth, A Life*.